A
GRAVE
MISTAKE

Roger Whale

Roger Whale

Orca Publishing

First published in 2013 by Orca Publishing
Ponsworthy

www.orcapublishing.co.uk
roger@orcapublishing.co.uk

Printed by
Short Run Press Ltd

A
GRAVE
MISTAKE

By the same author

THE DAMSON TREE
THE YELLOW SAPPHIRE
THE OAK APPLE
OLIVES AND WHORTLEBERRIES

ONE

For Clive Luscombe it had been a hard day. Every appointment had seemed to go on longer than the last, longer than he had anticipated and he had grown weary of the heartfelt but seemingly minor problems and complaints that he had had to listen to. In an attempt to free his mind of work related problems he had chosen to drive home across the moor. The peace and solitude of the rolling open spaces, the rock-topped tors and the steep-sided green valleys seemed miles away from the pressures of the modern world. He stopped for a while on a high point and looked down to where a fast flowing steam twisted and turned as it tumbled from the high ground to the valley floor. A farmstead, seemingly embraced by the hills around it, with small stone-walled fields nestled in the shadows. A gravelled track led down to it from the road and Clive wondered if the hard existence experienced by those eking out a living there was less stressful than his.

He drove on, eventually dropping down into the valley of the Redacre Brook, now dark in the late evening light. He crossed the granite bridge and powered up the hill bursting out into the last rays of autumn sunset as he neared the top. As he rounded the bend a small bunch of Dartmoor ponies ambled across the road, causing him to brake suddenly. One of the mares paused and looked at him with scorn. It was as if she was well aware that she had possession of everything in this her natural domain. Clive waited for them all to cross and then drove on across the crossroads and into the centre of the village.

He stopped outside the old village school, now converted into a busy village hall, and climbed stiffly out of his car. In front of him a boy of about twelve came out of the door of the nearby café and stood looking at him. His white school shirt was hanging outside his trousers and his tie was loose, the rebellious fashion of the young against school uniform, which ended up being a uniform of youth.

"I'm looking for Grimstone Court, is it far from here?" asked Clive, walking a few paces towards the boy.

"No, go on through the village and take the first right turn and then right again. It's about a twenty minute walk."

"Thank you" said Clive, noting with pleasure how polite the boy had been and also that his accent was not local, judging by the way he said *abaht* with a flat 'a' rather than *abowt* with a rounded Westcountry second vowel. He got back into his car and drove on out of the village passing the Church on his right as he headed for home. There was still a mountain of paper work for him to see to which would take up a lot of his time, so much so that he might not get to see his mother until much later that evening, if at all.

The silver grey Range Rover coming towards him was the only other vehicle on the road and in the setting evening sunlight it looked bronze-coloured with bright golden flashes reflecting off the shiny trim. But before it drew level with Clive it turned off the road into a small lane and disappeared from view. Clive stretched, pushing back on the steering wheel easing his tired back muscles. He had been driving for too long, but with a bit of luck and the light behind him he felt sure that he could be home before dark.

It was Mark Bosworth who had driven off the road and up the small gravelled lane, the bushes on either side almost meeting overhead to form a tunnel. On his left he passed the remains of a small-holding. All that was now standing of the house was the ivy-covered gable end with its chimney and most of one wall. The few out-buildings were hardly more than moss covered mounds of granite stones with clumps of nettles and a small thorn bush growing through the dereliction. On the opposite side was a gate leading into a field and at that point the lane turned left. Mark followed it and parked behind the buildings in front of a field gate that was almost as dilapidated as the buildings and held together with bits of bale cord. Inside this gate the lane only continued for a few yards beside what had once been the farm-yard wall, before ending in a pile of gravel. Beside this pile was an upturned wheelbarrow, a few odds and ends of what looked like building materials and a long-handled Devon shovel. Beyond was a large, flat topped granite rock.

Dotted across the field were white wooden pegs about two feet tall that were driven into the ground in orderly lines. Running down through the centre of the field were a few hawthorn trees, red with berries and a small stand of hazel, their leaves almost all gone, showing where many years before a hedge had once divided the field into two.

Mark walked up the slight incline across the field and passing the clump of hazel made his way some three hundred yards up to stand under the tallest of the ancient beech trees that graced the top hedge. Its leaves were a beautiful reddish gold, made more so by the light from the fast setting evening sun. He turned and looked down across the field. But his eyes didn't see the beautiful unspoiled ancient hay meadow or the rolling hills and tors of the moor beyond. He smiled because in his mind's eye he could see his plan for the area coming into fruition in a very short while, and he felt good. He had always liked a challenge and this had certainly been one. First there had been the objections from several of the local people, not that that had bothered him. Then his planning application was turned down by the National Park Authority. But that hadn't stopped him either; it had only fuelled his desire to succeed. He had appealed, and that afternoon he had just heard from his legal team that his appeal had been successful, albeit with a few minor modifications.

He was by no means a large man; in fact he was only five foot eight inches in his shoes and less than ten stone in weight. But what he lacked in stature he made up for in sheer determination. He had a round face with slightly over full lips which gave him a somewhat effeminate appearance. His wavy hair was dark brown, which he dyed to conceal the onset of grey at the temples, and he wore blue contact lenses with which to enhance the colour of his pale blue irises.

To the west the darkening sky was turning from light yellow to red with a few wispy clouds of various shades of orange adding to the beauty of the evening. The vapour trail of a trans-Atlantic aeroplane looked like a blood red cut through the dark blue velvet of the sky. He walked back down across the field towards his Range Rover, taking care as to where he put his feet. Having looked at the bright sunset he found it difficult to pick out the details of the dark ground in front of him. When he reached the pile of gravel he was surprised to see a figure in a dark waxed, hooded jacket sitting on the large rock with its back towards him.

"What d'you think you're doing here?" he asked with more than a hint of anger in his voice.

The figure stood up and turned around, face still invisible in the shadow of the jacket's hood. Hung over its forearm was a twelve-bore shotgun open at the breech. The shiny brass ends of the two cartridges plainly visible.

"I've come to see you" said the figure in a quiet voice. "Lovely sunset isn't it? Take a good look at it while you still can.... "

"What do you mean?" said Mark "and what the hell are you doing with that gun; that's my shotgun?"

"Nice gun isn't it, must have cost you a packet. I found it in your Range Rover. Rather careless of you, leaving your vehicle unlocked with a gun in it, don't you think?"

"Never mind that, what is it that you want to see me about?"

"I've come to tell you just how much I hate, loathe and despise you and everything you stand for; you're a brutal vicious bully. You seem to take a delight in hurting and upsetting people, including those nearest to you. So now I've decided I'm going to put an end to all that."

"Oh yes" said Mark sneering "and how do you propose to do that?"

"You're forgetting this" said the voice as the breech of the shotgun was clicked shut. The gun lifted and pointed unwaveringly straight at Mark.

"Don't be ridiculous" said Mark with a laugh as he took a step forward, but the sneer had gone from his tone, replaced with nervousness.

5

"Nothing ridiculous about it......I'm going to kill you."

"But ....that's murder.....you won't get away with it......you'll be arrested and go to jail.... probably for life."

"True, that is a distinct possibility. And if I were to be found guilty of murder I might be sent down for life, which could be for twelve years. With good behaviour I could be out in six, if not less" said the voice calmly.

"But think of your family...."

"You're missing the point. I may go to jail; I may have to spend several years in jail away from friends and family. But you....you will be dead. Just think of it....dead.....And all your money and all your so called position and all your power will be of no avail.......You will be finished.....You will be dead."

Down in the village half a mile away Charlie Blundell stepped out of his garden shed. He had been putting away the canes that had held up his crop of runner beans and was about to go indoors for his supper. He looked up at the sky, a few splashes of orange in the dark blue and a reddish glow to the west. Down in the valley behind him a mist was forming, creeping up the stream dulling the sound of the water tinkling and lapping at the stones.

'Be a fine day 'morrow I reckon....bit dull and misty to start with maybe.'

He walked up the path between the neat beds of his vegetable garden, all empty but for a few winter greens and some turnips, and stopped at his back door to take off his boots. As he did so he heard a shot.

'Young Stapleton after a rabbit by the sounds of it' he said to himself. 'I doubt if Mr High and

Mighty Bosworth will take kindly to him shooting on his land'.

TWO

Charlie's forecast turned out to be right. The mist that had formed in the evening was still filling the valleys the next morning. Up on Braggator, Mick Cribbett was riding his grey horse, Osprey. Mick was the local blacksmith who lived in the valley below, in what used to be the old mine captain's house. Braggator mine was one of many tin mines scattered all over Dartmoor that had closed down over a hundred years before. All that was left was the house with a few outbuildings and two small fields; an oasis of flat ground in a valley whose steep, heather-covered sides were scarred with deep ravines and piles of rocky waste, the remains of the open-cast mining.

All around him the low ground was full of dense white mist, giving the impression that the tide had come in. The hills and tors stood out like islands and below him he could just make out the four pinnacles of the church tower; the only sign showing of the busy little village that was there.

Mick wouldn't be working that day; in fact most of the villagers would be taking the day off for the funeral of their late vicar, the Reverend Quentin Russell. Although in a way he would be working because Cecil Webber, the undertaker, had asked him to be one of the bearers at the funeral. He turned Osprey and galloped up the long, wide grassy path to the top of the tor. Once there it gave him a good feeling to be sitting astride his beautiful horse up on the open moor, looking around at the scenery of which he never tired. Osprey, who was blowing a little after his exertions, gave a violent shake that was more like a shudder. It went right through Mick almost making his teeth rattle, at the same time the tremors made the leathers creak and the bridle jingle. Then he had a short ride along the ridge before going back down, taking a different path towards his home. As he did so the sun began to burn off the mist, thinning it enough for him to see more of the buildings in the village.

The funeral was scheduled for twelve noon, but before half past eleven the church was full and already people were standing wherever there was a space. Neighbours looked around and quietly nodded to one another. The organist had played Handel's Water Music right through and had started on a piece by Bach. The notes gently filled the air, though barely covering the odd cough and whisper from the assembled mourners.

Finally the funeral cortege entered led by the new vicar. Behind him Cecil Webber led the four bearers carrying the simple pine coffin. Quentin's widow Grace, looking even smaller than usual, in a dark grey two piece suit led the principle mourners. When they reached the chancel steps the bearers stopped and turned the coffin around before resting it on two trestles. Although it is more usual for the coffin to be turned after the service, in the case of a departed vicar he is customarily placed to face his congregation for his last service.

It was a short service with a brief but honest eulogy given by Sir Harold Edworthy, the lord of the manor. Quentin, he said, had been a good friend to all his parishioners for many, many years; knowing them all by name and following their progress through life. He had baptised, married and buried them, in some cases all three. Then the last hymn, which seemed to epitomise Quentin's approach to life,

9

"Forth in thy name, O Lord I go;
My daily labour to pursue."

The bearers took their places and followed the vicar and the undertaker out into the bright sunlight and the peace of the churchyard. At the grave the coffin was placed on two stout pieces of wood resting across the open grave. The two wooden carrying handles, which had been clipped onto the rings at the head and the foot of the coffin, were removed and in their place long webbing straps were threaded. Then at a nod from the undertaker the bearers took the strain, the pieces of wood were removed and to the words of the committal the coffin was lowered into the ground.

Cecil stepped forward with a small basket in his hand in which were small sprigs of heather. These he offered to the mourners who wished to drop something in on the coffin as they passed and took a last look into the grave. Grace then thanked the bearers and the undertaker and led all those who had attended across the green and into the village hall for refreshments. It was then that the mood changed from being sombre to happy reminiscing of times spent with Quentin and the joy and comfort that he had brought to their lives.

At the back of the hall were the four bearers. Charlie Blundell was talking to his opposite number, Ben Fuller, a retired policeman. They had been at one end of the coffin while the other two bearers had been Mick Cribbett and Frank Narraway, who lived with his widowed mother at Wistworthy Farm and earned his living as a mechanic.

"You're looking puzzled Charlie" said Ben "what's up?"

"I don't rightly know; something wasn't quite right just now, but for the life of me I can't think what." He paused, staring up at the ceiling as if as if he could get help from there. "Never mind, 'twill come to me later no doubt."

"Did you hear that phone ringing?" said Ben.

"No, can't say as I did, when was that?"

"In the churchyard, when we were at the graveside, I heard it.....clear as day 'twas.....good job it didn't go off during the service in church. Some people....I dunno.....This modern age, it don't sit well with me. Any way, let's go get a cup of tea and some of those sandwiches" said Ben "there's nothing we can do now even if you reckon there was something that wasn't right."

They moved across the hall to where Charlie's wife Sal with her best friend and next-door neighbour Edna Marriott were serving cups of tea. Grace meanwhile was slowly and methodically making her way through the crowd, thanking people for coming. Grace was a small, bird-like woman who had an unfortunate habit of getting very close to the person with whom she was having a conversation. She would stand with her head tipped back slightly right under the other person's chin, and this had resulted in her being given the nick-name of 'Close up'. She had just finished talking at some length to Blanche, Frank's mother, and had moved on to talk to Hilary Bosworth.

"How nice of you to come Mrs Bosworth, we don't see you very often in the village. Is your husband not with you today? Away on business I suppose, yes.... a busy man I realise."

"Oh, please call me Hilary. I felt I had to come and offer my condolences, Mrs Russell. Your husband was a very well liked man and will be greatly missed.

11

And you're right, Mark is away at the moment, but my brother Jeremy" she turned and reached to touch the arm of a man standing slightly behind her "has come to accompany me."

"Pleased to meet you" said Grace.

"I do hope that you will come up any time you feel the need for a bit of company, Mark is away quite a lot and it would be nice to get to know each other a bit more. I feel a bit guilty that I haven't joined in village life very much since we moved here, but I realise that many locals don't approve of pushy incomers." At this she gave a small laugh and looked down at the floor.

"That would be lovely, I shall be sure to take you up on that kind offer within a day or two.....Mmm yes....." she turned to go and then almost as an afterthought said "so nice meeting you Jeremy."

She moved on through the crowd, getting friendly words from everyone she stopped to talk to.

Sal and Edna were watching her progress with interest, noting the people Grace stopped to talk with and for how long.

"Grace is looking up very well considering. She could have just sat in a corner and let folks come to her. Instead she's going round the room talking to everyone. Not an easy thing to do," said Edna "I know, I've been there, when my man passed away."

"Haven't seen Hilary Bosworth here in this hall before" said Sal.

"No, she don't come into the shop much either" replied Edna, "but then, I s'pose it must be a bit difficult for her."

"How d'you mean?"

"Well, with her husband wanting to build that huge shop in his field."

"Yes, but that's a new thing this year; she never came into the village much before he started on that. Besides, didn't I read in the local paper that the National Park's turned down his plans?"

"Yes, but he's appealing against them. He'll get his way, you mark my words; he's got money and money talks."

"Have you noticed.....she don't look very comfortable here?"

"No" said Edna "Then 'tis hardly surprising, she don't know many folks here."

"I don't think it's just that, she's all the time looking at the door when anybody comes in."

"Really?"

"Yes, and the look on her face, sort of guilty like, as though she shouldn't be here. Or like she's half expecting her husband."

"I feel a bit sorry for her myself. I reckon he keeps her on a pretty tight rein."

"You could be right" said Sal "d'you think he doesn't trust her, with money I mean? Perhaps she's like Dolly Palmer used to be, if she had money on her she couldn't help herself, had to spend it."

"Yes, I mind she said to me once 'If I've got a sixpence in my purse Cheel, I just got to spend it'. Must be terrible that."

"I can't think that Hilary has that sort of problem; any road, her old man's got plenty of money".

"That's probably how he came by it Sal, making sure she didn't get a chance to spend it" said Edna laughing. "No, I reckon he's a bossy beggar, one of they there control freaks, always got to be top dog and in charge. I don't suppose the poor woman has a life of her own, stuck up there in that big house with no one to talk to. Like I say, I feel sorry for her."

"Still, it seems odd that he isn't here, he don't often miss an opportunity to lord it over the village. Just cos he's got a bob or two don't make him a gentleman and never will, all cash and no class. Not like Sir Harold, now he's a real gent, born to it see, generations of them up at the manor.

THREE

Hilary had in fact been more than a little worried by Mark's disappearance the evening before. It was so unlike him to go off with some business acquaintance or other without telling her. Normally he would have had left a list of instructions for her as to what he would need on his return. She had arrived home, after visiting her mother, to find the place in darkness. She had assumed that he had had to go off with somebody in a hurry because he had left the Range Rover parked outside the front of the house. There had been no phone calls or messages from him and so after watching television until after the ten o'clock news she had gone to bed to spend an uneasy night, awake more than asleep.

There had been no call from him the next morning and then when Paul, his PA, had come to work at half past eight she had gone into the study and asked him if he knew where Mark might have gone. He had said that he had no idea either and had looked in the diary to check.

"The only thing noted in his diary for today is the Reverend's funeral" he had said. "Maybe something to do with the fact that he won his appeal yesterday caused him to leave. I know he wants to put things in motion regarding the start of the work, clearing the site etcetera. And I know that he has to do that himself, for some reason he arranged it so that legally no one else can."

"Well, I shall have to go to the funeral on my own, if he hasn't come home by then" she had said, "I know he would want me there, if only to represent him."

15

"Have you tried phoning him?"

"Yes, I tried his mobile earlier; it rang for a while and then went to voice mail. So it's switched on but he isn't answering it."

"How long ago was that? Perhaps I ought to try again."

"Yes do, it was probably over an hour ago."

Paul had tried calling Mark again but with the same result. Then he had gone over to the smaller desk in the study where he worked, and sitting down had taken out several papers from the drawer. He was a strange looking man. Thin and tall, over six feet, with thinning mousey brown hair that had at one time been curly. His neck was long and together with the fact that he stooped, it gave him the appearance of a tortoise poking its head out of its shell. He wore small wire-rimmed glasses and always looked as though his elderly mother had dressed him.

"I'll try calling him from time to time, but it seems as though he doesn't want to be contacted. Either that or he's left his phone somewhere, like in his hotel bedroom, and forgotten it."

"I must say that that sounds very unlikely, he hates being without the means to keep in contact with people" Hilary had said, remembering only too clearly, how upset and annoyed he had been with her one morning. She had put his clothes out and inadvertently had left his mobile in the pocket of the suit that she had put away in the wardrobe the night before. Ever since then she had made sure that he would have his phone with him, no matter what clothes she had put out for him to wear.

She had then gone to make a coffee for them both, and not long after that her brother had arrived. Jeremy didn't drive, he went everywhere on his bicycle. It wasn't that he couldn't drive, just that he preferred to cycle. But it meant that when he arrived Hilary sent him upstairs to the bathroom where he could shower before changing into the suit that he had brought with him.

Later, when they were leaving to go to the church Hilary had looked in on Paul and asked

"Have you been able to get in touch with him?"

"No" he had replied "I rang not five minutes ago, I'll try again d'rectly"

"Thank you Paul. We're off now, we'll see you later."

From time to time during the course of the day Paul had interrupted his work to try contacting Mark again. At Hilary's request he had contacted all the people and places that he could think of where Mark might have gone. But to no avail.

FOUR

When Paul arrived for work the next day Hilary was waiting for him, considerably concerned by Mark's prolonged and unexplained absence. She had tried ringing his mobile several times during the evening and in the end there had been no ring tone as if the battery was down.

"D'you think we ought to contact the police?" she asked.

"I'm not sure if that would be appropriate. It's not as if he's a child or a minor. He may be a missing person as far as we are concerned, but the police might say that he's old enough and perfectly entitled to go off on his own somewhere without telling you or me."

"I've looked to see if there is anything in his diary for today, any appointments. The only thing there is G with CC 10am. I've no idea what or who that is. D'you know?"

"I think that's golf with CC. Give me a minute or two, I'll see if I can find out who CC is."

Hilary left him and returned some time later with a cup of coffee for Paul.

"Have you had any luck?"

"Well" he said "I'm not altogether sure but I think that CC could be Charles Cannon."

"The Assistant Chief Constable?"

"Yes."

"You could be right; he's been here for dinner on more than one occasion. And I think he shoots pheasants with Mark as well. D'you think we ought to ring him?"

"No, I think that the best thing to do would be to wait. If he's supposed to be playing golf with ACC

Cannon and he doesn't turn up, no doubt we'll get a phone call from the ACC asking where he is."

During the course of the morning there had been several phone calls from people asking for Mark. The contractor who had been engaged to do the work on the new building site had called twice. He had heard that Mark's appeal had been successful and was itching to get on with the job. It was a big contract and with the economy as it was, he was only too pleased to have won it. To all callers Paul had said that Mark would call back later.

Finally just before lunch Charles Cannon rang. Hilary took the call.

"Charles Cannon here, is Mark about, something wrong with him? We were supposed to be playing golf this morning but he never turned up. I waited for about an hour, and then had a few holes with Colonel Jameson. Not the same though, man's useless, got no idea. Anyway, where's Mark."

"That's just the point, we don't know."

"Don't know, what d'you mean don't know? What about that secretary fellow of his, doesn't he know what his boss is up to? Keeps his appointment diary for him doesn't he?"

"Yes, but your appointment was the only thing noted in Mark's diary. You see, I came home the night before last to find the house empty and Mark nowhere to be seen. His Range Rover was parked outside and I assumed that he had gone off with someone, a business colleague or something like that. We tried contacting him all day yesterday. Paul has been on to everyone he can think of. Mark has just disappeared. It's very worrying."

"Oh I am sorry Hilary, I didn't realise. There was me getting all wound up over a missed game of golf and all the time you are worried sick as to where Mark has got to. Have you reported it?"

"No, Paul thought that it was hardly urgent enough to bother the police, Mark being a grown man and all that......"

"Nonsense dear lady, I'll get someone on to it right away, that's what we're here for. Can't have you worrying, leave it with me."

FIVE

Detective Sergeant Shirley Ashton had just finished her canteen lunch when she was called into the office of Chief Inspector Collins. Shirley Ashton was a motherly looking woman of thirty nine. She was of medium height with mid brown hair that was beginning to show a few strands of grey. She was slightly overweight, due she said to too much desk work, though it was more likely due to her passion for clotted cream on anything sweet.

Collins was a neat dapper man, a typical admin type. His uniform was always neatly pressed, tie neatly tied and his shirt a gleaming white. He would have made a good manager in any profession; it just happened that he had chosen to join the police when he left college. He rarely mixed socially with the other officers in the station and his nick-name was Mullet, after the character with a similar personality on a television police drama.

"Close the door Ashton, I've got a job for you, seems a bit of a waste of resources at first glance. You see, I've had a strange request from the ACC. One of his golfing pals has apparently gone missing. According to the man's wife the circumstances are somewhat unusual and she's very worried. It's probably a storm in a teacup and will blow over in no time, but it seems we ought to investigate it."

"Who is this man Sir and where does he live?"

"He's a business man, lives up on the moor, here's his address" he said handing over a piece of paper. "You'd better take DC Chaffe with you, his family are farming folks, it may help you to get through to the locals. I understand from the ACC that our man was not very popular with the rest of the village. Could be nothing.....just feel your way Ashton."

"D'you want me to go right now Sir? I've still got that business with the stolen boat at Teignmouth, I would rather like to clear it up first. It's only paper work, should have it done by this evening."

"Fine, do that and start on this missing person case tomorrow first thing."

"One other thing Sir, what sort of business is this missing man involved in?"

"No idea Ashton, look him up on Google. I will contact his wife and tell her to expect you tomorrow morning."

SIX

So it was that at quarter past nine the next morning DS Shirley Ashton and DC Newman Chaffe set off from the station to drive up onto the moor. It was a dull autumnal morning, cold but dry with a thin mist that added to the seasonal feeling. As they climbed up from the low ground and crossed the cattle grid that denoted the start of the moor they seemed to burst out of the gloom and into bright sunshine.

"Wow!" said Shirley "What a difference. The weather's beautiful up here."

The road wound across open moorland where patches of rust-brown bracken and dark green gorse bushes covered most of the ground. Sunlight sparkled on the dew drops throwing back millions of tiny rainbows. All around there were gossamer spiders' webs, perfect circular creations that looked as though some magic glass blower had been at work, weaving reflective threads during the night. As they drove even higher these bushes gave way to light sandy coloured dead grass that stretched away to either side like an African savannah. They reached the top of a hill and looked across the valley, where the village that they were about to visit nestled, to the line of tors beyond.

"That is probably one of the best views in England" said Newman. "I often drive this way when I go to visit my folks."

"They farm up here I understand" said Shirley.

"Yes that's right, over towards Tavistock. It's a lovely drive at any time of year, but naturally its best if the sun's shining like today."

They drove on down towards the village and eventually pulled up on the wide gravelled area at the end of the long tree-lined drive that led to Grimstone Court. The house was an imposing two storey pile built by a Victorian shipping magnate in a mock Elizabethan style. A large granite porch with a heavy oak door stood out in the middle of the wall that faced them. To either side were mullion windows with leaded panes, while above a cluster of ornate chimney pots graced the roof.

"Bit posh, wouldn't you say" said Newman.

"Not quite my style I admit. It must cost a fortune to heat a place like this."

They got out of the car and before they reached the door it was opened by a slim, attractive looking woman with dark brown wavy hair, dressed in a dark green skirt, a cream long sleeved blouse, done up to the neck, and a pale green cardigan. After they had introduced themselves she said

"I'm Hilary Bosworth, do come in. It's a lovely sunny morning but too cold to stand outside."

She led them through the porch into a large hallway the floor of which was covered with a pattern of black, red and white tiles. Against one wall was a long narrow mahogany table with two brass handled drawers. On the other side was a beautiful brass-faced mahogany grandfather clock, and at the far end was a staircase. This led up to a half landing where it divided, going both left and right. A stained glass window above this half landing depicted a clipper ship in full sail.

Hilary took them into a relaxing lounge on the left of the hall and invited them to sit in one of the sumptuous soft armchairs.

"It is so good of you to come. I fear that I'm making an awful fuss but.....it just seems so out of character of Mark to leave like this."

Newman took out his notebook while Shirley said

"Perhaps you could start at the beginning and tell us just what happened.

"Well, I was out that night"

"Sorry, which night was that Mrs Bosworth" interjected Newman.

"Oh, Tuesday night. I always visit my mother on Tuesdays; she's in a home near Dawlish. Well, I left here at five o'clock and when I got home at about half past eight everywhere was in darkness. I wasn't unduly worried at that, Mark is occasionally out of an evening. But his Range Rover was parked outside so I naturally expected to find him at home. I came in and called, thinking that he might have fallen asleep before the need to switch on any lights, but he obviously wasn't here so I watched a bit of telly and then went to bed."

"Does he often stay out at night?" asked Shirley.

"No...well... if he's away on business he does of course, but then I know that he's going to be away. I have to get all his things packed for the journey, if you know what I mean. I must admit I didn't sleep very well that night and when Paul came in the morning...."

"Sorry, who's Paul?"

"Oh, he's Mark's PA. He works here every day in the study. All of Mark's business is run from here these days. Anyway, when he came I asked him if he knew where Mark could have gone. He had no idea and then looked in the diary to check."

"What attempt did you make to locate your husband Mrs Bosworth?" asked Newman.

25

"Well, I had tried ringing him on his mobile several times, it rang but he didn't answer. Both Paul and I tried ringing several times that Wednesday, eventually the ringtone stopped so I guess that the battery had run down. Paul and I also spent a good deal of time ringing everywhere we could think that Mark might have gone, but to no avail."

"It may sound a bit morbid Mrs Bosworth, but have you rung any of the local hospitals to see if your husband has been admitted?"

"Yes, Paul did yesterday, in the late afternoon I believe it was, but again nobody has heard of Mark."

"So what happened next?"

"Well, Charles Cannon, your Assistant Chief Constable I believe, rang to see where Mark was. They were supposed to be playing golf together. When he heard what had happened he said that he would sort it and ....well....here you are."

A noise from the hallway caused Hilary to look in that direction, an anxious look on her face. Then a knock on the half open door and Paul put his head round saying

"Can I make you some tea or coffee?"

"That would be lovely Paul. These are the policemen who have come to help us find Mark."

"One other thing Mrs Bosworth" said Shirley. "Do you know if your husband changed his clothes when he came back in the afternoon, before he disappeared?"

"I really don't know."

"You said earlier that you put out his clothes for him to wear on occasions. Do you remember what he was wearing when he left here on Tuesday?"

"Yes, I think so. Yes, he was wearing his blue pin-striped suit and a white shirt. He changed at lunch, I remember now."

"A white shirt, you say."

"Yes, he always wore a white shirt. He would change sometimes as often as twice a day, liked to be seen in a clean white shirt."

"So could you look and see if he's taken anything else."

"I'll certainly go and have a look, but there was nothing in the laundry basket that needed washing."

She left the room and while she was away Paul came in with the coffee. He put the tray on the coffee table in the middle of the room and then Hilary came back in.

"I can't see anything to suggest that Mark changed or took any other clothes."

"Thank you, that information could be valuable. If you should think of anything that is the least bit unusual, no matter how small or insignificant, please let me know."

Then while they were all drinking their coffee Shirley asked Paul a few questions, but there was nothing that he could add to what they had already heard from Hilary. Newman said that they would need details of his credit card and banking and a list of the companies that Mark owned and was connected with. Shirley said that they would no doubt have to come back and ask them some more questions but for the moment that was all. They would call back if that was alright whenever they had reason. Hilary said that that would be fine and went with them to the door.

Sitting in the car afterwards Newman said

"What d'you think Sarge, d'you think he's done a runner? Gone off with his lady love."

"No....somehow I don't think that Mark Bosworth would do that. If he had a mistress he would just tell Hilary to pack her bags and go. I can't see him running away in the dead of night."

"She's very anxious...."

"Anxious or nervous. Did you notice the way she almost jumped when she heard Paul moving in the hall. She had the look of a startled rabbit, and then when she saw it was him she looked relieved. I can't make it out."

"I'd like to question that Paul chap on his own,"

"Really, why?"

"Well, he knows all about the business side of things. People who do well in business like Mark often make enemies. Mark left here in somebody's car, not his own 'cos that's still standing in the drive. Did he go of his own free will or....?"

"Was he kidnapped you mean?"

"Yeah, something like that."

"I think we need to look in his car, I should have thought of that before" said Shirley. She got out of their car and with Newman following made her way to the front door again. This time the hall door was slightly open and Shirley was able to see Hilary coming in answer to their ringing the bell. The nervous look on her face turned to relief when she saw who it was.

"I'm so sorry to bother you again Mrs Bosworth. Do you think we could have a look in your husband's car?"

"Certainly, I'll go and get the keys, they're in the study."

They walked over to the silver-grey Range Rover pulling on their latex protective gloves as they went. Shirley unlocked the car and opened the driver's door. There was a very slight smell of something which she recognised but couldn't place.

"There's a smell in here Chaffe, I can't place it. Newman opened the rear door and took a sniff. Though rapidly fading, he recognised it at once.

"Its cordite Sarge, and here's where it comes from" he said, moving the waxed jacket on the back seat that was covering a twelve bore shot-gun. "I'm surprised that there's still any smell left. The new cartridges don't leave much, not like the old black powder cartridges that my grandad used to use. You could smell them for days afterwards."

"Would you say that this was recently fired before being put here? You seem to know a bit about shotguns."

"Possibly."

He carefully lifted the gun and looked at it.

"This is some piece of kit Serge; this is a Holland and Holland gun, one of a pair I would say. A gun like this costs thousands of pounds. Mr Mark Bosworth has got expensive tastes sure enough. Perhaps he took a shot at a rabbit before coming home."

"Yes, and a gun like this, or any shot-gun should not be left out here in a car. He should have locked it in his gun case. We need to have another word with Mrs Bosworth about this."

They went indoors again and found Hilary in deep conversation on the telephone. As they entered she said "....that will be lovely, I look forward to seeing you tomorrow." With that she hung up and turning to Shirley said

"That was Mrs Russell, widow of our late vicar whom we buried on Wednesday...."

"I was hoping you might be able to tell me about your husband's gun. We have just found it on the back seat of his car covered by a waxed jacket in the pockets of which are some cartridges."

Shirley held up the gun while Newman was holding the jacket.

"Well....yes....that's Mark's gun, I believe. Well I know it is, he has a shoot, you know. A pheasant shoot somewhere in the South Hams. I thought that it was always locked in the cabinet in the study. The jacket is definitely his; I gave it to him for his birthday last year."

"Do you have any explanation as to why he might have left it in his car?"

"Not really....I know he was always on about the number of rabbits around here...."

"So he might have been rabbit shooting before he disappeared."

"Yes.....I suppose so.....I really don't know Sergeant, I'm sorry."

"Not to worry Mrs Bosworth. But we will have to take this gun and the jacket with us for testing, finger prints etc."

"Of course, I'm sure Mark will understand."

"I'll give you a receipt and we will call in and see you again as soon as we have something to tell you. Also you must leave the car untouched and locked. We may need to test it as well. Meanwhile if you should think of anything, anything at all, don't be afraid to contact us."

With that, Shirley handed Hilary her card and thanked her for all her help. The two police officers then left and drove off and down into the village.

SEVEN

Hilary's brother Jeremy lived in a small two up two down semi in a new estate on the edge of town. It was not exactly what he wanted; he would have preferred to be out in the country, ideally on the moor. But when he had left the army three years before, it was the only accommodation that was available at a price that he could afford. However, the estate itself was clean and tidy and those living there obviously took a pride in the place. There was no litter and no unwanted cars or old fridges and the likes dumped at the side of the road, as there were in some estates. Storage space in the house was limited and Jeremy was glad to have a reasonably large wooden shed in his small garden in which he kept his bicycles.

This morning he took out his road bike and set off for the five mile trip to visit his sister. Although he had talked to her on the phone several times since the funeral, he had not been to see her. This morning he felt that it was high time that he did. He knew that she would be lost without Mark. He had always been the dominant one in their household, making all the decisions for them both. Paul would be able to run the business side of things but without Mark to wait on, Hilary would probably feel that she had no routine or purpose.

About a mile out of town he left the main road and took a small side road that led through woodland and past two small farms up onto the moor. He pedalled strongly, revelling in the exertion, feeling the blood pumping around his body. No visits to the gym for him, although keeping fit was important. He cycled everywhere and enjoyed walking on the high moor whenever possible. He was of medium height and build, with short cut light brown hair and a tanned, lined face that looked lived in. His green eyes had that half shut look, as though he was searching for something in the far distance and he moved with the cat-like grace of an athlete.

When he left the army he had little idea as to what he was going to do. He had toyed with the idea of joining one of the many mercenary armies that seemed to have sprung up all over the world. But having served two tours of duty in Afghanistan he felt that he had seen enough active service. On a visit to his sister, Mark had told him of his plans for the water bottling factory and Jeremy had taken the job of setting it up and running it. The plan was to house the bottling plant in the proposed new building below Grimstone Court, with the water piped directly from the spring. As a stop gap measure, and to see if the idea was viable, the plant had been set up in a small unit in the industrial estate just outside the town. That had meant that the water had to be taken from the spring to the plant in a small tanker once or twice a week. The only drawback had been the resistance of the local people to Mark's plan.

Jeremy had felt in agreement with them, he couldn't understand why Mark hadn't opted to re-build the near derelict Glebe Farm; a plan which he felt sure would have met with approval from the National Park Authority and most of the local people as well. But he had discovered, in the short time he had spent working for Mark, that he was a very single-minded man who was determined to have his own way. In fact, there were times when to get his way he would often employ tactics that bordered on the illegal.

Hilary was Jeremy's only living relative, apart from their mother who was in a nursing home in Dawlish. Although his time spent in the army had meant that they had seen little of each other over the past fifteen years, they were close and he cared greatly for her. On recent visits to her he had felt that she was not entirely happy, and there was a slight nervousness that he couldn't understand. He knew that Mark was inclined to boss her around; he had witnessed that sort of behaviour occasionally. But he had thought that it was just an example of Mark showing off his authority over her, childish though that was.

There had been one occasion recently when he had been invited to join one of Mark's pheasant shoots. The day had gone well until in the last half hour the heavens had opened and within minutes everywhere was soaking wet. The ground had rapidly turned into a sea of mud, people were slipping and falling, and tempers got a little frayed. By the time they got back home to Grimstone Court most of the people were feeling better, and the spread of food that Hilary had laid out for them all was truly wonderful. Mark however was still in a hideously bad mood and had found fault with nearly everything, doing his best to make Hilary look small in front of his friends. She had just put her head down and taken his tirade without saying a word, though she was nearly in tears. It was most embarrassing for the guests and Jeremy had wondered what they thought of it all. He knew that Mark had money, though how he had come by it he had never discovered, and thought that he could buy position with it. So were these people who had been invited to join in the shoot real friends or purely steps in Mark's climb up the social ladder?

Finally after ten minutes of hard pedalling he rode out onto the open moorland above the fields. He stopped and looked over the vast expanse of wild country towards the high moor. It always reminded him of days spent training near Cranmere pool, crawling through heather and rocks, along rain soaked peat-black sheep tracks. Nowadays when he walked those hills he stayed upright and returned home almost as clean as when he left.

He rode on down towards the village and into the drive that led to Grimstone Court. Hilary answered the door and threw her arms around him. After a long embrace she stepped back saying

"You've got a new outfit" looking at his light blue and yellow Lycra cycling suit. "It's very bright isn't it? I think I preferred your old black and maroon one; it was a little more sober.

"But that's the whole idea, winter is coming with the darker days and this is more visible. Anyway, more to the point is there any news? Have you been able to think of anything that might help?"

"No, I can't think where he can have gone or why. It's so unlike Mark to go off without telling me. I mean, he usually wants me to get his case ready, with all his clothes and that, if he's going away. And Paul has no idea either."

"Have the police got any ideas?"

"No, they haven't a clue. They had a good look round, looked in the Range Rover and took his gun and coat that were in there. Said I was to leave the car locked and not touch it."

"Gun, in the car? That's odd; surely it should have been in the gun locker."

"Yes...Oh I don't know...I don't know anything these days."

They went indoors, into the kitchen where Hilary put on the kettle to make them a drink.

"Well, I'll do anything I can to help; you just have to say the word."

"I don't know what you can do, really. All we can do is wait and hope. And you mustn't neglect your job at the factory, I don't want you getting into trouble, we both know what Mark can be like."

"That's alright; I'm on nights again most of this week. We've had a few big orders lately."

They took their drinks into the lounge and sat making small talk, mostly about their past. Jeremy hoped that by reminiscing it would take her mind off Mark's disappearance, but he noticed that she was constantly looking towards the door as if expecting him to appear at any minute. He found it awkward just sitting and talking, he wanted to do something, but there was really nothing that he could do. He felt it was like visiting someone in hospital. There the first ten minutes were alright, but then, having eaten the grapes and run out of things to say about the weather and the local gossip, it was time to leave. So, embarrassed at having nothing better to add, he got up saying

"I'll be getting back now, if you need me for anything, just give a shout. I'll call in again soon."

"Thanks, I'll be alright. I'm sure Mark will be back soon. It just feels so strange without him."

"I know you'll be alright"

They embraced again and he walked out into the autumn sunshine. As he got on his bike and rode away he thought

'I've no doubt it feels strange without him, but it probably feels a lot better'

EIGHT

Shirley and Newman parked outside the pub. The village centre was a large triangular open space surrounded by houses and a shop, a village hall, a pub and the village Church. Three roads came into this area forming the surrounds. At one time the centre had been a small grass meadow and was called the village green. In mediaeval days it had been known as Butt Park, being the area where the local able bodied men had to practice their archery skills. Now that the whole area had been covered in tarmac the name didn't seem so appropriate. In the centre was a large old horse chestnut tree with wrought iron seats surrounding it, a peaceful and shady spot to rest on a hot summer's day.

They walked into The New Inn to be welcomed by Bob Peters who, with his wife Julie, ran a pub that had a reputation for good home cooked food. As it was nearing midday she had suggested to Newman that they have their lunch there.

"Good idea Sarge, it looks comfortable and inviting here. I'll get us some drinks."

They went up to the bar and Shirley, taking out her warrant card said

"I'm Detective Sergeant Ashton and this is Detective Constable Chaffe. We are here to investigate the somewhat unusual disappearance of Mr Mark Bosworth. It seems that he left his home sometime on Tuesday afternoon and he hasn't been seen since. His wife and his secretary have tried in vain to locate him, both through friends and acquaintances and by trying to get him on his phone; but to no avail. We are hoping that someone may have seen him that afternoon. It is important that we learn

36

of his last movements. I don't suppose you can shed any light on the matter, can you?"

"I don't think I can. I was out at the wholesalers that afternoon, shopping; didn't get back until just after dark. My wife Julie was here, she opened up at six o'clock. I'll get her."

But Julie was unable to add to what Bob had said. Bob suggested that they talk to any of the locals who worked in the area like Mick Cribbett, the local blacksmith, or Sidney Turner who drove the school bus, as they might have been on the road at the time.

"Thank you, if you see anyone who might be able to help perhaps you could ask them to contact me, either at the station or on my phone." Shirley passed a couple of her cards across the bar.

"Meanwhile we would like to have something to eat while we're here."

So taking a menu and their drinks they went and sat in a window seat. As they waited for their food Shirley said

"There's a girl I know who lives here, local vet. I've had to call her out more than once to put down animals that have been injured on the road. She may not be at home today but it might be worthwhile looking her up after we have had our lunch."

So an hour later they knocked on the door of Cathy's cottage and were both pleased and surprised to find her at home. With a warm smile she asked them in and after a brief girly catch-up Shirley explained why they were there.

"I'm sorry I can't help you. I was working until late that afternoon, an operation on a Labrador dog. It took a lot longer than I had anticipated and I didn't get home until half past seven."

37

"I understand that Mark Bosworth was not exactly a popular man. I have a feeling that that fact will mean that people are less likely to help me?"

"You could be right. Also people will be careful not to say anything too derogatory about the man. He may come back and on hearing what has been said, take action against them."

"Really?" said Shirley.

"He's a hard man and likes his pound of flesh."

"But how would he get to know what's been said?"

"In a village like this Sarge" interjected Newman "there's always someone who's prepared to run with the hare and hunt with the hounds. You have to be careful what you say and who you say it to. In fact it's generally best to say nothing."

"Sidney Turner the school bus driver might have seen him on his travels, he lives just opposite. He'll be home in about an hour" said Cathy. "Then there's Frank Narraway, my cousin over at Wistworthy. He's a mechanic, so he's often out and about collecting or delivering a car that he's seeing to."

"Sidney; isn't he the chap who was wrongly accused by that young girl of assaulting her on the school bus?" asked Shirley.

"That's the fellow. And he's a very reliable man. If he told you that he saw something then you can count on it as being genuine. Another man who might be able to help is Phil German, he farms the Manor Farm."

Armed with the names of those three men Shirley and Newman left Cathy and set off to question them. Neither Phil nor Sidney could shed any light on the matter. The few people that they thought they saw were just one or two locals, nothing out of the ordinary. They certainly couldn't remember seeing Mark that day at any time let alone in the evening.

So they drove out of the village, leaving the towering mass of Brown Tor on their right as they dropped down to the Redacre Brook. They crossed the bridge and turned right to follow a single track lane that ran upstream beside the brook in a pretty moorland valley. After a short while they came to a place where a small clapper bridge crossed the water, and at that point the stone walls of fields began on their side of the valley. The lane ran between these fields and the brook for several hundred yards until it ended in a tidy farm yard. Granite buildings to either side enclosed the yard with the dwelling forming a third side. The fourth side was open giving a view across the brook to a small copse of trees beyond. In front of the house was a small enclosed garden and beside it was a granite paved path leading up to the door.

Shirley and Newman climbed out of their car and looked around. To Newman it was a traditional Dartmoor farm, very like the one his parents had, if a bit tidier, and where he had grown up. While to Shirley it was a step into another world. As a town person Dartmoor was a mysterious place and this isolated habitation seemed a bit frightening.

They walked up to the door and before they had chance to knock it was opened by a small girl of about four.

"Who is it, Jasmine?" a voice from inside called.

"It's a man and a lady," said the girl, turning as she did and running back into the house.

With that, a young woman with dark, wavy, shoulder length hair came out of the kitchen to meet them. Shirley introduced herself and Newman.

"You must be Cathy's friend, I'm Linda and this little imp is my daughter Jasmine."

"Is your husband Frank at home?" asked Shirley and went on to explain the reason for their visit. As she did a van pulled into the yard and a man in a boiler suit jumped out.

"There he is, you're in luck."

When he joined them in the front hallway Shirley once again told him why they were there.

"Come in and sit down a minute" said Frank. They went into a typical farm kitchen dominated by a large wooden table at which they all sat.

"That evening, that would be the evening before Reverend Russell's funeral. Let me see now, I got home at about seven or just after. I can't recall seeing Mr Bosworth on the road, no."

"Did you see anybody suspicious or unusual?" asked Newman.

"No, can't say I did, it was just the normal crowd going home from work."

"And they would be?" asked Shirley.

"A few cars and vans and the odd bloke on a push-bike."

"Push-bike?" said Shirley, "what's that?"

"That's what we around here call a bicycle. When I was a boy they didn't have all these wonderful gears on bikes like they do nowadays. With our hills here, we spent a lot of time pushing the bike; seemed like we did that more than ride the thing." He laughed at the memory.

"Well, if you do think of anything else please let us know" said Shirley getting up from her chair to leave. Then turning to Linda she said "You have a lovely home here, though I doubt if I could live in such an out of the way place."

"You should come and visit some day, when you are off duty. We could show you around and then you might realise why we love living here."

"Thank you, I might take you up in that" and with that they were gone, heading back to the station. Though a pleasant time had been spent talking to nice people they had to admit that the afternoon had been wasted as they had learned no more of the missing man's movements on that Tuesday afternoon.

"We'll come back on Monday" said Shirley "maybe we'll have more luck then."

NINE

That evening in the pub the talk amongst the locals was naturally about the police investigating the disappearance of Mark Bosworth. One or two felt that it would be just as well if he remained disappeared but all felt sorry for his wife Hilary. For some time the conversation had been around the need to have a police search for a grown man who had gone missing. Frank Narraway said

"I would have thought that at his age he would be allowed to go off on his own, if that's what he wanted to do. If it had been a child, well that would be different."

"From what I could gather from the police sergeant" said Bob the landlord "he was supposed to be playing golf with the Assistant Chief Constable and when he didn't turn up he rang Hilary to find out why. She then said that he hadn't come home the night before and she had no idea why, or where he might be. She naturally told him that she was worried and that started it all."

"So it obviously helps if you have friends in high places." said Frank with a grin.

"People go missing every day, according to the papers" said Ben Fuller, joining in the conversation. How many cases of missing people from this village can you remember Charlie?"

Charlie, who had been sitting quietly, listening to the others talk put down his pint and said

"D'you mean people who have gone missing for a while and then come back of their own free will? Or d'you mean those who have gone and been been found by others searching for them. Or those who have disappeared and have never been heard of again?"

"Both, don't tell me that there have been several cases."

"Well, there was that girl who ran away from home; the one who falsely accused Sidney of molesting her in the school bus. But she was only gone for a day really. Caused enough fuss she did. Then there was that young chap who used to live where Cathy's sister Jenny now lives. Steve, I think he was called. He ran away to Corfu when his mum took a man friend, after her husband died. Jenny's friend John bumped into him and persuaded him to come back; although it was only for a short while. Still it did put his mum's mind to rest, and she's been out there to stay with him I understand. Just for a holiday like."

"But has there ever been a case where the person who disappeared was never found?" asked Ben.

"Yeah....come to think of it there was......a young boy, 'twas way back during the war."

"What, a local lad?" asked Frank.

"No, he was one of they evacuees, sent down from London to get away from the bombing. He had a funny name, let me think.....Zab....no Zach....that was it, Zach. Nice lad, he was a year older than me but we were in the same class, well there were only two classes in the school in those days. He lived down the old mill with the couple there. They were a strange pair and no mistake; don't know where they came from, they certainly weren't local, and they left the village shortly after the end of the war. We chillen were afraid of them, always ran when we passed the mill. I don't think Zach was very happy there. Mr and Mrs Wilson, that's what they were called. I think he

43

used to beat the boy a bit. Mind, in they days some folks was a bit heavy handed with their chillen; brought 'em up by hand, if you know what I mean. We kids always thought she was a bit of a witch, she could have been Irish, see in those days I didn't know much about accents from other regions. I suppose I would have been about ten, maybe eleven, when they left. "

"So what happened to this boy Zach?"

"Well he went missing one day, Mrs Wilson came to the school and told the teacher that he wouldn't be coming in to school that day because he had disappeared. Asked us all if we knew where he could have gone to. She didn't seem over worried about it mind. I think the police were involved, I don't really know, I was only six at the time, see. Any road, he never came back to the village; he probably wanted to go home to his mum and dad. 'Twas silly sending them down here to get away from the bombing, after all Jerry bombed Plymouth, Exeter and Newton Abbot so he was probably no worse off back home." He laughed and took another drink from his pint.

"The Wilsons weren't the only odd folks to live in the mill" said Ben. "Wasn't there some artist chap who had two women living with him living there for a while?"

"Oh, that was years later; that was in the sixties in the flower power days, they were all at it then. That was the time of free love and all that. But 'tis true, there have been some odd folks there. It's a good job young Terry has bought it, he's sensible enough. Although I reckon he'll have plenty of work to do to get it in a reasonable state; the last lot had several dogs and cats and it always looked a bit rough from the outside."

44

"Dad always told me that it was haunted" said Frank, "but that was when it was empty for a long time and he probably wanted to scare me off from going in it."

"They always say that about empty buildings, it's no more haunted than my cottage" said Charlie.

"No wonder, your missus would frighten any ghost away" said Ben.

TEN

Grace Russell had been the wife of the vicar for over fifty years. She came from a long line of vicar's wives and parochial duties were almost embedded in her genes. But for far too many years she had been seen by the villagers as 'The Vicar's Wife'. Eventually, she had decided that it was time that she was seen as Grace, a person in her own right. This had started with her rescuing a girl whom she had met in hospital while visiting a friend there. After that her self-confidence had grown and although she continued her parochial duties, helping her husband, she started several friendships in the village but particularly with other elderly ladies in the village.

She had not been to Grimstone Court since Mark and Hilary had moved in. She drove her little car up the tree-lined drive and parked outside the stone porch of the imposing house. She rang the bell and waited, looking up at the windows and wondering if she had come at a bad time. But Hilary had invited her and she felt sure that she had seen a movement in an upstairs window. Finally the huge oak door opened a little and Hilary, somewhat nervously, looked around it. She was wearing a long skirt, a cashmere cardigan with long loose sleeves and around her neck she had a fine silk scarf.

"Oh do come in Mrs Russell. I'm so sorry if I kept you waiting, this is such a big house and sometimes it takes rather a long time to get to the door."

They went into the lounge and Hilary immediately asked how Grace was managing on her own.

"Well, as a matter of fact I'm not finding it too hard. Yes...well of course I miss Quentin; the house feels very empty without him. But....there's so much to do....forms to fill in and people to see....I hardly have time to think that I'm alone. I suppose the worst is at night....I lie there thinking and there's no sound of him breathing....he didn't snore you know.....yes....I suppose that's the worst time. But that's enough about me, what about you? I hear in the village that Mark has disappeared and you've got the police out looking for him."

"Well, I didn't get them out; they came because the Assistant Chief Constable told them to."

"I say, that must have made you feel important. Have they been able to discover anything, and how and when did Mark disappear?"

Hilary told her how she had come home and found the place empty and Mark nowhere to be seen. How the next morning she had asked Paul if he knew anything and then next day of the subsequent visit by the police. All the while she seemed uncomfortable and kept glancing at the door as if expecting someone to come in. Then she said

"Let me get you a cup of tea or coffee."

"Thank you" said Grace "a cup of tea would be lovely."

While Hilary was out of the room Grace looked around her. All the furniture, the pictures, the ornaments, the curtains and the carpet spoke of luxury and money. Wealth and comfort, but not necessarily warmth and love. It was neat and tidy, like a photograph from an interior design magazine and Grace wondered why and whose idea it was that a home should be like that. She thought of her husband's study, the walls lined with bookcases full of books and church magazines. The old brown leather armchair by the fire, the arms worn almost white from years of wear. His desk, a battered old oak kneehole desk with two handles missing, where he would sit as he wrote his sermons. And the dust, she knew there was dust; she just couldn't reach it on the tops of all the books. But it all gave the room something, gave it a feeling of cosiness. It was like an old pair of shoes that were really fit only for the bin, but which were much too comfortable to part with.

Hilary came back into the room with a tray of tea things and a plate of biscuits. As she reached over to pour Grace a cup, her scarf slipped a little and Grace saw an ugly bruise on her neck. As they sat talking and drinking their tea Grace watched her carefully. She had asked why Mark had decided to move to the village and whether Hilary liked it. It was obvious that Mark had moved there from the London area to get away from the 'rat race'. But it was so peaceful and quiet, and that was what Hilary said that she liked most.

"And did you do the décor here; did you design the layout and dressing of this beautiful room?"

"No it was Mark's idea" she said "it isn't really my sort of room; it's a bit too formal for me." As she said this she looked anxiously at the door again, almost as if she had said something she shouldn't have and was afraid lest someone was listening and heard what she said.

"Well....yes....it is very impressive even if it is a little formal....but very comfortable" said Grace with a smile. Hilary sat back in her chair; the friendliness and the kindness of her guest making her feel more relaxed. Resting her elbows on the arms of her chair she clasped her hands together.

"It is so nice of you to call, so nice to have someone other than Mark's business acquaintances to talk to. With them I always feel I have to be on my best behaviour; it's as though I'm on show. I feel I can be myself with you, and I've only really known you properly for a few minutes."

"I'm so glad that you feel that way Mrs Bosworth."

"Oh please, you must call me Hilary, please."

"Very well, but only if you agree to call me Grace."

"Of course" she paused and then laughing said "We must sound like a couple of old maids from a Victorian drama saying 'you must call me Hilary'....."

She giggled, raising her hands to her mouth and as she did so the sleeves of her cardigan slipped down towards her elbows and Grace saw angry bruise marks just above each of her wrists; marks that were beginning to fade but bruise marks and no mistake. Though concerned at the sight of so many bruises now was not the time to make any mention of them, so she just smiled and nodded. They carried on talking, reminiscing about the days when as children they always had to call their elders by their formal names. Then the talk moved on to their school days and although there was a considerable difference in their ages they found many aspects of their early lives similar. Eventually Hilary said

"This has been nice Grace, so very nice, do please call again, Mark is often away all day on some business thing or other and I have so enjoyed your company."

"Its nice of you to say so, I'll be happy to call again at any time. We all need someone to talk to from time to time, someone with whom to share a confidence. Mmm....yes.....well....perhaps its time I was going, do let me know if and when there's any news of your husband."

With that she struggled to get out of the deep comfy armchair and as Hilary rose from hers she said

"I'm sure that you will soon have him back here again."

She walked out to her car and as she drove away thought to herself 'That house is cold, emotionally cold; there's no love there, not for that poor girl anyway. For her I fear that there's only pain'.

ELEVEN

Terry Cooper was a plumber. When he left school at the age of sixteen he had joined the local builders and worked for them for several years, learning a lot of general building skills as he went. He had married young and had a son and then he had seen an opportunity to advance himself by joining a national firm and specialising in plumbing. The training had meant being away from home a lot and during that time his wife had found herself some company with another boyfriend or two.

Once his training was over he returned home, but he found that the spark had gone out of his marriage. Thinking that he should give her a bit more freedom from looking after their baby son he took to staying home baby minding while she went out for the odd evening for a drink with her friends He was at home on one such a night, looking after the baby while she was out, supposedly with a group of girls on a hen night. In actual fact she was in pub in a nearby village with another man. A friend had seen this and, knowing that it was not the first time she had carried on in this way, had rung Terry and told him what was going on. Terry went down to the pub and had a row with her. He said

"You should be ashamed of yourself; you should be at home helping to look after our son." To which she had replied

"What d'you mean, our son? He's not our son; leastways you're not his father." And she had laughed at him and turned to her new friend for support. Terry said no more, he left the pub and went home. There, he took all her things out of the wardrobe and chest of

51

drawers and where ever else he could find them, and put them into black bin liners. Then he put the baby in its pram and into his van, together with all her things, and drove back to the pub. He walked in and told her that he never wanted to see her again and that all her belongings, including the baby, were outside for her and her new boyfriend. It caused quite a stir and was the talk of the village for several days.

But the whole sad affair had shattered Terry's confidence and made him rather bitter where women were concerned, so it wasn't surprising that he had remained single ever since. He had concentrated his life on work, which he did very well, and now at thirty two he had a good little business and was in demand locally.

He had just finished servicing the central heating system in the Old Rectory for Giles and Nancy Cameron-Hyde. As he carried his bag of tools out to his van Nancy called after him

"You'll come in for a cuppa before you go."

He turned, smiling and said thanks and that he would be in in a minute or two. He was a big man, six feet four, though at fifteen stone not overweight. At twenty five he had started to go bald and now he cut what hair he had very short. It gave him the look of a prize fighter, though he was in fact the most gentle of men.

He went back into the house and sat at the kitchen table where Nancy had a large pot of coffee and a plate of ginger cake.

"When do you move into your new home?" asked Nancy.

"Soon I hope, I got the keys yesterday. It's going to need a bit of work done on it, but all I can do at the moment is give it a good clean, and there's a lot of that needed."

"Why don't you ask Lisa to give you a hand?"

Lisa had a small cleaning business, going around several of the houses locally cleaning and doing other helpful jobs for those less able. She rode everywhere on a bicycle with a small trailer behind it containing the necessary tools and equipment for her work. At that moment she had just finished cleaning the downstairs rooms for Nancy and walked into the kitchen as if on cue. Jerry looked up as she came in and saw a short woman of about thirty with short dark hair cut like a boy. Her face was expressionless, almost severe. Despite the time of year she was dressed in shorts and a sweat-shirt and looked a picture of health and fitness with her athletic figure. Though he knew of her and had seen her riding around the area on her bicycle he had never met her socially.

"Terry hopes to move into his new home soon and needs to give it a good clean before he does. I suggested that he might ask you to help with the cleaning. What d'you say?"

"Yes, I probably could, I'd need to look at it first, when could we do that?" she asked, turning towards Jerry.

"Well, I'm free after lunch" he said. "If we could meet there you could see what is needed and tell me if you want to do it. It's not a big property but it's old and needs a good clean."

"Fine, I'm not doing anything until four. Remind me where your new place is."

"It's the Old Mill down below Home Farm."

"Right, I'll see you there."

The Old Mill had not worked for a hundred and fifty years. The leat that had brought water to power the wheel was dry and overgrown with small trees, and the wheel itself had long since collapsed and been burned. Inside, the mill itself was empty; all the old milling gear like the wheel had gone. But Terry considered that it would make a very useful workshop and store.

The living quarters consisted of two reasonable sized rooms. In the kitchen was an old solid fuel stove, a Belfast sink stood under the window and there was room for a large table. The other room downstairs had a nineteen-fifty's tiled Devon grate that had been put into the old hearth fireplace. Behind a door, as in many a Dartmoor cottage, was the staircase that led upstairs. There, what had originally been two rooms was now three; one big bedroom, the other having been divided into a small room and an even smaller shower room.

"Are you going to do much before you move in?" asked Lisa.

"All I need to do is upgrade the plumbing which I should be able to do in the next couple of days. There's a lot more I wanted to do, like rip out that modern fire place, expose the old hearth and put a wood burner in, but thanks to Mr 'High and Mighty' Bosworth I'm a bit short of cash so that will have to wait."

"What did he have to do with it?"

"Oh, it's a long story....."

"So, tell me. I've heard that Bosworth has a habit of upsetting people, how did he upset you?"

"Well, shortly after he moved in to Grimstone Court he called me one night to do what he called an emergency repair job. It was eleven o'clock at night and I didn't really want to turn out, but he was new to the village and seemed to have plenty of money and I thought it would be silly to turn him down. Well the job wasn't an emergency at all, and could have been left until the next morning. So when I put in the bill I added fifty pounds for 'late call out charge'. He didn't seem to object and paid me by cheque, although he did say that he noted I had added the extra sum.

Then when this place came up at auction it seemed just the place for me. I set myself a top figure that I would go to, which would have left me about ten thousand for repairs and renovations. There were only three people bidding and my last bid seemed to have got it. The auctioneer said 'Going, going....' and then Bosworth said a figure five thousand more than my bid. You can imagine the auctioneer was surprised and said 'Did you say...?'Well, I still had a bit to spare and I thought I can go on, but it will mean that I won't be able to do all the renovations just yet. So I put in another bid of five hundred pounds more. Again nobody bid against me and again the auctioneer got as far as "Going, going....' and again Bosworth bid another five thousand more. I was devastated, he didn't want or need the property, he was just showing off that he has plenty of money and can get whatever he wants. Well, I decided to go once more. It would leave me with virtually nothing to spare but I had to try. After all, if he did want this place he would bid again and I would have made him pay a bit more for it. I couldn't afford to go any higher. If he didn't want it, well I would have it although at a higher price than I really wanted to pay. So I bid another five hundred and that was it, end of story, at least end of auction. I got it and here we are. As I walked out of the auction room I met Bosworth who was obviously waiting for me. He had a big smile on his face and said to me

"That's what I call a 'late call out charge'".

"He didn't; the bastard. You mean to tell me he made you pay an extra ten thousand pounds to pay you back for charging him fifty pounds for turning out at eleven o'clock at night. Well, you must have felt like killing him, I know I would."

"That's the sort of guy he is. But now I hear he's disappeared."

"Yes, and if you're lucky he may never return, who knows. Anyway, I'll certainly give you a hand with the cleaning. Just let me know when you are ready. I can also give you a hand with moving in if you like."

"Sounds great, I'll give you a call tomorrow to fix a day and time. I will have done some of the work by then and will know better where I am."

With that he walked with Lisa to the door. She turned and looking back at him smiled and for a moment it felt as though his heart had stopped. Her stern, expressionless face had been transformed into one of amazing beauty by her wonderful warm smile. He stood transfixed, not breathing. Then with a wave she mounted her bicycle and rode off up the hill towards the village.

TWELVE

When Shirley got in to work on Monday she found two messages waiting for her. The first was from Mick Cribbett to say that he had some information for her regarding Mark Bosworth. He said that he wasn't sure if it was important, but that he would be at the riding stables that morning. The second message was from Beatie Silverton, the district nurse which just said that she would be at home in her cottage next to the Old Smithy Café until midday.

So, having checked with Chief Inspector Collins she and Newman left for the village. It was a rather cold dull day and as the drove up onto the moor they met a fine drizzle that even though they were in the comfort of a car seemed to chill them.

"Different world up here Sarge, my folks always said that it's one coat different up on the moor, and two coats on the high moor where they run their sheep during the summer."

Shirley leant over and turned up the heater a little and then said

"We'll visit the district nurse first and then go on down to the stables."

They stopped in the centre of the village as before, and walked the few steps to Beatie's cottage. The door was opened to them by a young woman with a trim figure and chestnut hair tied back in a pony tail. She was wearing a pale blue nurse's uniform and in answer to her question Shirley explained who they were and why they were in the village making enquiries.

"Do come in, it's miserable out today. I didn't know when to expect you after leaving that message.

When I saw Bob in the pub the other day he said that you hoped someone might have some information regarding the disappearance of Mark Bosworth, so that's why I called."

They followed her into a cosy sitting room that was furnished with a small cottage style settee and chairs to match. Prints on the wall depicted scenes of Dartmoor and over the fireplace was a painting of a ranch in California. Beatie asked them to sit and offered them tea or coffee.

"Coffee would be nice" said Newman, looking with a questioning glance at Shirley.

"Yes, if its no trouble" said Shirley, "black for me please."

When she came back into the room with mugs of coffee they all sat down and Shirley said

"We need to find out, if we can, what Mark Bosworth was doing on Tuesday afternoon. We know that he left home on business that morning. His wife Hilary left home that afternoon, she was visiting her mother, and he hadn't returned home by the time she left at four o'clock. When she returned at half past eight his Range Rover was parked outside but he wasn't at home and he hasn't been seen since. Not only that but all attempts to contact him have failed."

"I see...well, I was driving home, I'm not sure exactly what the time was but it was just getting dark. You know, that awkward time when it's between lights and you have to switch on your headlights but they don't really seem to help. I wasn't far from here when I saw Mr Bosworth's Range Rover coming toward me. He wasn't that close, but I still thought that he was taking a bit of a chance pulling across the road in front of me to turn right into the lane that leads up to his place."

"So how far away was he when this happened?" asked Newman.

"Probably fifty yards, but it felt nearer because of the fading light. I was driving towards the west and there had been a very impressive sunset. That had passed, and the sky was nearly dark but my dipped headlights didn't help a lot."

"Did you definitely see Mr Bosworth driving the car?" asked Shirley.

"No, but then how often even in broad daylight can you see who's driving a car? It's either too dark in the car or the windscreen reflects the sky or something. All I know is that it was Mark Bosworth's car."

"You can be sure of that?" asked Shirley.

"Oh yes, he's the only person around here with a brand new Range Rover. Besides, up here we get to know most of the vehicles belonging to the locals."

"I know what you mean" said Newman. "My parents farm on the other side of the moor and they always know whose vehicle it is that goes by, sometimes just by the sound of it."

"Well" said Shirley "thank you very much for that. It seems that we can assume that Mr Bosworth arrived home just after dark, which would be about two hours before his wife got home. OK, thanks for the coffee; we'll be on our way now. We've got to see Mr Cribbett; apparently he's at the stables this morning."

"Yes, he's there every other Monday. My sister runs the stables and he sees to all their shoeing needs."

"Oh right, this is a real country community" said Shirley with a smile.

"Oh yes, we all know each other here, and each other's business, or think we do" said Beatie with a laugh.

Back in the car Newman said

"Well, we know what time it was when he got home. He had plenty of time to meet up with someone; some person who gave him a lift and took him off to his secret destination."

"Yes, but I still think he would have changed out of the clothes he had been wearing all day if he was going off with a business acquaintance or a girl friend or whatever. Mrs Bosworth is sure that he hadn't changed, and she seemed to be in charge of his wardrobe."

"I don't know about in charge of it Sarge, to me it sounds like she was expected to be his valet."

"Yes theirs is a strange relationship and no mistake."

They drove down to the stables and into the yard. Two lines of white-washed horse-boxes with neatly stained stable doors faced each other giving the impression of a well run establishment. They parked beside an aged Land Rover and got out. A door marked office was nearby and as they went toward it, it opened and they were met by a young lady. She looked the typical horse lover in jodhpurs, boots and gaiters, and a pale blue jumper with the name of the stables embroidered on it. Her blond hair was cut short giving her a youthful appearance but her hand shake as she welcomed them was confident and assured.

"Hi, I'm Pippa. I believe you've come to see Mick, he won't be long, he's just finishing the last one."

"You obviously know why we are here" said Shirley as she introduced herself and Newman. "Did you by any chance see Mr Bosworth on Tuesday afternoon?"

"No I didn't. Is it true that he's just disappeared, gone off without telling his wife or anyone where he was going or why?"

"That's how it seems at the moment."

"Has he run off with a mistress or something, or done a Reggie Perrin and just walked out of life?"

"We really don't know, but any information may help us to find out what has happened."

At that moment, Mick came over to meet them from the far corner of the yard and Pippa suggested that they go indoors. Although it was sheltered in the yard it was not very warm. They went through a busy tack room with saddles lined up on racks and bridles hanging from hooks below them. The smell of well soaped leather was strong and everywhere was neat and tidy and well cared for. Beyond the tack room was the office with a well worn desk and several chairs. This room was not nearly as tidy as the other; papers of all kinds were strewn over the desk top showing that Pippa was more interested in the horses than the paper work.

Shirley repeated her question to Mick and after a slight pause he said

"Yes I saw him on Tuesday, late afternoon it was. I had just pulled off the road into my turning. I got out to open the gate, drove through and when I got out again to shut the gate I saw him. He was walking down through that field of his where he's going to build his emporium. The sun was lighting up the beech trees at the top of the field, beautiful 'twas; looked just like they was on fire. I might not have seen him as he was in the shade, but his white shirt and pale face caught my eye."

"Did you see anything else, his Range Rover for instance?" asked Shirley.

"No, you can't see much down at the bottom of that field and in the lane. The bushes and the remains of the old buildings screen it like."

"And you couldn't tell what he was doing there?" said Newman.

"No; well I wasn't bothered really, I was going home for my tea. He was just walking down over his field; probably thinking of what he was going to do with it now that he's got permission to build there, and what it will look like."

"From your tone of voice it sounds as though you are not in favour of his plans."

"I don't think that many people around here are."

"Would you care to elaborate on that?" asked Shirley. Mick looked straight at her with the beginnings of a smile on his face and said one word

"No."

Shirley looked back at him and she also started to smile.

"Very well, Mr Cribbett, thank you for your time and for the information you've given us. We may need to speak to you again some time, if that's alright."

"Fine".

The two officers got up and after shaking hands all round made their way out to their car.

"Well we seem to know what Mr Bosworth was doing just before he went home, but not much more" said Newman.

"It certainly is a funny business and no mistake."

THIRTEEN

As they drove back to the station Shirley and Newman went back over all they knew of the case. Mark Bosworth was by no means a popular man, as far as his neighbours were concerned. Did this feeling extend to his business partners and competitors? From the information they had gleaned from Paul, his PA, Mark was equally hard in his business dealings. But like so many of those they had interviewed, Paul was very careful not to say too much about his employer. It was as though everyone in the village was a little scared of Mark and didn't want to say anything too strongly against him. As if they feared that when he returned he might in someway take his revenge on them.

"Do we know exactly what his business is?" asked Shirley.

"Well, he has a small plant bottling spring water from his estate. Also it seems that he has a lot of property, certainly more than one block of flats" said Newman. "Then he has an import business, general fancy goods as I understand it."

"That could be perfectly innocent, or it could cover a multitude of dodgy or even illegal items coming into the country, couldn't it?"

"Yes Sarge. The other enterprise that he started just over a year ago is one of those 'pay-day' loan companies."

"What are they?"

"They're on-line loans that are intended to be for a very short period. You borrow a hundred pounds just to tide you over until next pay day. The trouble is that the sort of people who go in for such loans are very often people who can't get a loan any other way. For the first week or two, leading up to the next pay day, the interest is modest. But if you go beyond that period the rate goes up tremendously and is soon unaffordable. It often ends up with people not being able to pay their rent, their fuel bills etcetera. The only ones to win are those lending the money."

"Isn't that always the way. Does he have any other lines that you know of?"

"Probably, but that's all that Paul has told me about. I can't say that I entirely trust the man; he could well be hiding something. Once we're back at the station I hope to find news of his credit card spending since he disappeared."

"That's assuming that he used his card" said Shirley. "I'm still not convinced that he left voluntarily."

"You think he could have been kidnapped Sarge?"

"I don't know; it just doesn't seem to add up. Here we have a man who has just won his appeal to go ahead with his new building. He's probably very pleased to have won; he sounds that sort of a man. But he leaves his house and his wife with no warning and no explanation of any kind, either to her or his PA. He hasn't changed his clothes or locked his precious gun away in its gun cupboard. He's left no note, which most people would do even if they had to leave in a hurry. No, I can't help feeling that Mr Mark Bosworth left here on Tuesday night against his will."

They drove on in silent thought and after they got back to the station they found, as Shirley had predicted, that Mark's card had not been used since Monday afternoon when he had bought a lunch for two in a pub outside Exeter. Newman immediately

65

rang Paul to find out with whom Mark had lunched that day. After a short wait Paul was able to tell him that it was an old friend and business acquaintance of Mark's and that he was a man who ran a debt recovery service.

"Well Sarge, he was obviously a friend, not the sort to kidnap Mark."

"No, but I wonder....these debt collectors can be pretty frightening; especially if they come and threaten to take away your goods and even the roof over your head. Could one of those poor unfortunates who took out a pay day loan with Mark's company have got into serious trouble and....?"

"What Sarge..... Come out and kidnapped him?"

"Actually, I was thinking worse than that."

"But there's no sign of violence, either in the Range Rover or outside it. If he left, surely it was because he wanted to. If he had been forced or frightened into going I'm sure he would have left, or at least tried to leave, some sign. Scrape marks in the gravel or something perhaps. And if he was under threat, why didn't he use his gun to frighten off those threatening him? No, I still think he's done a runner with his girl friend. Mark Bosworth is a fighter, if someone was trying to beat him or better him in any way he would fight back and then stand up and tell the world about it."

"Yes and as you say he's a fighter. If he wanted to start a relationship with a new girl friend, as you put it, he would not have skulked away like a thief in the night. He would have told Hilary that it was time she left and just kicked her out. It's obvious to me that she's scared stiff of the man, though quite why

I'm not sure. Did you find out if the local hospitals have admitted him?"

"No luck there Sarge. I did wonder whether I ought to ask the Dartmoor rescue group to keep an eye out for him, you know, when they are out training and that, but I don't think they will be able to help us. Mark Bosworth preferred to look at the moor through the window of his car; he wasn't one for putting his boots on and going out into it. Proper townie he is."

"But he's got his pheasant shoot."

"Yeah, but that's just him playing at being country gentry, that's how he got in with ACC Cannon and with a whole lot more influential people I'll be bound. It's how he lives, how he gets position and influence. He befriends the rich and famous; he's not the first to do it."

"Well, we'll just have to go through those papers Paul gave you and see if there's anything or anybody that we've overlooked so far."

FOURTEEN

Charlie was in his potting shed at the bottom of his garden planting hyacinth bulbs ready for Christmas. He heard the phone ringing and looked up the path towards the back door. He knew that he would never get indoors before whoever it was had rung off, so he just said to himself

'If 'tis important, they'll ring back' and went on with his potting. When he finished and had put the bowls of planted bulbs in the dark he went up the path and indoors for his lunch. Sal and Edna had gone into town on the bus for the day, so after a good wash Charlie had to get his own lunch. Well not really, Sal had left some bread and cheese covered with a cloth on the kitchen table and a jar of her homemade runner bean chutney. As he sat down a knock came to the door and grumbling to himself he got up again and went to see who it could be; it was Grace.

"Oh, I'm so sorry to trouble you" she said, looking up at Charlie "I hope I haven't interrupted your lunch.....mm....yes well.... I've brought a couple of magazines for Sal, there are some recipes she was interested in."

"Will you come in? Sal's not here, she's gone to town with Edna"

"Oh no no......I'll leave you to your lunch....I'm sure I can catch Sal later."

With that she was gone, scuttling almost mouse-like back to her car, a small lady who seemed to care nothing for herself and could always find time to think of others.

Charlie walked back to his lunch deep in thought. How much longer could Grace find the strength to carry on? He realized that it was a front she put on, that by helping others she was able to forget her own pain, but eventually......His thoughts raced on, thoughts of lonely people who had lost a loved one, and how difficult it must be for them to cope. He thought of old friends who, once their partner had gone, seemingly couldn't live without them and had very soon died as well. And then it came to him. That which had bothered him at the funeral and had been worrying him on and off ever since, at last he knew what it was. Grace would eventually be buried with her husband as was only right. It was a double grave.... but that was the point....it wasn't......that was what had been worrying him. He decided to eat his lunch and then go and have a word with Cecil Webber, the undertaker.

Cecil lived with his wife Betty in a house just outside the village. They were a remarkable couple, well into their eighties. She was crippled up with arthritis and he was really too old to continue his profession. But he saw it as providing a service for his departed friends and their surviving relatives and would probably continue until it was his turn to be buried.

Charlie had been acting as one of his pall-bearers for more years than he cared to remember, and he and Cecil were old friends.

"Come in, come in Charlie, come in and sit down. What brings you here? Sal's alright I hope."

"Oh don't get excited, I'm not bringing you any business today." They both laughed at their rather macabre sense of humour, knowing full well that they were good enough friends to be able to joke about almost anything, including death. Then they went into

Cecil's kitchen and sat on the two wooden chairs by the Rayburn stove.

"No, there's been something bothering me ever since Reverend Russell's funeral and for the life of me I haven't been able to think what it was. It came to me just now when Grace called and I felt I had to come and see you."

"So, what's the problem?"

"Well, s'far as I can work it out, the grave wasn't deep enough."

"Of course it was, what ever makes you think that."

"Well, you know how I've always been on at you to get new webbing straps, 'cos yours are too short. Every time we have to lower someone into a double grave we gets right to the end of the straps, right?"

"Yes, I know you grumble about it, but those straps are fine, they'll last longer that I will."

"Yes, but that don't alter the fact that they are short, right?"

"Yes."

"Well, 'tother day when we lowered the coffin it came to rest and I still had at least a foot of strap in my hand. I expect it was just the same for Ben who was opposite me."

"So what is it you're trying to say Charlie?"

"Well, I know you had to get a man from the council to dig the grave, 'cos young Dick who usually does it is away. All I'm asking is did he take out a double grave? If not, what's going to happen when Grace goes?"

The question hung in the air for a while as Cecil thought about it. Then with a frown on his face he looked at Charlie and said

"It definitely was a double grave; I went there on the Tuesday afternoon and measured it."

"With those drain rods of yours" said Charlie with a laugh.

"They're not drain rods, they're measuring rods. Just 'cos they screw together don't make them drain rods."

"And 'twas definitely deep enough?"

"Oh yes, 'twas a full eight feet. No doubt about it. Like you, I had to be sure, being as it wasn't Dick as dug it like."

For several minutes the two old men sat deep in silent thought. Finally Charlie said

"Well, there was something in that grave that stopped the coffin going down to the full depth. I know, 'cos I still had plenty of webbing strap in my hand."

"What d'you think it could have been?"

"I've no idea, I'll have a word with Ben, he may have know. In fact I'll see him tonight at darts, he owes me a pint from last time."

He got up to leave and as he got to the door he turned and said to Cecil

"Silly isn't it, it's been worrying me ever since the funeral that something wasn't right, but I couldn't think what it was. Trouble is, now that I know what 'twas....it's still a worry, if not more so."

But Ben couldn't add anything to solve the mystery of the shallow grave, although he agreed that he also had a fair length of strap in his hand when the coffin came to rest. All he did was to make light of the matter, leg pulling Charlie most of the evening about it. In fact, his final shot as Charlie was leaving to go home that night was to say

"I know what was in that grave Charlie."

"What?" said Charlie, expecting another silly and supposedly amusing reply.

"I reckon that missing chap Mark Bosworth is hiding in there."

FIFTEEN

Grace was finding it hard. The brave face that she put on when in company slipped once she was at home and alone. She had tried to work out just what it was that she was missing. Oh of course she knew that she was missing Quentin, it would have been hard not to after being his wife for over fifty years. She couldn't help but miss the closeness, turning over in bed at night and just knowing that he was there beside her. His touch when they passed in the corridor, his call of 'Grace dear' from the next room. But what in particular did she miss? Getting his meals? But that was for the both of them. Sorting out his paper work when he got it in a muddle, as he sometimes did? It wasn't as though they had done a lot of things together as a couple. He had had his job, and where she could she had helped with it. But most of her time had been spent doing her own things to help in the community.

It was, she realized, all the little things that she missed. Things she had already thought of and more. Like when she walked into his study he always used to be there, slumped in his old leather armchair with a book. As she entered he would look up and give her a smile and a nod before returning to his book or whatever it was that had his attention. And she hadn't realized that he had made her an early morning cup of tea every day for, who knows how many years. Now she had to make it for herself, or go without. When they sat down for a cooked meal he would always serve her, never the other way around. Yes, it was the little things.

They hadn't been able to have children. Both would have liked to have been parents, but she had a niece, a nephew and several grand nephews and nieces. She was also god-mother to a number of local children and although most of them had moved away she kept in contact with them at least once each year and followed their progress in life. Although she didn't have the hands on experience of bringing up a family of her own, she felt that sometimes, seeing things from outside and from a different perspective, she was able to make a valid contribution and help families with their problems.

For too many years she had felt that she was looked upon as just the vicar's wife, almost like an appendage. She had even felt at times a little jealous of the attention that his flock received. But she knew very well that it was she who was putting herself in the position of vicar's wife, not he.

And then about five years ago she had found herself. It had started with the girl in hospital and her boyfriend, for whom she had found a home and a job in the village. After that she found that she could do all the things that Quentin did to help others, but on her own rather than as his little helper. And the expertise she had gained, without any conscious effort, had been from watching him. No doubt it was what he had wanted for her all along. How sad it would have been if she had never found herself as she had done. She would still have been the vicar's wife; well no.......even worse.....the vicar's widow.

And now she was on her own. So was Hilary, sad unhappy Hilary. Except that in Hilary's case she didn't know when her man was coming home, or worse still, if he was coming home. Grace thought back to a dreadful case of a woman in the nearby village whose husband was a helicopter pilot. His job had been to service the oil rigs out in the North Sea.

One day his plane went down and was lost. Wreckage was never found and that poor woman was left in a sort of limbo land waiting all of seven years for her husband to be declared officially dead. How awful it would be if Hilary had to wait that long.

Then the other matter that concerned her greatly was the obvious fact that Mark was a violent man and, judging by the bruises on Hilary's arms and neck, a wife beater. All the time that Grace had been in the house, Hilary had been on tenter hooks watching in case Mark came in. She wanted him back because she was lost without him, and yet......

"Oh Quentin, why did you have to go....I need you now....I need to help this poor woman and I need you to show me how. You were always so good at helping others....but you could do it....sort of quietly.....without them realizing that you were doing it."

She slumped down in his old armchair and looking around the room cried softly to herself. The warm familiar surroundings with the peaceful air that had always been a feature of the room eventually calmed her. She wiped her eyes and smiled, beginning to feel his presence near her. Finally she stood up and straightened the cushion in the chair, then with one last look around the room she walked to the door and turned.

"Thank you Dear" she said "I think I know what to do now."

SIXTEEN

Charlie had heard Sal's account of her day in town with Edna. Well, he had heard, but not really listened. Most of the talk was about those whom Sal had met that day and gossip about them and their families. It really didn't interest him greatly and his mind was elsewhere.

That night he slept soundly as he usually did, but woke suddenly out of a vivid dream. Not accustomed to dreaming he remembered it in every detail. He had been walking across the churchyard, carrying the webbing straps in his hand and calling to Cecil who was walking in front of him. All of a sudden a shot rang out, a shot that was loud and woke him up. Was the noise of the shot real, or in his dream? It certainly had been particularly loud and almost a double bang. Like 'b-bang'. It was getting light, then carefully so as not to disturb Sal, he got out of bed and taking his clothes from the chair by the bed made his way downstairs.

For a long time he sat in the kitchen with a cup of tea thinking. Was he making a mountain out of a molehill? Could what he had been thinking about for the last fifteen hours or more be possible? It seemed more like something off the telly. Should he contact that nice Sergeant Ashton? Would he be just wasting her time? He still had her card that she had left in the pub. Yes, he'd give her a ring later and if she didn't want to hear what he had to say......well......he wouldn't have to tell her, would he?

But Shirley Ashton did want to hear what he had to say. After all she had precious little else to go on in her search for Mark Bosworth.

SEVENTEEN

Sal and Edna were just leaving to go to the weekly coffee morning in the village hall when DS Shirley Ashton and DC Newman Chaffe arrived the next morning. They hesitated for several minutes, hoping to be involved and find out a bit more juicy gossip to pass on to their friends. But Charlie quietly but firmly sent them on their way.

"He'll tell me all about it later" said Sal to her friend in a conspiratorial tone as they walked across the green to the hall.

"What's it all about, d'you know?"

"No idea, he just told me that he had something to pass on to the police and that he couldn't say what 'twas. When I asked him why he couldn't tell me, he said 'twas because it might be a load of nonsense and my head was full of that sort of stuff already."

"Cheeky toad" said Edna, laughing and nudging Sal. "He's got you weighed up hasn't he?" And giggling happily they went on their way.

Meanwhile Charlie had invited Shirley and Newman in and shown them into the sitting room. Like many a Dartmoor cottage front room it was small and cosy. A two-seater settee was under the window with beside it in the corner next to the fireplace a new television set. Two recliner armchairs faced the fire and the TV and were obviously where Sal and Charlie usually sat. There were several pictures around the walls, mostly Victorian scenes of Dartmoor seen through romantic eyes, and one very good painting by F.J.Widgery over the fireplace. This last had a small brass plaque attached to the frame with Charlie's name and a date on it. Shirley thought it was probably a retirement gift or something of the sort. Pointing to the settee he asked them to sit. He then went into the kitchen and put on the kettle, calling over his shoulder as he did so that he was making tea or coffee and which would they prefer. With a tray of drinks on the low coffee table in the middle of the room he sat back and said

"I hope I haven't brought you pair out here for nothing."

"I'm sure you haven't. Believe me we are no further on in our enquiries than we were last week. So anything that you can tell us may be of use."

"Well it started at the funeral see..."

"The late vicar's funeral?" asked Newman.

"Yes.'Twas a big affair, well he was a well liked and respected man. So is his wife... well...widow I suppose. Any road, it had to be done proper and Cecil the undertaker had asked me to be one of the bearers. He is really retired, fact he retired some time ago. But he'd worked with the vicar so many times in the past and felt that he wanted to see him off. And I would have been vexed if he hadn't asked, 'cos I've been bearer for him many, many times over the last thirty years or so. It all went well, beautiful service and Sir Harold gave a nice eulogy. But when we got back to the hall for the bun fight afterwards, I kept thinking that something was wrong. Something kept niggling in my mind but I just could not think what.

Well yesterday, Grace, that's the vicar's widow, came here with a magazine for Sal. She's wonderful; a little old lady who's just lost the man she was married to for all those years and yet all she seems to think about is helping other folks. I couldn't help but marvel at her. Then for some reason I thought 'how long is she going to last?' You know how it can be sometimes, you get these devoted couples. One dies and the other soon passes away, like they just can't live without each other. And I thought 'well she'll be in with him again' because 'twas a double grave and that see. And then it hit me, what had been worrying me after the funeral."

"What exactly was that?" asked Shirley.

"The grave wasn't deep enough. You see, for a double grave it has to be eight feet deep. When we get to the grave the coffin is placed on the two wooden bars that are across the grave. Then the wooden carrying handles are unclipped from the rings on the front and back of the coffin and webbing straps are put through the rings and we lower the coffin down with these straps. For years I've been moaning at Cecil that the straps are too short for a double grave; they'm only just long enough, see. Well this time, when the coffin came to rest I still had at least a foot of strap in my hands.

I thought that the grave digger had got it wrong. Dick, the local chap that usually does the grave digging is away, so the council sent out some fellows from town to do it. But when I went and saw Cecil yesterday and told him what I was thinking how the grave hadn't been dug proper depth for a double like. Well, he said that he had measured the depth of the grave and that it was correct."

"When did he measure the depth?" asked Newman.

"On the Tuesday afternoon. He has this set of rods that screw together, I call 'em drain rods and Cyril gets annoyed with me for calling them that."

"So what you are saying is that between Tuesday afternoon and midday Wednesday when you buried The Reverend Quentin Russell, somebody or something had raised the level of the bottom of the grave. Am I right?" said Shirley.

"Yes, that's about it" said Charlie.

"And what else do you think?"

"Well, you're looking for a man who's gone missing; and not to put too fine a point on it, a very unpopular man. He's a man who seemed able to do whatever he wanted and in the process rode roughshod over all those who opposed him. He is probably the most disliked man that ever came to live in this village but a man with money and power and influence. In fact, I reckon if it had been me that had gone missing you wouldn't be here looking. But Mark Bosworth knows your boss and that's why you are here, am I right?"

"I really can't comment" said Shirley.

"Alright....well....there's something else. Mick Cribbett tells me that he saw Bosworth walking down across his field at sunset on Tuesday, right?"

"Yes, he told us the same."

"At about that time I had been packing away the canes I had used to support my runner beans this year. Well, I had just come out of the shed and as I was going indoors I heard a shot, sounded like it came from Bosworth's fields and I thought that Jimmy Stapleton was out after a rabbit. One odd thing, it sounded like a double shot, like who ever was shooting had pulled both triggers. Sort of like 'b-bang' if you get my meaning. Then when I heard that Bosworth was in the field at that time....."

"I'm not quite sure that I get what it is you're trying to tell me" said Shirley. "I know Mr Bosworth was far from popular, although few people seem willing to speak out against him. Are you suggesting that he was out shooting or that the shot you heard could have been more deadly. In other words you think that maybe somebody may have killed him?"

"Could be....Correct me if I'm wrong, but as I understand it, you can't have a murder without a body.....so if no body ever turns up there's no murder, right?"

"Sort of, it doesn't always work like that."

"But if Bosworth never turns up, you'll never know if he's alive or dead. Like Lord Lucan."

"And?"

"The best place to hide an apple is in a bowl of fruit."

For several minutes nobody spoke and Charlie lay back in his chair with a questioning look on his face and a smile playing on his lips. Shirley looked across at Newman and finally said

"If I understand you rightly, what you are suggesting is going to open a right old can of worms. We will have to get a lot more evidence before we can proceed." She paused, looking at Charlie with a certain amount of admiration, yet dreading what she would have to do next.

"If you don't mind I would like you to keep this idea of yours to yourself for the time being. We certainly need to investigate it further. Meanwhile, thank you for your input. One other thing, have you any idea of the exact time that you heard this shot?"

"'T'would have been about half past six, maybe a bit before. 'Cos when I went indoors, the local weather forecast had just started."

"Thank you, six twenty five or thereabouts, that's a great help. Come on Chaffe, Mr Blundell has given us plenty to think about, we had better start acting on it." She stood up and shaking Charlie's hand led Newman out into the crisp autumn morning.

"What are we going to do now Sarge?"

"I think we ought to go and look at that field, after all that is where Mr Bosworth was last seen."

"I'll get the car then."

"No, we'll walk, it's not very far and you can explain the layout of the land as we go."

EIGHTEEN

The two police officers set off along the road leading out of the village. The churchyard with its neat stone wall was on their right and The Old Smithy Café and two other cottages, one of which the nurse lived in, were on their left. After that they were soon beyond the village, with fields on either side. A lane with a gate across it led off the road to the left.

"That's the road to Mick Cribbett's place" said Newman "you can see how he would have been able to watch Bosworth walking down across his field from there."

A field with a tidy trimmed hedge was next to the churchyard, a narrow field that stretched for several hundred yards up the slight incline ending in a group of trees.

"That's the glebe meadow" said Newman pointing across it "and at the top you can just see the roof of Grimstone Court. It's the only field left that used to be part of the Glebe Farm and is still owned by the Church."

"What's the Glebe Farm?" asked Shirley.

"The Glebe Farm was the farm that belonged to the Church. It used to form part of the vicar's stipend." At that point they turned into the lane and walked up and around the ruined buildings.

"These ruins were the farm house and its buildings. All the land from here on to the next road used to be Glebe land but is now owned by Bosworth. I can't understand why he didn't apply to renovate these buildings for his shop. I'm sure the National Park Authority would have been delighted to give him permission. It seems like he was only happy when he was upsetting people."

They walked on to the gate leading into the field and stopped. The tyre marks of a large vehicle ended in front of the gate, indicating where Mark Bosworth had parked that Tuesday evening. Three weeks of an Indian summer meant that the weather had been unusually dry and the normal autumn rains had not come and washed these marks away. Ahead of them near a big flat rock two magpies were pecking at something on the ground. Seeing Shirley and Newman they bounced across the grass and then took off to fly into the bushes a hundred yards away. Sitting high they screeched and chattered their defiance at the two intruders.

Shirley stopped by the flat rock and looked around. To her it was just a field with a number of white pegs dotted across it. Newman had looked briefly at the ruined buildings and then at the old wheelbarrow and the odds and ends beside it.

"What's that brown mark over there? Is that what those two birds were interested in?" asked Shirley.

Newman walked over and stood looking down at a large brown patch on the ground. The grass was thin and short and the dry grey soil had soaked up a lot of whatever had caused the stain. A few large maggots were wriggling into the grass at the side, probably what the magpies had been feeding on. Bending down Newman touched it with his finger and felt it to be slightly sticky.

"This is blood Sarge, a lot of blood. When my folks used to keep a pig, in the good old days when you could keep a pig and kill it at home for your own use, I remember a pool of blood just like this. We used to take the pig out into the orchard and Dad would stick it and it would bleed to death. There was always a fair drop of blood, six or seven pints I suppose. Mum used to catch a jug-full for black pudding but most of it went to waste."

"Oh my god, how disgusting, whatever did your folks want to kill a pig for?"

"To eat of course, what d'you think?"

"I think you had better go back and get the car. There are some specimen bags in there. We need a sample of that blood, if that's what it is, to take back to the lab. I can't believe that anyone has been killing a pig here, but if it turns out to be human blood....wow....Charlie Blundell could well have got the answer."

While Newman went to get the car Shirley walked back down the lane and through the gate into the glebe meadow. She looked across the short distance to the churchyard, noticing the small gate in its wall. A country person would have seen where the path led in a slight arc to this gate. Being unused to rural living she walked in a straight line towards the gate and found, when she had got about half-way, that the ground beneath her was getting soft and her heels were sinking in. In the winter months water from a small spring would have been running in a little trickle out of the ground, but now it was just damp and squidgy. She stopped and looking at her feet saw marks in the soft ground that could have been made by something that had been dragged across the field.

Back by the ruins she looked at the old wheelbarrow lying on its side and wondered if it could have made the marks in the field. But then this was the country and every cottage had a garden and most likely, every garden would have a wheelbarrow. Still it was another thing that would have to be checked.

Her phone rang, disturbing her thoughts. It was Hilary who said that there were one or two things that had come to her mind since they last spoke which she thought might be important.

"I'm in the area and I can be with you in a short while" said Shirley.

When Newman returned he collected a sample and Shirley put blue and white 'Police Don't Cross' tape across the gateway. Then they drove to Grimstone Court.

Hilary met them at the door and invited them into the large comfortable lounge. Grace was sitting there and as they entered she got up saying

"Oh....well....perhaps I had better go. I can see that you are going to be busy....you don't need me here....."

"No, please stay Grace" said Hilary. "After all it was partly your thoughts that made me realize that I had forgotten to tell Sergeant Ashton about the car."

"What about the car?" asked Shirley.

"Well you see, Mark was always very particular about where the car should be parked. He always parked it beside the house, facing outwards. He never left it in front of the house. I suppose I was too concerned as to where he was and didn't give it any thought, but for him to leave it where it is now.....well it just wasn't what Mark would do, if you see what I mean."

There was a pause as Shirley and |Newman looked at one another, Newman with a questioning look on his face as if to say 'Is this really important?' While Shirley was thinking 'Yes, I can well imagine, Mark Bosworth was very particular about everything'.

"Then there was the bunch of keys" said Hilary. "They were on the hall table. He would never leave them there; they always had to be kept in the study. In fact when I saw them on the table that evening I took them straight into the study and put them in their proper place."

'Yes' thought Shirley 'I bet you did, you didn't want Bosworth to find the keys in the wrong place. You were afraid that he would tell you off....or worse.'

"What Hilary is trying to say" said Grace leaning forward and almost getting out of her chair to get nearer to Shirley "is that it seems as though....well....it must have been either somebody other than Mark who parked the car and put the keys on the hall table. Or Mark was being forced to do so....under some form of duress....perhaps?"

"We have considered the idea of a kidnap, but if Mark had been taken by person or persons unknown, why have we not heard from them. He's a very wealthy man, as I understand, and kidnappers usually demand a ransom or some form of payment after a very short while. Otherwise what would be the point of the kidnap?" said Shirley.

"So judging by what you've just told us" said Newman "the other possibility is that the car was parked by somebody other than your husband. Who ever that was then opened the front door, put the keys on the hall table, thinking that that was a perfectly normal thing to do, and shut the door behind them as they left."

"Yes, I suppose so" said Hilary.

Newman stood up and asked Hilary

"I wonder if I might make use of your toilet?"

"Oh certainly, it's at the end of the hall. Give Paul a shout, he'll be glad to show you I'm sure."

Newman left the room and as instructed called out to Paul, who came out of the study with an enquiring look on his face. With his head sticking out on his long neck and his jacket collar raised up behind it because of his stooping posture, he looked even more like a tortoise. Newman's mind instantly went to an old TV commercial where a tortoise extolled the virtues of electric heating, and the phrase 'turn off and on-able'. However he managed to keep a straight face as Paul asked

"Yes, can I help you?"

"I was looking for the toilet..."

"It's to your left."

"Thank you, there is one other thing. Do you by any chance have a record of your boss's blood group?"

"Yes, it's in his file on the computer."

With that he went back into the study and almost immediately said

"His blood group is AB negative, which I understand is rare. He was rather proud of that fact for some reason."

"Did he give blood?"

"Yes, once a year. In fact he is due to give blood in" he paused and looked at the computer screen again "three weeks time."

"Thank you."

Newman left him in the study, and after a brief visit to the loo rejoined the others in the lounge. As he entered Grace was asking

"You still have no further news.....as to....Mark's whereabouts?"

"No, but we have just come across a new line of enquiry which may or may not prove useful. I can't say anything just now, it may lead nowhere. But you can be sure that as soon as we have anything to report I will be in touch."

They left Hilary and Grace and walked out into the autumn sunlight. Shirley went around the side of the house and stood where she imagined Bosworth would have normally parked his Range Rover. She looked down over the fields to where they had just been by the ruins and could clearly see the lane and the gate into the field with all the pegs in it.

Immediately in front of her was a small gate leading into the glebe meadow, similar to the one at the bottom of the same field that led into the churchyard. Beside it a thick thorn hedge divided the meadow from Bosworth's land, a hedge that was loaded with dark purple berries.

"What are these fruits Newman? are they damsons....good to eat?"

"No, you don't want to eat them Sarge, They're sloes, the fruit of the blackthorn, they're bitter as gall." He laughed. "The only thing you can use them for is making sloe gin."

"And this gateway, what d'you know about this?"

"There always used to be a footpath through here, a short cut to the village for the people in the cottages over there" he said pointing beyond the house. "Bosworth closed it, saying that it was never a public right of way. He was quite within his rights to do so, and I can understand him not wanting the world and his wife wandering through his garden. But he upset several people by doing so, then as I said, he seemed to take a perverse delight in upsetting folks."

"Yes, a strange man and no mistake. We need to get back to the station and get that sample off to the lab. Come on."

NINETEEN

Shirley was whacked. She walked into her flat and picked up the junk mail inside the door. Then putting her keys and her bag on the worktop in the kitchen diner she sighed and went into the bedroom. For several minutes she sat on the bed. Then she stood up, undressed and went and had a long shower. She shampooed and stood under the flow of hot water, a small stream of bubbles running off her nose and collecting in the tray around her feet. Slowly but surely the water with its warmth calmed and relaxed her exhausted body and she felt revived.

Dressed in her favourite old pair of trousers and a comfortable sweater she went back into the kitchen and looked in the fridge to see what, if anything, there was to eat. Eating in the station canteen most days meant that she didn't cook very often. However, there were three small rashers of streaky bacon, two rather sad looking mushrooms and a carton of eggs. She decided on an omelette and as she cooked it sipped a glass of white wine. Then, sitting in her favourite armchair with a cushion tray on her lap, she ate her supper.

The afternoon had not been that good, which accounted for her mood. She had reported to Mullet how they had found the stain in the field and that a sample had been taken to the lab. She had made no mention of Charlie Blundell's idea; she felt that until there was more evidence, he would probably consider it to be too much of a wild theory. However, knowing that all relevant information should be passed on and to cover her back, so to speak, she did tell him that she had heard a strange story that might be related, from one of the local inhabitants. Until more evidence turned up she felt that it was not an idea that needed to be pursued. But she assured him that if anything did turn up to validate the idea she would let him know straight away. He seemed happy with this, saying

"I leave that to you to judge Sergeant."

She then went on to relay Hilary's account of the unusual parking of Bosworth's Range Rover and its possible implication. The rest of her afternoon had been spent writing up her reports and she had been glad to leave the station and get home to her cosy little flat, her bolt hole and refuge from work.

It was a flat that she had moved into shortly after it had been built seven years ago. The décor was plain and simple, neutral colours and very few ornaments. An aunt had died and had left her a small legacy, and rather than put it in a bank she had decided to buy herself a property. 'Minimalistic', Martin called it. He was an estate agent whom she had met while working on a case and a sort of friendship had grown from then. So it wasn't really surprising that when she started looking for somewhere to live, she had called on him to find her a place. He was a few years older than her, divorced with a grown up daughter and, as one might expect for an estate agent, a very nice house. As time passed they had met occasionally, specifically when Shirley needed the specialist knowledge relating to property and property values.

But not for the first time lately she had begun to wonder for how much longer she could live the life she was leading. So far she had been happy with her life as a career woman. The job with its challenges, variety and the occasional surprise had been fulfilling. But now she found herself wondering. This particular case was going to be difficult. Maybe more than she would be happy with. Mullet was bound to put an inspector in charge of the case and if it was DI 'Storming' Norman Smith, well....he would spend most of his time in the incident room, shouting a lot and making her and Chaffe do all the work......and then he would take all the credit.

But was she ready to leave the force? Probably not, but retirement would come eventually, in fifteen years at the most, and what then?

She thought of her friend Cathy, the vet who was happily dedicated to her career, and compared herself to her. She seemed to be able to work all the hours God gave without any thought of the future. Then she was a good bit younger. And then there was Beatie, the district nurse, recently married with two grown up step-children. She had made the change, reduced her days of work and had got the work/home balance right.

She poured another glass of wine and switched on the telly, aimlessly flicking through the channels, not really seeing what was on the screen.

"Oh, sod this, I'm going to bed" she said out loud to the four walls.

But it wasn't to be a night of sleep; she tossed and turned, too many thoughts churning around in her head, too many unresolved problems.

TWENTY

The next day it all kicked off. The results came back from the lab and the news was that the sample was indeed human blood of group AB negative.

Not relishing the next few minutes, Shirley went to see Mullet and put the facts and more to him. He immediately agreed that the whole area by the ruins of the Glebe Farm should be treated as a crime scene and ordered the 'Scene Of Crime Officers' team sent in. She had wondered whether to put Charlie Blundell's theory to him because she felt sure that he would pooh-pooh it as ridiculous. So she decided that she would see if she could get one of the SOCOs boys to check the path through the glebe meadow and, if possible, the ground around the grave.

When, some time later, the results of the extensive finger-tip search of the site came back, a picture began to immerge. Beyond the large blood stain, probably caused by several pints of blood, there were several fragments of human tissue, specs of blood and woollen fibres. The wheelbarrow also had traces of blood in it, although some attempt had been made to clean it. Though not conclusive, it did appear that there were several marks in the glebe meadow which could have been made by the same wheelbarrow.

But the most conclusive piece of evidence, as Shirley saw it, was the fact that two small traces of the same type of blood were found on the grass beside the grave of The Reverend Quentin Russell. So armed with all this information Shirley went in to see Mullet again.

"Yes Ashton, what is it?"

"I hope you will bear with me Sir, what I am about to suggest might sound far fetched to some, but I am not sure that it would be wise to dismiss it as totally ridiculous."

"Well, try me."

"You may remember Sir that I mentioned that I had heard a strange story from one of the locals, a story which I felt needed more verification before we pursued it further."

"Yes."

"Well, I think that we no longer have a missing person, I think we have a murder."

"Really, and by that you mean that Mr Mark Bosworth is the victim, am I right."

"Yes Sir. As I see it he was killed near the ruins of the old Glebe Farm, which would explain the blood."

Shirley paused, watching Mullet closely, trying to judge the effect of what she had just said. He sat back in his chair, elbows on the arms of the chair, the finger-tips of his hands formed into a steeple with the index fingers touching his nose. He looked at Shirley with no expression and nodded as if to say carry on.

"Later, probably after dark, maybe even in the early hours of the morning, the body was moved in the wheelbarrow that was on the site across the adjoining field into the churchyard and deposited in the newly dug grave. It was then covered with a layer of soil. If it hadn't been for the experience of one of the pall-bearers it would have stayed there unnoticed for ever."

"I agree with you it does sound preposterous. What makes you so sure that it isn't?"

So Shirley went on to explain in detail all that Charlie had told her. How he had been worried that the grave hadn't been dug deep enough for a double grave; possibly because it had not been dug by the usual local man. Then later, when Shirley had questioned Cecil Webber the undertaker, he had assured her that the grave had been dug deep enough. He had made the point that because the grave digger was not the usual man he had measured the grave on the Tuesday afternoon to make absolutely sure that it was deep enough. She also explained that the grave would have been covered with a sheet of corrugated iron and the surrounding area, including the pile of excavated soil, would have been covered with Astra-turf.

"Several points of query Sergeant. First of all, if the body had been left for several hours where it fell, wasn't there a danger of somebody finding it? Would the murderer have taken that chance?"

"His plan to bury the body in the late vicar's grave may not have been his first intention. He may have been happy to leave it where it was to be found eventually. But remember, this is a field in the country, well out of sight of the road. It is private property, and just like a garden in a town it's not open to all and sundry to go walking in. I doubt if anyone would have gone in there for days, maybe even weeks. Country people don't go wandering in their neighbours' fields without good cause....or permission."

"Alright, what about the risk of being seen, he would have had to have a torch wouldn't he, to see what he was doing? After all, if he moved the body later, as you suggest, it would have been in the dead of night."

"I doubt if he would have needed a torch Sir. There was a full moon that night, what the locals call a 'poacher's moon'. That's to say it was misty and the light was bright but diffused casting no shadows. Good to see by, but less likely to be seen. I agree he might have needed a light to see what was going on in the grave, as far as covering the body with soil was concerned, but that light would have been in the grave and might not have shown."

"Surely the undertaker, or the man who filled in the grave after the burial, would have noticed that the pile of soil had been disturbed?" said Mullet thoughtfully, but there was a note of interest in his voice now and Shirley felt that he had begun to take her seriously.

"I thought of that Sir, but it seems that the team of men who filled in the grave were a different pair from those who dug it. As to his or her (we mustn't assume that it was a man who committed this murder) plan to bury Bosworth in another man's grave, that may well have been his intention all along. He just wanted to wait until it was dark before he did so. And as Mr Charlie Blundell suggested, like the case of Lord Lucan, if the body had never been found and there was no corpse....there's no murder."

"Clever, deviously clever, I'm beginning to think you are right about this case. But you do realize what a furore this will cause. We will have to get Home Office permission to exhume the coffin." He paused, staring out of the window for a while, deep in thought. Then he said

"Is there any way of determining if there is a corpse under the coffin before we actually dig it up? I appreciate that the small trace of blood beside the grave is fairly conclusive, however....."

"I understand that there is a gadget that is used after earthquakes to find survivors under the rubble of fallen buildings. I think it's a sort of probe with a light and a camera on the end. It must be rather like the thing that a doctor would use when doing keyhole surgery, but a bigger version."

"Well find out and get it organised. Meanwhile, you will have to get permission from the late vicar's widow. This will be a major upset for her on top of her recent bereavement. Is she likely to be difficult?"

"I don't think so Sir; she's a quiet lady but very sensible and remarkably worldly wise. She has also befriended Mrs Bosworth, the missing man's wife, so she would probably see it as helping her friend as well as helping us."

"Good, well I'll have a word with DI Smith. If you are right, and there is a body in that grave, then this becomes a murder enquiry. He will take over the case and you and Chaffe will be working under him. Right that's all."

Shirley turned and just as she was opening the door to leave Mullet said

"Good work Ashton."

TWENTY ONE

Terry was enjoying himself, he had moved into his new home and every evening, after he had made himself a bit of supper, he worked at the renovations that he had to do to bring the place up to the standard that he wanted. Lisa had been a great help, first with the cleaning and then she helped him to move his few things in. For this she had refused any payment and so he had asked her if she would like to come for dinner with him one night. He could still see, in his mind's eye, the somewhat quizzical look on her face at this suggestion.

"It's alright" he had said "I can cook; I've been looking after myself for years. Is there anything you can't eat?" To which she had replied that she could eat anything except tripe.

Now he had finished the basic alterations to the kitchen and so he felt confident that he would be able to prepare and serve a decent meal for them both. Lisa had agreed to come the next evening and he had planned a simple dinner for two. He would start with a mushroom soup, then roasted lamb chops cooked with roasted vegetables, a simple rhubarb and ginger crumble to follow and then cheese and biscuits and coffee to finish. He was getting quite excited and he realized that he was treating the forthcoming evening almost as a date. He had absolutely no idea as to Lisa's feelings for him. She was a very new friend who had been kind enough to help him. As a friend he found her good company and a good work mate. Did he want more from her, it was too early to say, maybe having dinner together might help him to decide. And what if anything did she want? He didn't even know if she was already in a relationship. Did she have a boyfriend, or maybe a girlfriend?

There wasn't going to be time to paint the walls, but as he still had to install several more cupboards he knew it would just have to wait. As to the sitting room, they would have to sit in front of the Devon grate, that reminder of a bygone age. Taking it out and cleaning up the old traditional hearth fire place would take a lot of time and would have to wait. Besides, he had plenty of firewood, and what could be nicer than sitting in front of an open fire watching the flames go up the chimney and the fox and hounds, the burning specs of soot, running up across the fire back.

TWENTY TWO

Although the two police vans had been parked well out of sight behind the ruins f the Glebe Farm, the villagers were aware of their presence soon after their arrival. Mick Cribbett saw them arrive as he was riding Osprey on the slopes of Braggator. As the figures climbed out of their vehicles and donned their protective white coverall suits he was reminded of a previous disastrous occasion, an occasion that had changed his life forever. Before Mick had returned to Devon to live at Braggator Mine he had been the Master of a Hunt in Cheshire. It was at the time when there was a great deal of anti hunt feeling, before the ban on fox hunting. Coming home late one night Mick found his house on fire. A young student had put a lighted firework through Mick's letter box. The subsequent blaze had engulfed the house in minutes and Mick's wife and young son had perished in the inferno.

After the firemen had left the police had swarmed all over the place trying to find evidence as to how the fire had started. The how had been the easy part, they had discovered chemical traces of the firework. But despite their best efforts they had been unable to find the arsonist. However, the young man had obviously been unaware of the catastrophic human damage that his prank would cause. He may not have realized that there were people in the house at the time. Once he had found out just what he had done he couldn't live with his guilt. His parents came home to find him hanging in their hall from the upstairs banister, and a suicide note in his bedroom.

So the lives of two families had been blighted and changed forever.

Mick rode home deep in thought, he recalled spotting Mark Bosworth walking down through the field. The Sergeant had told him that he was, as far as the village was concerned, the last person to have seen him before he disappeared. And now the police were searching the area.

What goes on in a small community is rarely a secret for long. And if the exact reason for the occurrence is not known, well, somebody will have a bright idea and a rumour will get started that will do until the truth is known. Charlie's nephew Jim, who was married to Pippa, took a delight in leg pulling Sal and Edna, largely because he knew how they loved to gossip. He had been in the shop that morning to get his paper and overheard the two women speculating on the reason for there being so many policemen in the village. As he left the counter he dropped the remark

"Looked a bit like the bomb squad to me." And winking at John Hunt, who ran the post office and general stores, he left and went on his way. This probably explained why for the next few hours many thought that there was an unexploded bomb in Mark Bosworth's field. In a way it helped the police because it kept the curious from getting too close and in their way.

"I can't understand why anybody would put a bomb in Bosworth's field, 'tisn't like he's put up his building yet. There's nothing to blow up, is there?" said Edna as she and Sal walked back from the shop to stand outside her house.

"I don't suppose it's in the field at all. It's probably in the ruins of the old buildings."

101

"Why would there be a bomb there, who would want to blow up a ruin?"

"During the war the army commandeered Glebe Farm. They might have left something there and it's turned up now. That's the only thing I can think of" said Sal. "Are you coming in for a bit, I've got the kettle on?"

"Near's well" said Edna with a smile.

Charlie meanwhile had gone into the churchyard and was approaching the Reverend Quentin Russell's grave. When he was about thirty yards from it he saw a young couple with a bunch of flowers standing beside the grave. The girl crouched down and the young man handed her a plastic glass with water in. She put this on the grave, moving a bit of the newly placed turf so that it would stand, and arranged the bunch of flowers. They both then knelt down beside the grave. On seeing this Charlie turned around and left the churchyard, not wishing to embarrass either them or himself.

He walked away from the green to visit his friend Ben and found him in his kitchen washing his breakfast dishes.

"Come in Charlie, fancy a cuppa?"

"Thank you, that would be nice. Tell me Ben" he said as they sat down at the kitchen table "all those men in white boiler suits, what d'you suppose they're looking for? You used to be in the force, you know don't you?"

""It's such a long time since I was in and times have changed so much in the last few years. I doubt if I could give a sensible guess as to what they're doing."

Charlie sat quietly sipping his coffee. He felt sure that the police presence must be connected to his suggestion that he had made to Sergeant Ashton. But after the leg pulling that he had received from Ben when he had put the same thought to him that evening in the pub, he didn't want to mention it again. He felt it would be better to wait and see if Ben had possibly changed his mind.

The two men sat with their arms on the table, both deep in thought. After several minutes silence Ben finally said

"Could be that Sergeant took note of your daft idea; in fact, maybe it wasn't such a daft idea after all."

"You think so?"

"Well, there was an item on the news the other day. It was to do with some young girl who had gone missing fifty years ago in Scotland. They were going to exhume a grave because they thought that the fella who had raped and abducted her had probably killed her and put her in an open grave. Then she had been covered with the coffin of the person who was meant to be buried there. So you see, your idea isn't so daft after all."

"It just shows, there's nothing new is there?"

TWENTY THREE

Grace had seen all the activity in and around Glebe Farm as she drove over to visit Hilary. Her mind raced over all the possibilities and exactly what she would say to her friend. As she got out of her car she looked down over the fields and could clearly see the white figures, some on their hands and knees, busy at their task. Looking up towards the house she saw Hilary's face at an upstairs window, an anxious expression on her face. When she saw Grace looking her way she smiled and left the window, pointing downwards to indicate that she would come down. She met Grace at the front door and led her in to the lounge.

"What's going on Grace?" she asked "Is it the police down there? I presume it is. What have they found, why are they there?"

"I really don't know my dear. Sergeant Ashton did say that they had another line of enquiry to follow. We'll just have to wait and see."

"But all those people, they must think they know something for them all to be there."

"Yes...well.....it doesn't do to imagine.....you'll only upset yourself. I'm sure that when they finish they will let us know if they have any news."

"I hope so, all this waiting, it's so unsettling."

"I realize that, and so I have come up today, not just to see how you are and keep you company for a while, but to make a suggestion."

"Oh, what's that?"

"Well, I wondered if you would like me to stay here for a few nights.... keep you company like."

"Oh no, that would never do" said Hilary; her agitation at the idea plain to see. "If Mark were to come home and find you here he would not be at all pleased. It's very nice of you to offer, but no."

"Then....perhaps you would prefer to come and stay with me for a short while?"

"Oh no no, that would be even worse, Mark wouldn't like it at all if I were to leave the house. He would be very upset to come home and find me not here" said Hilary, half rising from her chair and looking towards the door with a near terrified look on her face.

Grace, concerned at the reaction that her suggestion had evoked got up from her chair and went over to sit on the broad, well padded arm of Hilary's chair. She thought to herself 'Quentin, I do hope your advice is going to be right' and then, putting her arm around her friend's shoulders she said

"I didn't mean to worry you my dear. I can see that.....how shall I say it....Mark has very strong ideas as to how things should be....doesn't he?"

"Oh yes."

"And he's a stickler for you getting things right I should imagine."

"Very much so."

"And if you don't get things right....?"

"Well.....I have to learn the right way.....and sometimes I still get it wrong."

"And then he gets cross with you."

"Yes......"

"And......he......shouts at you."

"Oh, he never raises his voice. He's always very calm, like a school teacher with a silly child....which is what I am to him I suppose."

105

"And then.....like an old fashioned school teacher, he......hits you?"

"No" she almost shouted as she looked up at Grace with a look of fear on her face.

"It's alright my dear; it's not your fault. There's nothing for you to be ashamed of."

"But what makes you think....?"

"I've seen the signs so many times and in so many households. It is so sad that so many women are battered by their men. And very often by men whom nobody would ever think could be violent to their wives. Yes....you see it isn't just the simple, uneducated man who comes home from the pub drunk and finds something that he sees as wrong and then beats his wife. I remember a case.....yes...he was a solicitor, a pillar of the community with a lovely wife. But he had to dominate her and run her life his way. If she didn't.....he would hit her. It started with just pushing and pulling her around but it got worse. Eventually from somewhere she managed to find the strength to leave him......I was so pleased for her when I met her in a refuge for battered wives. Understandably, she had been too frightened to do so at first, but she did.....he tried to get her back......then it all came out....."

"But Mark isn't....."

"Then of course, when I saw the tell-tale bruises on your arms and neck the other day....well it was obvious.....I am so sorry my dear."

Hilary broke down in floods of tears, sobbing and shaking and Grace held her tightly in an attempt to give some comfort.

"It all started so well, when we were first married" said Hilary, sobs punctuating her sentences. "He seemed so pleased with every thing I did. And of course I was so pleased to be married to him because he was so confident and knew everything and I felt protected. Then when he started correcting me I was glad, glad to be taught by this clever, powerful man. But then the lessons got harder and the punishments too.

"I expect he explained so carefully where you had gone wrong and just why he had to punish you" said Grace.

"Yes, he always managed to make me feel that I should be grateful for his showing me the right way."

"And last summer, when you had that broken collar bone......you said that it happened when you fell......going down the steps in the garden...."

"Yes, he did that....."

"Oh you poor girl.....you poor girl....I'm here as your friend to help you in any way I can.....I do understand your predicament and I won't do or say anything until such time as you ask me to."

Grace paused, thinking that in view of what was going on down in the field below the outcome might have been already settled. But at this stage she couldn't say anything.

TWENTY FOUR

Mullet had called Shirley into his office the next morning. She knew what it was he was going to tell her to do and had been thinking about it for most of the night. Telling anyone of the death of a close relative was never an easy or pleasant job. In this case it was made even more difficult because as yet there was no body. In fact the evidence was purely circumstantial. Some, but not all, of the test results had come back from the lab. There were some smudged finger prints on the end of the barrel of the shotgun, but the rest of it was clean. It had probably been wiped and also the killer had probably worn gloves. The same applied to the Range Rover. They were still waiting for results of DNA testing but that usually took a little longer and in any case there was doubt as to whether Bosworth had ever given a DNA sample and if it had remained on the police files. Shirley wanted to wait until they had probed the grave and had definite proof that the body was in there. But that of course meant that they had to get Grace's permission to do so and that in turn meant that Grace would have to be told of Bosworth's death before they told Hilary. She feared that Mullet would not allow this.

To her surprise and relief Mullet was not as strongly against the idea as she had thought he might be. His only concerns being that Grace might be upset at the thought of disturbing her husband's grave and that she might tell Hilary of what was happening before the results of the probe were known.

"I don't think you need worry on that score Sir" said Shirley. "Mrs Russell is not only a very sensible woman, but she has become a very good and supportive friend to Mrs Bosworth. The last thing that she would want to do would be to raise her friend's hopes wrongly."

"Difficult job Ashton, I leave it to you, I'm sure you will be the soul of discretion. You'd better take WPC Newton with you as well as DC Chaffe when you do break the news to Mrs Bosworth."

So they had set off up onto the moor. Rain during the night had refreshed the parched ground after nearly a month of dry weather and the air was full of the scent of newly wetted earth. The car tyres swished and splashed through small puddles and although the rain had stopped some time before, little rivulets were running beside the road. The clouds were beginning to lift and patches of blue sky had appeared between them.

"Not enough rain to do any real good" said Newman as he drove up onto the higher ground. "It's all run off and down in the streams to Dartmouth."

"I preferred it when there was no rain" said Shirley, "I have enjoyed our late summer, but then I'm not a country man like you."

As she spoke a flock of birds burst out of a small tree beside the road nearly hitting their car and then flew ahead of them, finally settling in a hawthorn bush by the road.

"What are those birds?" she asked, startled by their close encounter.

"They're fieldfares, they're a sort of thrush and they come here in the early winter. They love eating the hawthorn berries and can strip a bush in a matter of minutes."

"I didn't have you down as a twitcher" said Shirley with a grin.

"I'm not, it's just that when you grow up in the country these things are all around you and become a part of every day life."

They drove on over the moor, the dead bracken on the hillsides no longer russet but a much darker brown since the rain. A light mist hung in the lower areas, partially concealing the beautiful autumn colours of the wooded river valleys. Eventually they pulled up outside the Russell's house. Shirley got out and knocked at the door. She waited a while and was about to repeat her knock when Grace opened the door, busily drying her hands on a towel.

"O dear....Sergeant Ashton, so sorry to keep you waiting, I was in the kitchen....mm...yes ...do come in."

She led the way into her kitchen saying

"I expect you'd like a cup of tea or coffee."

"Thank you, coffee would be nice."

"Is this to do with the disappearance of Mr Bosworth? I saw so much activity the other day; I do hope you will soon have some news for Mrs Bosworth. She is so worried."

"Yes, I do have some news but it affects you Mrs Russell and that's why I'm here. I'm afraid you may find what I'm about to tell you difficult."

"How can it possibly affect me? I hardly knew the man and I have only recently become friendly with Hilary."

So Shirley told her almost word for word what Charlie Blundell had told her. Added to that was the evidence of the blood traces in the wheelbarrow and beside the grave.

"Oh my dear.....yes....I do see that you have a problem.......mmm.....yes....difficult."

"The last thing we want to do is upset you. We hate to disturb your late husband's grave."

"Oh you mustn't worry about that. He's not there....oh no....but if he were I think he might be highly amused at the drama of it all."

"Well there is a way we can have a look before we open the grave, but obviously we need your permission. I have a small team standing by who will send a probe down into the grave. It will go down the side of it, passing the coffin and they should be able to see if there is anything underneath it."

"And if there is?"

"Then, again with your permission, we have to apply for an exhumation order from The Home Office and the local Environmental Health Officer."

"Well poor Hilary.....she won't get any rest until then....so I couldn't possibly stand in her way or yours. But I have no idea how she is going to manage now...no...you see....she relied on him so much. He ran her life for her, so to speak...."

"That was the impression I got, in fact I thought he must have been somewhat of a bully" said Shirley, hoping to get some information from Grace.

"For some people who desperately need attention, any attention is better than none."

"She acted as though she was terrified of her husband; she was always looking towards the door when talking about him, as if she was half afraid that he would come in at any minute."

"Yes....she did do that rather a lot."

"Admittedly I didn't see any physical signs, but judging by her clothing, the long sleeves and high collars, I thought that he could be in the habit of physically harming her."

111

"I'm afraid you're right. It's very sad I know and even more sad is the fact that she will miss him. Yes.... she will need a friend now more than ever."

She sat at the kitchen table, her hands clasped around her coffee cup, gazing out of the window. Shirley watched her as she drank her coffee, amazed at this little frail looking woman who was quite obviously much stronger than she looked. From somewhere she was able to get the resilience to forget her own grief and put all her efforts into helping others.

"How soon would you be able to do this......probing did you call it?"

"Almost immediately, if we have your permission."

"And would I be allowed to attend?"

"Of course, I see no reason why not, if that is what you would like."

"I think I would, it sounds rather interesting....yes...."

"In that case I will go out and make the necessary phone calls and get things started. In the meantime" she said, taking a printed form out of her handbag "could you please sign this disclaimer that allows us to proceed?"

TWENTY FIVE

The small group gathered around the grave later that day were shielded from public gaze by a screen. Two experts were there to operate the machine, Shirley and Grace stood near and Newman and WPC Jane Newton stayed outside the screen to keep curious bystanders away.

Slowly but surely the probe was sent down through the slightly softer soil of the recently disturbed ground. When sufficient depth was reached the point of the probe was turned towards the centre of the grave. A few moments later Shirley was called over to look at the screen and she was amazed to see the wooden side of the coffin.

The probe then descended on its way down, stopping every few inches to look. All that could be seen was earth and stones and Shirley was beginning to worry. Had she brought these people out on a wild goose chase? Had she been taken in by the fantasy of an old man? Grace was standing quietly beside her and as if sensing her concern said

"The waiting is always the worst part.....you can't help feeling that you might have been wrong. But I don't think you are."

Then the sight of something dark blue appeared on the screen. On closer inspection it could be seen to be woven material.

"Well that certainly shouldn't be there" said one of the operators. "I would say that's a bit of cloth, probably from a pin-striped suit."

"Mr Bosworth often wore a suit like that" said Grace.

"It looks as though Charlie Blundell was right. Now I have to tell Mrs Bosworth the sad news."

"Not an easy thing to do at the best of times. I would like to help, but I realize that this is something that you have to do.... yes....official procedure and all that."

"If you were to go and visit with Mrs Bosworth now, we could tidy up here and then come to see her a little bit later. The mere fact that you are with her when I have to give her the sad news will help not only her, but me as well" said Shirley with a wry smile.

Shirley and Jane sat in one of the settees while Newman went and sat on an upright chair with its back to the wall beside the windows. With the light shining in beside him he was in relative darkness and less visible. He took out his notebook and waited. Shirley looked around the room; everywhere spoke of luxury and money. Beautiful soft furnishings, an expensive looking mahogany coffee and occasional tables had all been carefully placed to give the room the feeling of staged tranquillity. With pictures and ornaments to match, the room had the look of a film set. Glamour there certainly was, almost perfection, but Shirley felt that there was no warmth. Once again she found herself feeling sorry for this poor woman whose life she was just about to turn upside down.

"Have you any news for me?" asked Hilary, a look of hope in her eyes.

"Yes, although it isn't one hundred percent, the circumstantial evidence would make it seem so." She paused, not wanting to rush in like a bull in a china shop. Then in a quiet voice and looking straight into

Hilary's eyes she said "I am very sorry to have to tell you that we now feel sure that your husband is dead."

Grace immediately moved over to sit with Hilary and put her arm around her. For a few moments there was complete silence. No one spoke or moved as if frozen in time, except Hilary who sat wide eyed looking from Grace to Shirley and back again, her mouth open and a look of total disbelief on her face.

"When you say that you feel sure that Mark is dead does that mean that you haven't found......?" asked Grace turning to look at Shirley, as if she didn't already know the answer.

"Investigations are still ongoing and we hope to have a definite answer very soon" said Shirley.

"Oh you poor dear" said Grace turning back to Hilary "you've had a dreadful time already, waiting for news....and now this. But we must allow the police time to do their very difficult job."

Hilary was still looking completely lost as though she couldn't take in what she had just heard. She didn't cry or say anything, she just sat with her head bowed, staring at her hands clasped in her lap. After what seemed a long silence Shirley stood up and quietly said to Grace

"Perhaps we could go into the kitchen and get some tea. Meanwhile, WPC Newton will stay with Mrs Bosworth."

"Oh.....yes.....very well....good idea." She rose from the arm of Hilary's chair where she had been sitting saying "you will be alright? I won't be long I'm sure."

As soon as they were in the kitchen Shirley said

"Thank you for making out that you knew nothing, Mrs Bosworth had to be told first."

"To do with the whereabouts and identity of the body?"

"Yes."

"I had a feeling it must be...I could see that you were uncomfortable....yes..."

Picking up the tray of tea tings Shirley followed Grace back into the lounge where Hilary was talking calmly to WPC Newton about her early days with Bosworth. Grace poured the tea and then said

"Would you like me to....move in here with you for a few days, or perhaps you would prefer to come and stay with me?"

"I think I'd better stay here, Paul will be coming every day to keep things running. But yes please, it would be lovely if you could come. Thank you so much Grace, you really are a true friend."

TWENTY SIX

It was ten to six when John Hunt woke. For the first time in weeks he had slept through the night without waking. For the first time in weeks he felt refreshed and alive. He slipped out of bed quietly, so as not to disturb his sleeping wife, dressed and went downstairs. The papers wouldn't arrive for over an hour so, with plenty of time in hand he made himself a mug of tea and sat at the kitchen table enjoying it. Then pulling on an old fleece and a pair of boots he went out into the early morning November air and walked across the green. Two large police vans and several cars were parked by the churchyard wall and a policeman was standing in the lych gate. He said a polite good morning to John as he walked by. Was all this activity still to do with the disappearance of Mark Bosworth, wondered John. It had been the talk of the village for days with speculation and rumour running rife. Only the day before, Paul had been in the shop and John had asked him if there was any news. There being nobody else in the shop at the time, Paul had confided that he had overheard the sergeant telling Hilary that following their recent line of enquiry the police considered that Mark was dead.

John walked out of the village and through the gate leading to Braggator. After a few yards the lane dropped away toward the old mine buildings where Mick Cribbett lived but John turned off the lane onto the open moor and followed the grassy path up to the top of the tor. When nearly at the top he stopped and sat on a rock beside the path. All around the moorland stretched away looking grey in the early morning light. The warm greens of the summer were gone, as were the bright purple and gold of the heather and gorse of September, and the reds and browns of autumn. Now Dartmoor was resting, greys and browns would be the main colours until the spring, making dark splashes in the light almost white sand coloured expanses of dead grass.

He thought of how throughout the past six months he had been worried about the future. Many a night he had woken at two or three o'clock and had gone to the toilet. Then when he got back into bed he had lain awake for an hour or two unable to sleep, thoughts churning through his mind that he couldn't stop. Some nights he had gone downstairs had made himself a cup of tea. On more than one occasion he had gone out for a walk in the village and even up onto the moor, gaining some solace from the peace and quiet of the Dartmoor night. He had been amazed at how easy it had been to get around in the night, which had never been completely dark. After the first of such night wanderings, his wife Jane had said

"You were up a couple of times last night for the toilet, is anything wrong? You're not getting a prostrate problem are you?"

John didn't want to worry her and was happy to let her believe that he had got out of bed twice to go to the toilet, rather than that he had been up for several hours many a night worrying about the business.

"Perhaps I ought to cut out the last drink of tea in the evening" he had said.

But worried he had been and with good reason. Several post offices in neighbouring villages had closed, would his be the next to go under the axe? It wasn't just the loss of his income as postmaster, which was undeniably useful, that he would miss. Those who came to the post office counter also bought things in the shop. Then, added to that had been his concern over Bosworth's plans to build a farm shop. It would inevitably impact adversely on his business. But now; if what Paul implied was right, despite Bosworth winning his appeal, there was a chance that the development was unlikely to go ahead. The concern had gone and he had slept right through the night. For the first time in months it felt good to be alive and he was able to smile.

TWENTY SEVEN

Meanwhile in the churchyard, screens had been erected around Quentin Russell's grave and work had begun on the exhumation. As well as officers from the council and the vicar, Shirley was there with DI Norman Smith. She was wearing her usual trouser suit with an added layer of a well padded anorak to keep out the morning chill. He was dressed more for the city in a light grey suit and a camel overcoat.

"I'm surprised that Mrs Russell isn't here" he said. Shirley said nothing; she felt that she understood only too well why Grace had kept away. For her, all that was in the coffin was no more than a bundle of discarded rags. Her husband was in a much better place and she was happy to let the business of finding Mark go ahead without her. Her main concern was for her friend Hilary.

With the aid of the small mechanical digger, which had been brought into the churchyard to do the job, it didn't take long to uncover the coffin. Then with great care that was lifted out and placed on the ground to the side of the grave. It was at this point that Shirley felt her heart beat quickening with anxiety as to what would be found next. Had she made a terrible mistake? And yet the probe had shown a piece of blue material that looked very much as though it could be from Bosworth's pin-striped suit. With great care and by hand, shovel-full by shovel-full the soil was removed and placed to one side for scrutiny by the SOCOs team. Very quickly the gruesome truth appeared. The body was lying face down with only a very thin layer of soil covering the first piece of clothing to come to light. That was the left-hand side pocket of Mark Bosworth's jacket which had somehow flipped up onto the small of his back. Poking half out of this pocket was his mobile phone. Then with great care, and still with a certain amount of soil attached to the clothing, the body was bagged and taken in the police vehicle to the morgue where, Doctor Donald Hall, the pathologist would carry out a post-mortem.

"You see to the clear up here Ashton, I'll see you back in the incident room" said DI Smith as he got into his car.

Then the grave was cleaned out to the correct depth and finally after the necessary searches had taken place Quentin Russell was re-laid to rest. The vicar said two prayers and once again the coffin was covered with the dark granite Dartmoor gravel, and the black peaty topsoil.

When she got back to the station the first thing that Shirley did was to ring Doctor Hall and find out if the body was ready for Hilary to see and identify. On being told that it was, Shirley reported to DI Smith, knowing full well that he would tell her to do the unenviable task of accompanying Hilary. There was no doubt, some aspects of the job were better than others. So Shirley had gone once again to Grimstone Court and knocked on the huge oak front door. She hated herself when she saw the look of hope on Hilary's face as she opened the door, knowing how her hopes would be dashed.

"Do come in Sergeant it's so cold out this morning. We're just having a cup of coffee, would you like one?"

How often had Shirley encountered this sort of behaviour from someone expecting bad news? It seemed to be easier to make a trite remark when bad news was expected, rather than ask outright and face the unpalatable truth.

Stepping through the porch into the warm hallway Shirley followed her into the lounge where Grace was sitting.

"There is no way that what I am about to say can be dressed up to sound better. I'm sorry to have to say that we have recovered a body which we believe to be your husband. We therefore need you to come to the morgue, when you feel up to it, to identify him."

Hilary sat down beside Grace who took her hand. She didn't cry or say anything for almost a minute, a pause which seemed a lot longer to Shirley. Then she said

"If I am honest I have been expecting this after what you said last time you were here. Will it be alright if Grace comes with me?"

"Of course."

"Then the sooner we get this over the better. I'll get my coat."

"She seems to be remarkably calm" said Shirley to Grace after Hilary had left the room.

"Yes....well....we've talked a lot last night and again this morning. I think that she's accepted the fact that she won't see Mark again....well... not alive that is. How well she will manage to live with that fact is another matter. Grief affects people in many different ways.....no two people are the same. No matter what the circumstances of the death there is always a feeling of guilt."

"It's a good job she has you as a friend to stand by her and help through this difficult time."

TWENTY EIGHT

The incident room was buzzing with anticipation when DI Smith walked in. Shirley and Newman were there together with three other detectives.

"Right" he said "we have a murder enquiry. I haven't had a full report from the pathologist yet; in fact I don't expect one till tomorrow at the earliest. However, he told me that the deceased was killed by a shot from very close range, and that the weapon used was probably a shotgun. Details will follow. Now Ashton and Chaffe will continue enquiries in the village, they have already made contact there which should help them. I am of the opinion that we must look deeper into the man's business life and his relationships outside this area. At the moment we have no prime suspect, in fact no suspect at all. As to the widow, does she require a victim support officer? What d'you think Ashton, you've met her several times."

"Well, she's not the strongest of characters, but she has a good friend in the widow of the late Reverend Russell. She is an amazing woman, small and a bit mouse-like. Victorian, is probably the best way to describe her. But she seems to have a lot more strength than her small size would suggest. She is staying there with Mrs Bosworth so I think she'll be alright without the help of a support officer."

"Right, any other comments?" asked Smith.

"Doesn't the fact that the killer was aware of the open grave as a place to hide the body denote that this was a local crime?" asked Chaffe.

"Yes, that's what I thought" said Smith "but the death and funeral of Rev Russell was not solely reported in the local press, it was in one of the Sunday papers as well. Quite a big article as I understand, I didn't see it myself."

"Really Sir?"

At this point one of the other detectives who was sitting by his computer said

"Apparently in the early fifties Quentin Russell did his two years' national service in the armed forces, as all young men did up until nineteen fifty eight. He served in the Korean War and was awarded the Victoria Cross. Without any concern for his own safety he went out under heavy enemy fire and rescued three of his fellow soldiers who had been badly wounded. Three trips he made; I'd say the man was quite a hero. As I understand it, he then went into the church, partly as a result of his experiences on the front line. He kept his war record a private matter, maybe he wasn't particularly proud of his efforts, though I would guess he just didn't want to be looked upon as a celebrity. It would appear that one of those whom he rescued was still alive and had heard of his death. He must have contacted the paper and told them that the man was a hero."

"So you see why we must widen our search. It may seem unlikely but the news of Russell's funeral could well have reached a wider audience. Also, a man who has climbed the ladder of success as Bosworth did, may have made a lot of enemies. His sort tend to walk all over those in their way."

"And the motive Sir?"

"Several to choose from; financial gain, revenge, hatred...take your pick."

124

"Which means we will probably have an equally large choice of suspects."

"Exactly."

As they left the room Newman said to Shirley

"Quentin Russell VC, eh? He kept that quiet didn't he? I wonder how many people in the village knew of that, if any."

TWENTY NINE

The next morning Shirley and Newman drove up onto the moor to continue their enquiries. It was a cold, dull, though dry, November morning and when they reached the top of the hill overlooking the village Newman pulled the car onto the grass at the side of the road and switched off the engine. Beyond their destination, tor-topped horizon after horizon stretched into the grey distance. Beside them a narrow path of close cropped grass ran between the dead bracken towards the rock strewn top of a tor. A few black-faced sheep were grazing amongst the gorse and rocks and a lone buzzard was circling overhead.

"Wonderful view, don't you think Sarge?" said Newman.

"I suppose so. It looks a bit cold and forbidding to me; I wouldn't want to be up here after dark. I have to admit I find it rather threatening."

"Yet you would probably feel totally differently if the sun were out. I find Dartmoor very comforting in all its moods." He paused for a moment, staring out of the window at the vast empty expanse of wild countryside.

"So how do we proceed with this investigation?" he asked, changing the subject in a way that surprised Shirley.

"We need to go back and do a house to house enquiry. We need to find out if anybody from outside the area was staying here during that time."

"So you think the same as Smith, that it wasn't necessarily a local person that killed Bosworth."

"Suppose whoever killed him had walked through the churchyard to get back to the village, he would have seen the newly dug grave wouldn't he?"

"That would imply that hiding the body in the grave was not a part of his original plan."

"Exactly, I'm not sure that it was. That idea may well have come later. What we have to do now is to find out if anybody local had enough of a motive to kill Bosworth."

"From what I heard in my earlier enquiries I should think that most of the population of this village hated the man with a passion. They were none too happy to voice their true feelings, but if they now know that he is dead.....well.....we may hear a lot more."

"So we check the guest houses and B&Bs first."

"And then?"

"We could do with talking to someone who knows the people and can give an honest appraisal of the characters here."

"So you need to talk to a local person, one who has lived here all his life. There aren't many of them left; almost ninety five percent are blow-ins, sorry....newcomers."

"You sound as though you don't think much of newcomers, or blow-ins as you call them. You're not biased by any chance are you?" She said, teasing him gently.

"Not at all, it's just that newcomers bring new ideas and different standards to the area, not all of which suit. They often want to change things, make it more like the towns that they came from. Then after a few years, generally about four or five, they pack up and leave. Some, like Bosworth, seem determined to impose their will on the area regardless of the damage they do. It's as though they have to show the world that they've got loads of money and because of that they can do as they wish."

"And you reckon that the local people don't act that way?"

"Most of them want to live and work **with** Dartmoor, not try to change it all the time."

"OK, who do we go to to give us this local viewpoint?"

"I can think of three or four; Phil German, who farms the Manor Farm, Frank Naraway at Wistworthy and Mick Cribbett the blacksmith who we've already spoken to. Frank is cousin to that vet Cathy that you know, and runs a business as a motor mechanic looking after the local vehicles. He also helps his mother on their small farm. And then there's Sir Harold Edworthy up at the manor. But whether any of them would tell us anything that would incriminate their neighbours.....I wouldn't like to say."

"Right then, we'd better get started with the holiday place down the hill from the pub, then the pub itself and finally the B&B beside the nurse's house."

"We can also ask in the pub and the café if anybody they saw at that time seemed to be acting strangely."

With that Newman started the car and drove on the last mile into the village.

Three couples had been staying in the holiday complex. Two of them had left on the Monday morning, but the third couple had left on the Wednesday. They were a middle-aged couple called Mr and Mrs Cash and they had arrived on the Friday.

"So, what sort of people were they?" asked Shirley of the manager.

"They seemed nice, quiet people, kept very much to themselves. In fact we didn't see much of them."

"And where are they from, you have an address I presume."

"Let me see" he said consulting his register. "Yes, here it is, Swindon, Mr and Mrs John Cash."

"And you wouldn't know if either of them was out during the early hours of the Wednesday morning?"

"No, I'm afraid not. But I rather doubt it; they didn't act like night owls."

As they climbed back into their car Newman said

"I fancy I recognize that name, but I can't think why."

"Are you getting mixed up with Johnny Cash the singer?"

"No, I'm sure there was something in the papers a while back concerning a Mr Cash and some scandal or other. I'll look it up later, if it doesn't come back to me.

The pub had had only two ladies who went walking every day staying at that time, and the B&B had been empty. However, in the Old Smithy Café, Jacqui had told them that her son, Timmy, had given directions to a man in a car on the Tuesday afternoon. He had wanted to know how to get to Grimstone Court.

"What time of day was that?"

"We were just closing; I suppose it would have been about six o'clock."

Could we have a word with your son?"

"He's at school."

"Right, we may want to come back and speak to him. D'you know if anyone else saw this man?"

"No I don't. Timmy may know; sorry I can't be of more help but I was in the kitchen finishing up."

"So we now have two possible people to check on who were in the area at the time" said Shirley as they walked back to their car. "They are probably totally innocent, but we have to eliminate them, one way or the other."

"We also need to go to the nursing home where Mrs Bosworth was visiting her mum and find out details of her visit" said Newman.

"You mean, check her alibi?"

"Yes, after all she stands to gain most from Bosworth's death. If nothing else we need to eliminate her."

"Perhaps tomorrow morning. Right now I think it would be good if you went and had a word with Ben Fuller, he used to be in the force. Get some of his ideas about the local people. We're starting from a new angle; we now have a murder, not a missing person. Also some people may be prepared to say more about their neighbours. I'm going to have another word with Charlie Blundell. Apart from anything, I need to thank him for telling us where to find the body."

THIRTY

Charlie was in the garden when Shirley called. Sal and Edna were in the kitchen enjoying a cup of coffee and asked Shirley to join them.

"Thank you, that would be nice" said Shirley "I need to speak to both of you and to your husband. Is he at home?"

"Yes, he's in the garden, I'll give him a shout."

While Sal went to call Charlie, Edna poured Shirley a cup of coffee. Anxious to know why Shirley had called she found it hard not to ask questions and hovered over her like a mother hen. Finally she could contain herself no longer and said

"So, how are your enquiries going, have you found Mr Bosworth yet?"

Shirley found it hard to believe that news of the murder hadn't reached Sal and Edna's ears. Admittedly the police had done their best to keep things quiet, but the village news network generally worked better than that. Before she could answer Sal and Charlie came in. Charlie washed his hands and then came over and sat at the table opposite Shirley.

"Morning Sergeant, what can I do for you?"

"I came to tell you all that we have found Mr Bosworth."

Charlie looked at her, saying nothing. For the time he was glad to play along with Shirley and act as though he knew no more than his wife.

"Where was he? Off with some fancy woman I suppose" said Edna.

"No, I regret to say that Mr Bosworth is dead. We found his body..."

"His body.....where?" interrupted Sal.

"I'm surprised that you haven't already heard. He was in a grave, buried under the late vicar, Quentin Russell."

"Buried under the vicar; how d'you mean, buried.....How on earth did he get there?" said Edna. "Oh, I suppose he was drunk and fell in and broke his neck. Serve him right, I never did like the fella much."

"We don't think it was an accident, he certainly didn't fall into the grave."

"You mean somebody put him there? He was.....murdered?"

"Yes. You will be able to read all about it in tomorrow's papers."

"Murder, well just think of it, we don't get that sort of thing here. Can you call to mind the last time there was a murder near here?" asked Edna turning towards Charlie but before he had time to answer she went on

"Course there was the young fella who shot that man through the pub window a few years back. He'd been having an affair with his wife, twas in all the local papers. But that was in Chudleigh Knighton."

"So that's what all the excitement was the other morning" said Sal "there were lots of policemen here early, remember Edna? There was a young man stood by the lych gate and several vans and things".

"Yes" interrupted Shirley "what I need to ask all of you is; do you remember seeing any stranger or unusual people here on the Tuesday. The day before the funeral that is."

"Can't say as I did, it's a job to remember really" said Edna.

"There was a fellow in a car, asking for directions from young Timmy" said Sal. "He got out of his car, most polite he was. I couldn't quite hear all he said 'cos he was facing away from me. Then Timmy told him where to go and he got back in his car and left."

"Did you hear where he wanted to go?"

"No, but from what Timmy said I am fairly sure he was asking for Grimstone Court."

"What time was this, d'you recall?"

"T'would be about six o'clock."

"Would you recognise the man again?"

"I doubt it. I'm terrible with faces. There's some I should know and don't recognise and others I think I know and it turns out I've never seen them before in my life. Like tother day when Edna and I went into Newton. You were going to meet your sister weren't you?"

"That's right. She was going down to Cornwall for a few days. Going to stay at a little place in Mousehole. She broke the journey, got off at Newton station and we had lunch together in The Queens Hotel. Very good it was too."

"Yes, never mind about that Edna" said Sal "As I was saying, I did a bit of shopping and then went for a bite to eat in that nice little coffee shop in Austins. I met up with Josie Tuckett and we had a table together. Well, whilst we were eating I saw this woman sitting at a table the other end of the room. The more I looked at her, the more I felt sure I knew her from somewhere. You know how it is. Then later on I could see her looking at me, and I could tell by the way she was looking that she probably felt sure that she knew me from somewhere too. I had finished my meal and was just sitting there. Josie was still eating, but then, she had been talking all the time, didn't have time to eat."

"That's Josie for you" said Edna "that woman never stops yapping, all a load of nonsense too. Nothing but gossip, got no time for it myself."

"Well, I saw this woman get up to leave so I got up too. I wanted to see if I was right, see if I did know her from somewhere. We arrived at the entrance together, I looked at her and she looked at me....and....d'you know what?"

"What?" said both Edna and Shirley in unison.

"It wasn't neither one of us."

Edna, who had been leaning forward in anticipation, sat back in her chair and roared with laughter.

"You're a case and no mistake" she said. "Twasn't neither one of us." And she laughed again.

"Maybe, but it just shows that I couldn't be trusted to recognise somebody that I had just seen for a few minutes."

"Were there any other people around that day, people that you didn't recognise, strangers to the area?" asked Shirley.

"No, not so far as I remember."

"Well thank you for your time. I get the feeling that Mr Bosworth was not at all well liked and that few will mourn his passing."

"Yes" said Charlie "A lot had reason to hate him....but to kill him...? I don't think so..."

THIRTY ONE

Shirley had arranged to meet Newman in the pub for lunch. Charlie had walked a short way with her as she left. He was glad to get the chance of a few words out of earshot of Sal and Edna but it was Shirley who spoke first.

"I wanted to thank you for your suggestion as to where we might find the body. I never would have thought of that, and if you hadn't told me, Bosworth would probably have stayed there for ever. His disappearance would have remained a missing person."

"It was the length of the strap, see. But it took me a long time to suss out what it was that was bothering me. Thank you for not letting on to Sal."

"I was surprised that she didn't know that we had found the body. There was enough activity around here that morning."

"Yeah, but Edna's grandchild was coming for her to look after that morning, so she had other things on her mind. You know how they are with little ones."

Charlie then said cheerio and Shirley went into the pub. She found Newman sitting at the bar talking to Bob, the landlord.

"What are you having Sarge?"

"Lemonade and lime for me, thank you" she said and taking their drinks they went and sat at a table in the window.

"So what if anything have you been able to get from our former policeman?"

"Quite a bit really. There's a chap called Steve Moore, lives in one of the cottages behind Grimstone Court. He lost his wife four years ago, breast cancer, very sad. He has a daughter aged nine. Well she always used to walk to school, to catch the school bus in the village. She used to go through Grimstone Court garden and then through that little gate, remember? That led down the path through glebe meadow and through the churchyard. When Bosworth arrived he closed the path, said it wasn't a right of way. He was right; it wasn't a right of way in law. But people had been using the path for years and it seemed very unfair. It also meant that Steve Moore had to drive his daughter to school every day, not a long journey, only about a mile, but time consuming and un-necessary. Caused a lot of bad feeling.

"I can imagine it did, but not really enough to justify killing him."

"No, but you can imagine that now that Bosworth is dead, several people remember just what Steve said in the pub one night when the conversation was all about how unpleasant Bosworth was."

"What did he say?"

"As far as Ben can recall he said 'I could happily kill the bastard'."

"Doesn't mean that he did though. Anything else?"

"Yes. His neighbour, chap called Joe Small, keeps a couple of horses. His fields adjoin Bosworth's. For years they have had water supplied from the overflow from the spring that rises in Bosworth's field. The spring that he uses for his famous bottled water. Again, when Bosworth moved in he turned off the supply to Joe's field, sent it across his garden to make a water feature. So now Joe has to fill a small water tanker and take it up to supply a trough in his field. Another example of a man who has a grudge against Bosworth.

"Well, we'll have to question them; if nothing else we must eliminate them from our enquiries. Was there anyone else?"

"Yes, Ben didn't tell me any details, he just said we ought to have a word with a plumber chap called Terry Cooper. He also mentioned John Hunt the shopkeeper, but then his phone rang and I thought it would be best to leave and follow that up another day."

"Well done, we've got plenty to work on. Now we'd better get something to eat, I'm starving."

THIRTY TWO

Five hundred yards beyond the drive that led to Grimstone Court was a small lane. This curled around the side of the hill eventually ending at two stone cottages nestling against a small copse of oak and holly trees. A plume of smoke was rising from the chimney of the right hand one and it was to its front door that Shirley and Newman walked. Beside the door was an old brass bell with a leather bootlace hanging from its clapper. Newman gave this a shake and smiled at the clear musical notes that followed. A dog barked somewhere within the building and after a moment or two the door opened. Standing behind it, stooping to hold the collar of a large grey lurcher was a tall man with long blond hair and a beard.

"Good morning, Steve Moore?"

"Yes."

Shirley took out her warrant card, introduced herself and Newman and asked if they might have a word.

"Yes, come in" said Steve, leading through a dark passage into a bright kitchen at the rear of the cottage. It was obviousely a new single-story addition to the building with a large window in the ceiling. Tidy worktops along two walls with cupboards above and below were clear of clutter. A large scrub-topped pine table with four old wooden chairs were the only other furnishings in the room. On the table were a laptop and a pile of papers.

"Please excuse the mess; I was trying to catch up on a bit of work. I seem to have got rather behind, looking after my daughter over half term. Please sit down; can I get you a tea or a coffee?"

"No thank you" said Shirley.

"What can I do for you, is it to do with Mr Bosworth's disappearance?"

"Yes, can you tell us what you were doing on the Tuesday the day before the funeral of the late vicar, Quentin Russell?"

"Well, I was working here as far as I can remember."

"And your work is....?"

"I'm a writer, I write novels."

"I see, we're particularly interested in the time between six and seven that evening."

"We would have been eating our supper then I expect, that's what we normally do at that time. I meet Evie, my daughter, off the school bus in the village and we get home at about a quarter past four. She has a light snack, a biscuit and a cup of milk or something like that and then she does any homework that she has to do. I generally get supper for six-ish o'clock and then we have a bit of play time together before her bath and bed."

"Is there any body who can corroborate this?" asked Newman.

"No, only Evie. Why, what's happened?"

"Mr Bosworth has been found dead, you will no doubt read about it tomorrow in the papers. We are treating it as murder" said Shirley.

"We understand that you had occasion to fall out with Mr Bosworth over the footpath through his garden" said Newman. "We need to eliminate you from our enquiries."

"That's a polite way of saying that I'm a suspect" said Steve with a laugh. "Yes I had an argument with Bosworth, jumped up little man. He's got far too much money, thinks he can do anything he wants. The man's a bully. I doubt if there's any one in this village who will mourn his passing, in fact many will be delighted that he's dead....including me. But that doesn't mean that I killed him. So when you say that you are particularly interested in the period between six and seven o'clock does that mean that he was killed at around that time?"

Neither Shirley nor Newman answered.

"Well, Evie is my only witness for that time, so that is my alibi for what it's worth."

"While you were out collecting your daughter from the school bus did you see any strangers in the village or on the road?"

"Not that I can recall."

"Thank you, you've been very frank. We have to ask every one these questions in order to build up a picture of what happened and to eliminate those not involved."

"So am I eliminated" asked Steve with a smile.

Again neither Shirley nor Newman answered, but then she asked

"Are your neighbours at home do you know?"

"I saw Joe down in the field with his horses about half an hour ago. He may have gone out for a ride, though he generally rides in the morning so he could be at home. I'm not sure about his wife Angie."

"Thank you again" said Shirley as she got up to leave. She and Newman said their goodbyes and once outside walked the few steps towards the front door of the neighbouring cottage. Before they reached it the door opened and a smart looking woman in riding breeches, boots and a yellow jumper stepped out.

"Can I help you?"

"Mrs Small?" asked Shirley introducing herself and Newman. "Is your husband at home, I wonder if we could have a word with you both?"

"He's in the stable, I'll give him a call. "

She went around to the rear of the cottage and shouted for Joe. Then coming back she said

"Come in, he won't be a minute." as she led them into a cluttered front room that was furnished with an old leather three piece suite that had seen better days and two tables that were covered with old copies of Horse and Hound magazines and the Shooting Times. A bookcase in one corner was laden with silver cups and colourful rosettes, while in another corner was an old wooden chair with a variety of coats thrown upon it.

At that moment her husband Joe came in followed by a boisterous Springer spaniel. Bits of hay fell off his loose woollen jumper as he walked. Again Shirley explained who they were.

"You may not have heard yet, but your neighbour Mark Bosworth has been found dead. We are treating it as a case of murder. We have to ask every body in the area what they were doing on the Tuesday before the funeral of Quentin Russell between the hours of six and seven."

They looked from one to another almost as if seeking inspiration. Then looking straight at Shirley, Angie said

"I was out visiting a friend in Bovey Tracey".

"I don't rightly know what I was doing" said Joe, looking first at his wife and then at Shirley. "At that time of day I would normally be seeing to the stock, putting them to bed for the night, so to speak. Isn't that so Darling?" He turned again towards his wife with a questioning look on his face.

"So you would have been on your own then, right?" asked Newman.

"Well, apart from the animals, yes."

"And what time did you get back Mrs Small?"

"In time for supper, Joe had cooked up a nice stew with dumplings and lots of nice veg. He used to be a chef, you know."

"And did either of you see anybody unusual at any time that day, strangers to the area?" asked Shirley.

"No, but then I never left the place all day, and you went straight to your friend's after lunch, didn't you?" Said Joe, looking at his wife.

"We understand that you didn't have a particularly good relationship with Mr Bosworth" said Shirley.

"No, not surprising really. I don't know anyone that did; he was a most obnoxious man. He turned off the water supply to our fields. Animals have to drink, not that he cares about a thing like that. He only did it because he could. It was an old gentleman's agreement that had worked well for years but it wasn't anything backed by law. It's not as if there wasn't enough for his bottled water and our stock, we only had the overflow."

"So how do you manage now?" asked Newman.

"I have a small water tanker that I fill up once a week or so, which I take over to a trough in the field. It was either that or run a long length of pipe."

"You're surely not suggesting that Joe might have killed him because of that are you?" said Angie, turning to Shirley with a look of horror on her face.

"We have to make our enquiries, that way we can eliminate those not involved. We will also have to

142

have the name and address of your friend with whom you spent the afternoon, to eliminate you Mrs Small."

At this with a certain amount of reluctance she told them where she had been as Newman took out his notebook and wrote down the details. Then with nothing more to be gained by staying any longer Shirley said

"Thank you for your time, if you do think of anything else please get in touch." She took a card out of her bag which she handed to Joe and then she and Newman said goodbye and left. As they drove away down the lane Shirley said

"Did you get the impression that they were both trying to convince the other of what they had been doing that day, as though they had something to hide. I had the distinct feeling that neither of them where were they had told the other they were."

"You could be right; their body language told me that they were both uncomfortable at having to explain in front of their partner. No doubt Mrs Small is on the phone now, talking to her friend and making sure that her alibi will be corroborated. As to the men, both of them could have done it I suppose, I mean they had the opportunity, but hardly a good enough motive."

"But Steve Moore was with his daughter didn't he say?"

"Yes, but he could have forgotten exactly what happened, and on which day. He would have been busy with his writing, off in a world of his own. He might well have overlooked that she was having tea with a friend that evening. I know my kids are always doing things like that; it's a job to keep track of them sometimes."

143

"We certainly have plenty of suspects, but none of them strike me as being the prime suspect."

THIRTY THREE

They set off back to the station with Newman driving. Shirley was silent for a long time, thinking over all that they had heard and all that had happened over the last few days. Finally she said

"I've been trying to work out in my mind exactly what the killer did. There seem to be too many alternatives.

"How d'you mean Sarge?"

"Well, did the killer go to Grimstone Court to meet with Bosworth, intending to kill him or did he just intend to have a row with him? Was he armed with a weapon of his own? Did he find, as I first thought, that Bosworth wasn't at home but then saw him in the field below. So he ran down through glebe meadow, out of sight behind the thorn hedge, picking up the gun from the car when he saw it there."

"Or did he see Bosworth turn into the lane and follow him in?"

"Exactly. Did he plan to kill or did he only mean to threaten Bosworth with the gun and Bosworth grabbed the end of the barrel, trying to take it away from him.....?"

"Yes, his finger prints were on the end of the barrel....."

".....and as he pulled, the gun went off and he....sort of....killed himself."

"I suppose it's possible, if the killer had his fingers on the triggers. But if he only meant to threaten surely the safety catch would still be on? And why hide the body in the vicar's grave? Did he think of that later, or was it something that he had planned to do all along? That would suggest that the killing was planned as well. And that would mean that he had not originally intended to use Bosworth's gun. He had taken that on the spur of the moment, bit of poetic justice, shoot the man with his own gun."

"So he then puts the gun back in the car, drives up to Grimstone Court; the nurse sees him going there, right. Parks the car, in the wrong place, puts the keys on the hall table, again the wrong place, and then goes off in his own vehicle."

"Or if he had followed Bosworth in from the road" said Newman "he would have walked back down through Glebe Meadow and gone.... where ever."

"Maybe back to the village through the churchyard...."

"Where he would have seen the newly dug grave, just waiting to be filled."

"Too many variables" said Shirley, frowning "and still too many suspects."

"Yes, and we haven't seen all of them yet. We still need to check on Mrs Bosworth."

"We'll go to the nursing home tomorrow, then if we need to, we'll interview her again. I would rather let her go for the time being, she's had a lot to cope with just lately."

THIRTY FOUR

Back in her flat that evening, Shirley was reading through her post. Amongst all the junk mail was a circular from one of the local estate agents offering to buy her house if she was ready to move and wanted to sell. It was something that she had considered of late, the flat had been her home for long enough. Now she found herself thinking in terms of a small cottage with a bit of garden. Perhaps going out onto the moor to the village had opened her eyes to a different way of life. No, she didn't want to live way out in the sticks, but something in-between her present home and a country cottage could be what she was looking for. Although she really didn't know exactly what she wanted she knew that when and if she saw it she would recognise it as the house for her.

Then, almost to her surprise, she picked up the phone and rang Martin, the estate agent. While the thought was fresh in her mind why not act? There probably was nothing on the market at the moment that would be suitable, but if she told him that she was looking.....

"Hello, Martin Travers."

"Martin, it's Shirley Ashton."

"Oh hello, how can I help you? Something to do with this murder case that you must be working on. It sounds fascinating, *'body found in grave under coffin of VC veteran'.*"

"No, it's nothing to do with work."

"What a shame, I've always liked detective stories. I had hoped that you might want my help and advice. *'Enthusiastic amateur helps police solve baffling crime'.*"

"Stop messing about Martin, what I have rung about is an idea that I've just had. I've been here, what is it now, seven years and I think its time for a change."

"Great, so what are you looking for?"

"I'm not really sure, a two bed-roomed cottage with a bit of garden, not too far from town and not too expensive obviously."

"Yeah, I know. I can't say that I have anything on my books at the moment that is quite like that. I do have a small barn conversion, it's more like one and a half bedrooms, it was a small barn. It might do."

"It could be interesting."

"What are you doing now? Are you working or have you finished for the day?"

""Why, were you thinking of showing me this place now?"

"Why not? You say that you have just had this idea, well let's follow it up and go and have a look. It will give you a better idea as to what is about and what it would cost you."

"OK, where shall I meet you?"

"Come to my office and park your car in the yard behind. I'll take you from there."

"OK, I'll see you in half an hour, alright?"

The property was two miles out of town. A gravelled track that ran down the side of a field led to what had for many years been an ivy-covered stone barn. It was now a small but comfortable dwelling, tastefully converted to include the amenities of modern living. Martin led the way through a small porch into the ground floor open plan space. A neat fully-fitted kitchen at one end led into a dining area while at the other end a wood burner took centre stage in what was obviously the lounge. The floor was oak boarding and a large Persian-style rug was in front of the stove between the armchairs.

Immediately in front of the door was a spiral staircase made of wrought iron with wooden treads made of the same oak as the floor. This led to a large bedroom over the lounge area and a bathroom and another bedroom over the kitchen diner. French windows in the gable end of the larger bedroom led onto a small balcony. Martin pointed out that this was the only access for taking furniture into the upstairs.

Outside there was a small garden area that needed attention. As Martin explained, the present owners had been using it as a holiday retreat, but since the summer they had not been down. He let Shirley have a good look around and then said

"Now that you've had a look at it you must have come to some conclusion as to whether it is anything like the sort of place you want. Why don't we call in at that nice little pub we passed on the way here and I'll buy you a drink and you can tell me your thoughts."

"That sounds like a brilliant idea. There are aspects of this place that I like very much, but I would really need to see a lot more properties to be sure that I picked the right one."

So they drove back towards town and enjoyed a drink together. As they sat on either side of a small table Shirley found herself looking across at Martin and studying him for the first time. His hair was light brown turning to grey and cut short. His face, like the rest of his body, was thin, with incredibly blue eyes that sparkled with good humour. When in conversation with her she noticed that his eyes never left her face, and he used his hands a lot, gesturing and emphasising his feelings.

They discussed the various types of property that Shirley might find suitable and then drove back to Martin's office. As Shirley got into her car he said

"I'll keep an eye out for anything that might be right for you and E-mail the details to you. Meanwhile let me know if you find anything. Oh and by the way, good luck with the case."

THIRTY FIVE

Cathy had just finished the second part of the TB test of Frank's cattle at Wistworthy Farm. One by one the beautiful Devon cattle, the Red Rubies as they were more popularly known, had gone through the cattle crush, which was the crate where they could be held and inspected without hurting themselves or anyone handling them. There she had felt and measured their necks for any tell-tale lumps that would denote that the animal was a re-actor. All were clear to Frank's great relief and so leaving her boots and overalls in the back of her car, amongst the boxes of medicines and other veterinary equipment, she went indoors with Frank for a well earned cup of tea.

As a small child she had stayed at the farm with her aunt and uncle for holidays, and had happy memories of days spent there. Her cousin Frank, though some years older than her, had been happy to take her to parts of the moor that he considered special, and had treated her and her sister Jenny as equals, not as silly little girls. And her uncle Stan had noticed her interest in nature and had taught her a lot about animals, which had no doubt influenced her decision to become a vet. Later, when she had qualified, she stayed there for several months until she managed to find a place of her own to live.

The kitchen was still the same as it had been in her childhood days, although some of the furniture had changed. The old settle that used to stand near the stove had long gone and so had Stan's leather armchair in which he had spent many a night during the lambing season. Sitting at the old scrubbed topped table it felt, as it so often did, as though she had stepped back ten years into the past. Frank lifted the lid of the Aga hotplate and there was the familiar hiss and bounce as a drop of water was trapped under the kettle. Linda, his wife joined them with their three year old daughter Jasmine who ran to Cathy to be picked up and made a fuss of.

"Well, that's over 'till the next time" said Frank pulling out a chair to sit down.

"All alright?" asked Linda.

"Yes, thank God, all clear."

"So what news from the village Cathy? As a friend of Sergeant Ashton I expect you to know more than most" said Linda with a smile. "I'm not privileged to any more information than you; all I know is that the police are treating Bosworth's death as murder."

"Sounds to me as though it must have been somebody local," said Frank. "Or at least, somebody who knew the area well."

"What makes you say that?"

"The fact that the body was put in Quentin Russell's grave."

"So who do you have as the most likely killer then?" asked Cathy.

"Just about anybody from the village, I should think" said Linda.

"According to Charlie, he heard a shot that probably killed Bosworth at half past six on the Tuesday evening. Who ever did it wouldn't have moved the body until later, when it was dark. So like I said, it must have been somebody local" said Frank.

"I always felt sorry for his wife" said Linda. "She didn't seem to have a life of her own, stuck up in that big house all on her own with only that bossy domineering man for a husband. You hardly ever saw her in the village, and when you did, she was as timid as a church mouse. Always looking over her shoulder as though she expected him to appear and tell her off for being there. Why is it that little men so often seem to have to make up for their lack of height by being so obnoxious?"

"I wouldn't be surprised if he beat her about" said Cathy. "She always wore long sleeves and high collars, if you noticed."

"Well I don't think that makes her the killer" said Frank.

"She certainly had motive, and she will probably inherit a vast sum of money, if he was as rich as he liked to make out."

"Perhaps she hired a hit man" said Cathy with a laugh.

"All I know is, it's a good job she's got Grace as a friend to help her through this terrible time" said Linda. "What ever her marriage was like, what ever he did to her, and we're only guessing, she will miss him....his death will have left a huge hole in her life now."

"John at the shop will be still worried by the threat of a rival business. I've no idea if Hilary is going to go ahead with Bosworth's plans to build, I read that his appeal was successful" said Frank.

"You don't think he could have done it do you?"

"It could have been anyone from this area, like I said; and that's what must make it a nightmare for the police who are trying to solve the case."

"She's got a brother hasn't she" said Cathy "he was with her at the funeral. He may be some help and support to her."

"Yes, but he works, or worked for Bosworth, at the water bottling factory. He also used to go shooting with him occasionally, so I'm not sure if he would be her friend or his. You know what men can be like, all lads together. Excluding you dear, of course" said Linda, turning towards Frank with a smile.

THIRTY SIX

The nursing home in Dawlish was a new building, purposely constructed for the job of caring for the elderly. Shirley and Newnan rang the bell by the security key pad and waited. They had to wait for a few minutes before a smart lady in a navy blue nurse's uniform came and opened the door.

Shirley introduced herself and Newman, and asked if she might speak with the manager. They went into a hallway where a small table stood against the wall. On it was a visitors' book which they duly signed, and then they were led down a wide passage with grab rails on either side and shown into an office at the far end. A brass plate on the door bore the name of T Salmon, Matron. A lady of, Shirley guessed, about fifty was sitting behind a desk working on a computer. There was a pile of paper work to one side of her, with a small tray of coffee and biscuits to the other. She rose from her seat as they entered and came around from behind her desk to greet them. She then placed two chairs in front of the desk and resumed her position behind it. After the necessary introductions Shirley said

"We are investigating the death of Mr Mark Bosworth. His wife was here on the evening in question, Tuesday the twenty fourth of October, visiting her mother. We need to verify that and also learn anything that you can tell us about Mr and Mrs Bosworth."

"I can't tell you very much about him, I think that I only met him once. He seemed very business like, almost abrupt. It was he who paid the bills and there was never any problem there."

"Did Mrs Bosworth's mother?....I'm sorry I don't have her name...."

"Mrs Armand....."

"Did Mrs Armand have any other visitors?"

"Yes, her son Jeremy. He used to come....usually on Fridays, though not every week."

"And do you have a security system of vetting or checking visitors?"

"Oh yes, we keep details of all visitors, including a photograph. That way, should we have a new member of staff on duty who hasn't met a particular visitor, identification is no problem."

"Would it be possible to speak to the person who met Mrs Bosworth on that Tuesday evening?"

"Certainly, I'll just get one of the nurses to check in the visitors' book to see who signed in and out that evening and at what times. She will also look to see who was on duty then and if she is available now."

She picked up the telephone and spoke a few words into it. After a brief conversation she said

"Hilda is one of our staff who has been here for several years. She took Mrs Armand's tea tray into her that day and would have met Mrs Bosworth. I've asked her to come here to speak to you. Ah, here she is."

A small lady with ginger hair and a smiley face covered in freckles knocked and came into the room. Shirley again explained the reason for their visit and asked if Mrs Bosworth had seemed in any way different from her usual behaviour.

"No....not so far as I could see. She was never what you might call very outgoing, if you know what I mean. Her mother was on good form that day though, 'twas definitely one of her better days."

"What exactly does her mother suffer from?"

"Old age" said Mrs Salmon. "She has become a little infirm and is safer in this environment. She is also beginning to show some early signs of dementia, not much as yet, but it is something we have to watch."

"I took in her tea tray like normal" said Hilda. "I like to take it in when Mrs Bosworth is here, see? 'Cos she helps her mum if it's necessary, and that makes my job easier."

"Anything else happen that day that you remember?" asked Newman.

"Yes, Mrs Bosworth had a phone call from her brother. Because it was one of Mrs Armand's better days Mrs Bosworth passed the phone over to her mum and they had quite a little chat, her and her son, see?"

"And at what time would that have been? The phone call I mean."

"Well, 'twas just after I took in the tea things, she always has that at half past six, see?

"And does Mr Armand often phone here when Mrs Bosworth is visiting?"

"No, 's far as I can recall 'twas the only time. Well, there isn't much need for him to phone, seeing as he visits his mum here most Fridays, see?"

"Thank you very much. And when did Mrs Bosworth leave here that evening? Did you see her go, by any chance?"

"Yes, she left at half past seven. I remember 'cos I was talking to Mr Luscombe in the hall at the time. He comes to visit his mum on Tuesdays as well.....very friendly with Mrs Bosworth he is. They often leave together...."

"I don't think the Sergeant needs to hear gossip Hilda."

"But it's true Matron, 'tisn't gossip. And that day Mr Luscombe was later than usual....so they just sort of said hello and goodbye like....see?"

"And how long has this friendship been going on?" asked Shirley.

"Oh, over six months I should say. They have something in common like, with both their mums suffering the same, see?"

"Thank you, that's very interesting." Shirley turned to Mrs Salmon and said

"Do you think I could see a photograph of Mr Luscombe please?"

"Er...yes of course." She got up from her desk and going over to a filing cabinet in the corner of the room got out a folder from which she produced a card. On it was a photograph of Clive Luscombe with his name and address. She passed it over to Shirley saying

"Here you are, it's quite a good likeness. You don't think that either he or Mrs Bosworth had anything to do with Mr Bosworth's death do you?"

"At this stage Mrs Salmon it's all a matter of elimination." As she said this Shirley took out her mobile phone and placing the card on the desk took a photograph of it.

"Well, I think that that will be all for now. We may have to come back again to ask you some more questions, but if in the meantime you think of anything else that is relevant, please give me a call."

With that Shirley stood up and taking a card out of her bag handed it to Mrs Salmon, shook hands with her and with Newman following left the room. Hilda walked with them to the entrance hall where they signed out. Then as she held the door open for them she said in little more than a whisper

"'Tisn't gossip, I don't care what Matron says. They'm an item, as they say. I was in The Duke of York about a month ago. 'Twas my sister's birthday party, there was several of us there, and Mrs Bosworth and Mr Luscombe was there too. Sitting at a table all hosey-cosy like. And 'twasn't the first time they'd been there either."

"Really, what makes you say that?"

"Well, by the way they was talking to the barmaid, see?"

"Thank you, we'll bear that in mind" said Shirley.

Hilda shut the door behind them as she gave them an almost conspiratorial nod. Once in the privacy of their car Newman said

"So that makes two more people we've got to interview; Jeremy Armand the brother and this Mr Luscombe, whoever he may be."

"Yes, but before that I think we need to have a quiet word with Hilary Bosworth."

"Are you beginning to think that she might not be the 'femme fatale' she likes to portray? She couldn't have done it, because she was here visiting her mum. But d'you think she might have engineered it?"

"I'm not at all sure. She is either a very sad and damaged individual, or an Oscar winning actress."

Before driving up onto the moor to interview Hilary they went back to town and to the morgue. Shirley said that she wanted to have a word with Doctor Don Hall, the pathologist. A written report was all very well but sometimes it was better to talk face to face and ask questions. They went into the building, all clinical white walls and stainless steel surfaces. Although there was no odour at all, Shirley always imagined that she could smell the smell of death and she never liked the place. They found Don Hall in his office and sat down to wait while he finished some paper work.

"What can I do for you Sergeant?" he said as he pushed his chair back from the desk a little.

"You can tell us in layman's words just what happened to Mark Bosworth."

"He was shot at very close range with a shotgun. Conventional five shot cartridges, most probably both barrels."

"That would agree with what Charlie Blundell said he thought he heard. He said it sounded like b-bang" said Shirley.

"The blast virtually took out his heart; there would have been extensive bleeding. Death would have been instantaneous."

"Judging by the amount of blood on the ground I reckon it was" said Newman.

"Also, the right cuff of the sleeve of his jacket had been torn, at a guess I would say, by shot from the gun. There was also some burn damage. That, together with his finger prints on the barrel of the gun, makes me think that he might have grabbed hold of the gun just before or as it was fired."

"To take the gun away from the killer; is that what you mean?" asked Shirley.

"I can't say what his motive was, or exactly when and how it happened. All I can say is that it looks as though he could have had hold of the end of the barrel of the gun when it was fired. Of course the finger prints could have been old, and it could be that he put up his hand in an instinctive movement to defend himself."

"Anything else?" asked Newman.

"Yes, although this may have absolutely nothing to do with it."

He walked over to a filing cabinet in the corner and pulling out a file took from it a clear plastic envelope. He came back to his desk and tipped onto it a small plastic disc, about the size of a five pence piece. It was dark red, almost maroon in colour, and had a small design in black on it. This looked like a three pronged fork with the letter S woven into it.

"I have no idea what this is or where it originally came from. It was in the soil and the blood that was stuck on the wound on Bosworth's back. It could have been on the ground where he landed when he fell. It could have been in the soil of the grave, or somewhere in between. So it might have belonged to Bosworth, or his killer, or one of the grave diggers or none of them. You had better take it with you, although as I say, it may have nothing to do with Bosworth's death."

Looking more closely at it Newman said

"It looks like it could be the cover of a button or something. The design could be a trade mark or logo of some sort."

"Once again, too many variables" said Shirley.

THIRTY SEVEN

They sat in the car outside Grimstone Court. A light drizzle was falling and the leafless trees, grey skeletons against the misty background, were dripping steadily all around them. After a short silence as they looked around them Newman said

"If the killer had come here to kill Bosworth, what weapon was he going to use? I mean, suppose as you suggested, that he came here and then, when he saw Bosworth down in the field below he changed his plan....Well, what I'm trying to say is that he wouldn't have planned to shoot him in the house. A pool of blood in the field is one thing, but here....? The only way of killing that wouldn't leave a trace would have been strangulation; garrotting. And then it's a lot further to take him to the churchyard."

"Exactly; so was the original plan to kill, or just to frighten? If it was to kill, did the plan include hiding the body in the vicar's grave? Or was that an afterthought? Come on, let's go and have a word with his widow."

Once again it was Grace who answered the door and led them into the comfortable lounge.

"I expect its Hilary that you want to see, she's with Paul at the moment....there's so much to see to and sort out. I really don't know how she would manage without Paul.....mmm.... yes.....well I'll go and tell her you're here."

With that she scuttled out of the room with her head down which made her look even smaller than she was, leaving Shirley and Newman standing in front of the welcome fire that was burning merrily in the grate.

She returned with Hilary a moment or two later. Hilary was looking pale and drawn, as though she hadn't been sleeping well for several days, and Shirley felt that to interview her again was not the kindest thing she could be doing. She leant over to Newman and whispered

"Softly, softly."

Hilary held out her hand and after shaking with the two police officers offered them coffee and asked them to sit down.

"Do you have any information for me, or do you want to ask me some more questions?"

"I'm afraid it's more questions, Mrs Bosworth. You visited your mother on the Tuesday evening before your husband disappeared. What time was that, can you remember?"

"I think I was there from about six o'clock until half past seven. I like to be there at that time, it means that I can help Mum with her tea, which is generally brought in at half past six."

"So that was quite normal. Did anything unusual happen while you were there?"

"Unusual, no I don't think so......oh yes, my brother telephoned while Mum was having her tea. They had a nice little chat, it was good, and then I had a word with him."

"What was that about, may I ask?" said Shirley.

"He asked me what I would be doing next day, I'm not altogether sure why. So I told him that I would be going to the funeral of the late vicar. Then he said he would come too, if I wanted."

"Do you know where he was calling from?" asked Newman.

"From the factory, you know, the water bottling place. There was a lot of background noise to begin with and I said that I couldn't hear very well. So Jeremy said 'I'll go outside' and it was a lot better then. It was a good job he did, because Mum would never have been able to understand what he was saying if he had stayed indoors."

"There's a lot of noise in the factory is there?"

"Yes, bottles clicking and the whirr of machinery."

"Is there not a phone in the office where it's quiet?" asked Newman, a puzzled look on his face.

"Oh yes, but Jeremy would never use that for a social call. He's a stickler for that sort of thing. He gets quite cross with people who help themselves to things from work, like pens and paper and using the copying machine. No, if he ever calls me it is always on his mobile."

"I see, thank you" said Shirley. "And how is your mother, is she happy there?"

"Oh yes, it's a lovely place, a real home from home. All the relatives that I have spoken to say the same."

"Do you get the chance to meet many of the other relatives?"

"The lady in the next room has become quite a friend to Mum, they spend a lot of time together, which is good. She has a very nice son who often visits on the same day as I do." She looked down at her hands in her lap, twisting her fingers together nervously, and then said

"We have become sort of friends. It's good to have someone to talk to who understands what it is like to have a mother in a home like that, with the sort of problems that she has."

"Of course" said Shirley "It must be a great comfort to you."

"He works for an insurance company I believe; he's called Clive Lucsombe."

"So, as friends, has he ever visited you here?"

"Oh no." said Hilary rather forcefully.

"So your husband didn't ever meet him, didn't know of him."

"No, he didn't have much to do with Mum. He was always too busy, I suppose."

"And you visited your mother again this last Tuesday, so you met Mr Luscombe then? I presume you will have told him about the death of your husband."

"Yes, of course."

"And did you tell your mother?"

"No, I thought it better not to. She was not having one of her better days, so I thought perhaps I'd leave it 'till later, when she's more receptive."

"I see, I'm sure that you're right. Well thank you very much Mrs Bosworth. You've been very frank. We may have to talk again, I don't know."

"One thing Sergeant, when will they release the body for burial?"

"That will be up to the coroner to decide. There will have to be an inquest first, but I don't suppose it will be very long after that."

Shirley got up out of her chair and she and Newman walked out into the hall with Grace accompanying them.

"I'm sorry we had to question her like that, with her being in such a raw state" said Shirley to Grace as they walked out into the open. "But I was glad to hear that she has made a friend of Mr Luscombe, we all need friends."

"Would you say that her brother is her friend, or more a friend of Mr Bosworth?" asked Newman.

"Well....I couldn't say. What a strange question.....He works, or should I say, worked for Mr Bosworth.....And he went shooting with him once or twice I believe.....mmm.....but I would think he would be Hilary's friend.....yes....he's very fond of her."

When they got back into their car Newman said

"I wonder how much Jeremy knows about his sister's marriage. I wonder if he knows that Bosworth used to beat his wife."

THIRTY EIGHT

Clive Luscombe had just finished his supper, his favourite Chinese take-away, Singapore Chow Mein. Since he had last spoken with Hilary, when she had told him about the death of her husband, he had read the sensationalized details in the papers. He felt that he ought to visit her at her home. He was after all a friend of several months' standing, but the last thing that he wanted to do was to cause her any embarrassment. She had obviously never told Mark about their friendship, perhaps she had never told anybody.

His thoughts went back to the meetings they had had and how their friendship had grown. At first it had been their mothers who had been friends. That had thrown them together and then they had often walked out of the nursing home to their cars together, talking about the problems faced by their mums and discussing their future.

Then one evening he had said that he was going to a pub for a meal and would she like to join him. He hadn't had the chance to eat earlier, being late home from work. To his surprise she said that she would be delighted and so they went to The Duke of York and that was when they really started to get to know one another. So it was that most Tuesday evenings, after visiting their mothers, they had a meal together in a pub. Sometimes Hilary was unable to join him because Mark would be home and would expect her to be there. But he seemed to have appointments of some sort on most Tuesdays, perhaps, thought Clive, because he knew that Hilary would also be out.

Clive had worked out, soon after their relationship started, that Mark was a demanding and domineering husband and that Hilary was more than a little afraid of him. Then on the third or fourth occasion, after they had had a meal together and he was helping her on with her coat, she had winced as he touched her. Not sure of what he had done, if anything, he said

"I'm sorry, did I hurt you, have you got a sore place there?"

"Just a bit of a bruise, I slipped and fell in the shower....silly thing to do."

But when a few weeks later he noticed a bruise on her arm, half concealed by her loose long sleeve, he feared that he knew what was going on in the Bosworth household.

Clive's father had been a dictatorial parent. He ran the house with an iron rod. Clive had been born when both his parents were relatively old. His father was nearly forty five and his mother forty two. In fact Clive often thought that his birth was a surprise, or more likely a mistake. That may have explained his father's behaviour. Discipline had been meted out with quiet, stern talk and frequent beatings, and Clive had soon learned to behave and keep out of his father's way. His mother would often warn him, saying

"Don't upset your father."

But it was she, he later realized, who was taking all the brunt of his father's wrath. He would hear them, when he had gone to bed and was in his room in the dark. His father's stern voice, not shouting, oh no, it was more of a menacing, quiet, whisper-like tone that was even more frightening. And his mother, whimpering, pleading, apologising, followed by the occasional sound of a slap. One morning, after his father had gone to work and Clive was about to go off to school he had run upstairs to get something that he had forgotten. As he passed the partly open door to his parents' room he caught a glimpse of his mother dressing. She had her back to him and was wearing only her panties. Her naked back was a mass of dark purple bruises. Not knowing what to do Clive stopped momentarily, should he speak, and if so what should he say? It was obvious what had been happening, but equally obvious that his mother didn't want him to know about it. So he ran on and made his way to school, a worried little boy of ten.

It was after that incident that he started to protect his mother when ever he could. It had meant that he often received the beating that might have been given to his mum, but he felt that it was the right thing to do.

As he grew, he learned some of the tricks that she had been using to de-fuse awkward situations and reduce the likelihood of a beating. He even, on rare occasions would stand up to his bullying father, but never did he let him know that he was aware of the way he was treating his wife.

Then one day when Clive was fifteen, his father didn't come home from work. They sat and waited, afraid to start their supper until he came home, and watched the television. The local news was dominated by the success of the local football team in a national competition. At the end there was a small item about an accident on the A38.

Two hours later, having finally eaten their late supper, there was a knock on the door.

"Answer that, will you dear" said his mother, and Clive had duly gone to the door. In the light from the porch were two policemen in uniform, one of them a WPC. Clive asked them what they wanted, to which they had asked if they might come in. Somewhat puzzled Clive had led them into the sitting room where his mother was hastily tidying the newspaper off the settee.

The police had then told them that his father had been involved in the car accident that they had seen on the television news earlier.

"Oh my God; is he alright?" asked his mother.

"He was taken to hospital in Plymouth. I'm very sorry to have to tell you that he was pronounced dead on arrival."

"I'm sure he didn't suffer, Mrs Luscombe" said the WPC.

It had taken his mother several months to come to terms with the fact that her husband was no longer there. Her self-confidence didn't seem to grow, as Clive had hoped that it might do, now that the bullying and beatings had stopped. But she was calmer and he could see that she was happy at last. He had slowly but surely adopted the role of the man of the house, looking after his mother. After he finished his education he managed to get a good job with an insurance company, with whom he had stayed. He had never married, not because his mother put pressure on him to stay and look after her, but because he had only once met a girl with whom he felt he would like to spend his life. Unfortunately, fate had decided that it wasn't to be. He had had a few girl friends before her, but they had all seemed too self assured and, in his eyes, too cocky. Perhaps because he had looked after his mother for so long, protecting her and caring for her, he needed a girl friend who was more like her. With Hilary he was beginning to feel that there was an understanding and a bond of friendship, a friendship that could possibly be built on.

Then, that evening in the pub when he had seen the bruising on her arm, he had told her of his childhood and of the way his father had treated his mother. She had listened in silence to his story, twisting her hands together and looking down at the table. When he finished he reached across the table and taking her hand said

"So you see, I know the signs, I've seen it all before. It isn't your fault, you are a victim. No doubt he has always told you that you are to blame, as my father did my mother, but I can assure you that you are not. If he won't stop, you must leave him; get out of this brutal relationship. I will do anything that I can to help you."

"Oh I wish...but he is so good to me in so many other ways....I have such a lovely house and...."

Clive knew exactly what she was feeling, he had seen it all before with his mother. The hopeless situation which the abused was afraid to leave, for fear that anything else might be worse. It was almost like an addiction to drink or drugs, she was aware that she should give up but she feared the alternative and so stayed with what she knew. She was also afraid that he would come after her and drag her back. And then there was the fear of being made to look a fool in front of others who might think that she was making a fuss about nothing.

He shook his head, rousing himself from his thoughts of their earlier meetings, stood up and carried his plate to the sink. As he washed up the few items he decided that he would go and see her, maybe tomorrow. He now knew where she lived and.....well....perhaps it would be better if he rang first.

THIRTY NINE

Back in the incident room D I Smith was holding forth. Shirley and Newman were sitting at the back of the room with the rest of the team at their desks.

"So far we have very little to go on. The deceased was a ruthless man, disliked by most of those who had any sort of dealing with him. Yet one could hardly call that reason enough to kill him. You've been looking into his business affairs Tom" he said, looking at one of the sergeants who sat in front of a computer, "what have you discovered?"

DS Tom Watson had worked with DI Smith for many years and was the only sergeant to be addressed by his Christian name. He pushed his chair back a little from his desk and turning slightly so as to talk to all those in the room said

"Quite a lot, though how much of it relates to this murder is hard to tell. He started several years ago with a small transport business, working between Europe and The Middle East. There was some speculation that he was involved in illegal activity, drug running and immigrants. But then about fifteen years ago there was a turf war and a bigger lot took over, putting Bosworth effectively out of business. Not long after that a combined operation involving police forces from France, Germany and the UK was successful in wrapping up that mob. I believe they were given some useful information. It was a big trial and the sentences were pretty harsh."

"Would that information have come from our friend Mr Bosworth?"

"Quite possibly."

"So have any of those finished their sentence? Could one or more of them be out for revenge?"

"That's what I'm looking into. The difficulty is that several of those sentenced are serving their time in foreign jails. Since then Bosworth has gone legit. He came down to the West Country about ten years ago when he got married. First of all to Exeter, and then he moved to where he is now, four years ago. He went into property in a fairly big way, a block of flats in Plymouth, mostly occupied by DSS tenants, and an up-market retirement complex for elderly people outside Exeter. He also has his water bottling plant but I think Sergeant Ashton is looking into that. But his main source of income now is his money lending website, 'Cash 4 U'."

"What exactly is that" asked DI Smith.

"It advertises itself as a no interest Pay Day loan service. It is true there is no interest charged on the first four weeks or until the pay day after the loan was taken out. But after that the rate of interest is horrendously high, something like four thousand percent. The thing is, the people who take out these sorts of loans are up to their eyes in debt already. When pay day comes all their money is already spoken for so to speak, so they have no chance of re-paying the new loan and then the interest piles up."

"So how does Bosworth get his money, you can't get a shirt off a naked man."

"He probably sends in his heavies, he wouldn't dirty his own hands. But he would probably wait until the interest had piled up; get a better return that way."

Turning to Shirley, DI Smith asked

"What have you been able to discover in the village, Ashton?"

"Not a lot Guv, there are too many people who had a good reason to dislike or even hate Bosworth, but whether any of them would have killed him....? We are still trying to check all their alibis. The trouble is, I get the feeling that most of them will cover for their friends and neighbours. They may well look upon the killer as a sort of hero, the man who saved the villagers from the evil Mr Bosworth, up in the big house."

"And who do you have as the most likely prime suspect?"

"At the moment, no-one."

They left the room soon after to continue their enquiries and as they walked out into the station car park Newman said

"I think I know what it was about that chap who was staying in the holiday complex. You know, John Cash. You said I was getting him mixed up with the singer fellow."

"What about him?" asked Shirley.

"I was talking to my missus about it last night. She remembers that sort of thing better than I do. Anyway, there was a piece in the paper about him. 'Cash blames Cash' was the headline, or something like that. This man was blaming Cash 4 U for his daughter's death. But my missus kept the paper 'cos there was a recipe that she liked the look of on the same page, so I was able to read the article myself."

"Really?"

"Apparently his daughter Ann was a very clever kid, won a scholarship to Cambridge, did well there and got first class honours. She then went on to get a good job in London somewhere. Bought herself a flat and everything seemed to be going well, according to her parents. The trouble was she was very clever maybe, but she had no common sense, at least not where money was concerned. You know how it is with some of these very clever people. Well, unfortunately the firm she was working for went bust and she was out of a job. She had overspent, like so many people, and had huge debts. She obviously thought that she would be OK with her good job and that. But sadly, she didn't manage to get another job and things went from bad to worse. When finally she did manage to get a job it was not a particularly well paid one and she was still short of cash. Then she fell into the trap of borrowing from Cash 4 U. Again the debts mounted up, but the silly girl hadn't told her parents. I suppose she was either ashamed or maybe she thought that she would be able to sort it out herself. Eventually it all got too much for her and she committed suicide. Naturally her parents were not only devastated but furious with the loan company and blamed it for sucking their daughter into the debt that she could never get out of. They went to the newspapers in the hopes that others might learn and not fall into the same trap."

"It all sounds dreadfully sad, that this young girl left home and communication between her and her parents seems to have completely failed. I suppose that's what can sometimes happen these days when youngsters go off to the big city to earn their living. But are you sure that the Mr and Mrs Cash who were staying in the holiday complex were the ones in the paper?"

"No, and even if they were, would they have known that the head man of Cash 4 U was called Mark Bosworth and lived nearby. It all seems very unlikely, that's why I didn't say anything when we were in there just now. I think I ought to try and investigate it

176

further before I say anything to Storming Norman. There was one thing that particularly interested my missus. The parents told the paper that the last time they spoke to the daughter she was all happy and excited because she had a new boy friend. Some chap that she had met at a friend's wedding. They hadn't met him yet and were looking forward to doing so, but he was away in the forces serving somewhere. They didn't know much about him except that he was a captain with a French sounding name. So you can understand that they were some surprised when their daughter killed herself a few weeks later."

"Would the daughter have confided in her boy friend?"

"Who knows, I get the impression that she was too embarrassed to tell anyone of her financial difficulties."

FORTY

Grace had gone into the church to check on the flowers. There were always a few that needed removing; nothing looked worse, she felt, than a couple of dead flowers in an otherwise fresh display. Coming in from the bright light of the sunlit outdoors, the interior of the church was dark. At first she thought she was alone but then she heard a sobbing sound coming from the darkest corner of the building. She carried on seeing to the flowers and then walked towards the sound.

Hunched in a pew, with head in hands was a small figure. With each sob the shoulders of this sad figure shook gently. Grace walked over, not sure whether to intrude or not, and said

"Can I help? I hate to see you sad like this."

The figure straightened and looked at Grace with tear-stained cheeks. It was Jane from the shop, and Grace almost ran over when she saw who it was and sat beside her.

"My dear Jane, whatever's the matter?"

"It's nothing, nothing."

"Oh dear......what you mean is you don't want to tell me.....am I right?"

Jane sobbed again clutching her wet handkerchief and looking at Grace with such a pleading expression that it was obvious that she really wanted to share her problem with somebody."

"All things in life are better for sharing, both good things and the bad ones" said Grace, putting her hand on Jane's arm. "And a problem shared is a problem halved, as the saying goes.....mmm....yes, I can assure you that you'll feel a lot better once you get it off your chest."

Jane nodded and after a short pause while she regained her composure she said

"It's John. He's been getting up in the night. At first I thought that he was going to the loo. I would hear him get up, but I would be half asleep and not notice if or when he came back to bed. Then maybe a couple of hours later I would hear him come back to bed; so I naturally thought that he had been out twice. I wondered if he was alright, did he have a problem that the doctor should know about, maybe to do with his prostate. You know how men are; they don't want to see the doctor, especially if it's anything to do with their water-works.

When I asked him he just said that he needed the loo and perhaps he ought to stop taking his last drink before bedtime. I assumed that he was getting out more than once. But then I woke on a number of occasions to find that he wasn't in bed and he didn't come back for a long time. In fact one time I got out of bed and went looking for him. He wasn't in the bathroom, he wasn't downstairs either, he had gone out somewhere. Why.....it was dark outside.....what on earth could he have been doing out there? I didn't say anything to him about it when he came back that night, but when it happened again a few nights later I felt that I had to ask him."

"And what did he say?"

"He just said that he couldn't sleep and that he had gone for a walk. He said it was lovely out in the quiet of the night, it was so peaceful and yet surprisingly easy to see. When I asked him why he couldn't sleep he said he didn't know, he supposed he just wasn't tired. But I'm sure that there's something that he doesn't want to tell me, something bad that he thinks it would be best if I didn't know about."

"And what do you think that might be?" asked Grace.

"Well, it could be the business. Things haven't been too good lately, what with the threat of closing the Post Office and then Mark Bosworth wanting to build his shop."

"Yes....I can see that might have been a worry....but the Post Office is not closing is it?"

"No, and I don't think that we would lose a great deal of trade to Bosworth's shop, do you?"

"Oh, I wouldn't know.....I don't suppose you would but I know nothing about business."

"Then when I heard this dreadful business about the murder and the body turning up in your late husband's grave. Oh that must have been awful for you, I am sorry. Well, John was out that night and......well.....they say that whoever did it, murdered Bosworth I mean, probably moved the body in the small hours."

"But it couldn't have been John.....surely you don't think that do you?"

"I don't know what to think. If only he would talk to me, take me into his confidence, tell me what it is that is making him unable to sleep at night. The trouble is that I'm afraid to ask.....I suppose because I'm afraid of what the answer might be."

She started crying again, heartfelt sobs racking her body. Grace sat beside her wishing that there was something that she could do to help. Finally Jane said

"I feel so guilty; I feel that I'm betraying John by even thinking that he could do something so terrible. But what if I'm not the only one, what if the police think it too?"

"What do you mean? Thinking what?"

"You see, I went to the wholesaler's that evening, after we shut shop."

"Which evening?" asked Grace.

"The Tuesday evening......when Bosworth was killed. I didn't get home 'till gone eight o'clock. I don't know what John was up to....don't you see....he could be the killer....."

FORTY ONE

The water bottling plant was in a small industrial estate. Because of the nature of most of the businesses there, the whole area was enclosed in a high chain-link fence topped with three strands of barbed wire. There was also a watchman at the entrance and he locked the gates at night and regularly patrolled the roads after the day-time units closed for the night.

Shirley and Newman checked in at the gate and asked for directions. As they drove on Shirley said

"We will probably want to have a word with him later, if he was the man who was on duty here that evening."

Next to the large metal roll-down door of the bottling plant was a small door on which was a white sign with office written on it. Under the window beside it was parked a bicycle, with a helmet hanging from the handlebars. They went in and were met by a young dark-haired girl with huge owl-eyed spectacles who got up from behind her desk and smiled at them.

"We are looking for Jeremy Armand" said Newman "is he here?"

"Yes, I'll get him for you. Who shall I say it is?"

"Detective Sergeant Ashton and Detective Constable Chaffe."

"Oh, right" she said and almost ran out of the office into the factory. As she opened the door their ears were assailed by the noise from the plant; a constant whirring and the musical clinking of glass bottles. She came back after a short while with Jeremy who was wearing a smart light blue boiler suit and wellington boots. He looked at them enquiringly and asked

"How can I help you?"

"We are investigating your brother in law's death, Mr Armand. We would like to ask you some questions."

"Certainly, come on through to my office, it's a bit cramped but a bit more private."

He led the way through another door into a room that was hardly bigger than a cupboard. In it was a desk on which were a computer and a basket with a few documents in it. Behind the desk was a swivel chair and in front of it a small wooden chair. On the ledge of the small window were two glass bottles with the inscription

Dartmoor
Dew
Natural spring water

written in red letters. They were a graceful shape, wider at the base then swelling slightly before tapering to a slender neck. The impression was of a drop of water and they were topped with crown stoppers, one blue for still water and the other green for sparkling.

"I'm sorry, there's only one chair."

"That's alright" said Shirley, sitting down. Newman stood beside her taking out his notebook.

"Could you tell us where you were and what you were doing on the evening of Tuesday October the 24th? That would be the day before the funeral of the late vicar. I believe you went to the funeral with your sister."

"Yes, well I was working here that day, or night I suppose it was. I was here from four o'clock

183

until eleven. We sometimes do a night shift if we have a large order to fill."

"Was there anyone else here working with you?"

"Not after five o'clock. It only needs one to keep an eye on things."

"I see, and how come you the manager does this extra shift?" asked Newman "I would have thought that you would delegate that to one of the other workers here."

"None of them wanted to do it, they all wanted to get home and watch telly that evening, it was the Barcelona match if you remember. I don't mind, I live on my own so I don't have to go home to a family, and I don't follow football. Then I can take time off another day, like I did to go to the funeral."

"So there is nobody who can vouch for your being here that evening?"

"Not really, no."

"And you were here from four 'till eleven you say."

"Yes. Come to think of it, the chap who mans the entrance gate spoke to me; I was outside having a five minute smoke break. Ought to give it up I know, but...."

"And when would that have been?"

"I can't say exactly, I suppose it would have been about six o'clock, it was still broad daylight I remember that."

"So you can leave the plant while you have a smoke break. How long can it be left unattended?"

"Well, it's not unattended, I leave the door open so I can hear if anything goes wrong, but I never leave it for more than a few minutes."

"And did you go out again, for a break that is?" asked Shirley.

"No I don't think so......oh yes I did, I remember now. I rang my sister; she was visiting Mum at the nursing home. In fact I had quite a nice long chat with Mum, it was one of her better days."

"What d'you mean by better days?"

"She doesn't always recognise me, even face to face. That day she knew my voice and it was lovely to have quite long conversation. Yeah, it was good" said Jeremy, smiling at the thought.

"So why did you go outside to phone her?" asked Newman.

"It's too noisy in the plant, Hilary said she couldn't hear what I was saying, so I went outside."

"But surely there's a phone in the office, isn't there?"

"Oh I wouldn't use that for a social call; I always use my mobile for social calls."

"And at what time did you make that call, d'you remember?"

"It must have been about half past six or just after. Mum told me she had just had her tea, so maybe it was nearer twenty to seven."

"Do you often ring your sister from here?"

"Not often."

"So was there any particular reason why you rang her that day?"

"I wanted to know about the funeral; what time it was to be etcetera."

"Did you have a personal reason for going to the funeral; I mean, did you know the Reverend Quentin Russell?"

"No, never met the man. But I heard about him from a friend of mine. As a fellow soldier I was

185

curious as to what sort of a man he must have been. After all, you don't find VC's in a packet of corn flakes. He must have been a truly remarkable man. I also wondered if the man who told the paper about his service days and getting the VC would be there. You know, the man who was one of the three that he rescued."

"And what branch of the services were you in?" asked Shirley.

"The Paras."

"And for how long did you wear the red beret?" said Newman, hoping to impress by showing off his knowledge of the Paras head-gear.

"Fifteen years; and although it is always called a red beret, in actual fact it is maroon. The colour was chosen by Daphne du Maurier the novelist, who was the wife of General Frederick Browning, commander of the First Airborne Division in nineteen forty two."

Shirley looked at Newman with a smile saying

"There you are, a free history lesson." Then turning to Jeremy she asked

"When did you hear that your brother in law was missing?"

"Hilary rang me, that morning, asking me if I knew where Mark was. I suppose she hoped I would know, but of course I didn't. He didn't confide in me, in fact I know very little about his life, private or public."

"So you went to the funeral."

"Yeah, I cycled over, Hilary let me use the shower and change into more suitable clothes."

"So what's going to happen now, to this place I mean?" asked Shirley.

"The idea was to transfer the business to the new building in his field. The set up here was always considered to be only temporary. Mark wasn't sure if the enterprise would be a success. So this was a trial run so to speak, both for the water and for me."

"And has it proved to be a success?"

"I think so; we seem to be getting plenty of orders. Our customers are mostly restaurants and hotels who want a nice shaped glass bottle to put on the table. Most bottled water is in plastic bottles, except a well known French one or two. As things are going it would be good if we did move, the new place would be bigger and the water would be on tap."

"But the move would mean a lot further for you to go to work wouldn't it?" said Newman.

"It's only fifteen, maybe twenty minutes on a bike, not much more than I do now from where I'm living."

"I take it that that's your bike outside; it looks a smart piece of kit. But you must be pretty fit; I would have thought it would take that long in a car."

"Yeah, well I like to keep in shape."

"Well, thanks for your time" said Shirley. "We may need to speak to you again. If you should think of anything that might help us to find who killed him, please get in touch."

They shook hands and as they passed through the outer office the girl with the owl eye spectacles gave them a cheery smile and a wave.

"There's one very happy member of staff here" said Shirley.

"So what d'you think Sarge, is he in the frame?"

"If he is, for the moment I can't think how. Before we leave lets have a word with the chap at the gate."

They pulled up by the entrance and went to the small office building beside the gate. A young man in a navy blue uniform met them, asking them their business.

"We need to know who was on duty here on October 24th" said Shirley after she had introduced herself. The young man went into his office and looked at the large chart on the wall which showed who was working and when.

"It wasn't me, it was Colin."

"When is he next on?" asked Newman.

"He's on tomorrow."

"And what about the CCTV tapes? I see there's a camera outside."

"They are all sent to head office at Exeter. Why, what's this all about, has Colin been up to something?"

"No, just routine enquiries, thanks for your time."

FORTY TWO

Shirley had left Newman at the station to see if he could find any further information on the Mr and Mrs Cash who had stayed at the holiday complex. Meanwhile she had driven over to the address Mrs Small had given them for her friend. Something had not quite rung true when she and Newman had interviewed Joe and his wife. They both seemed to be hiding something, and curiously they seemed to be hiding what ever it was from each other. As Newman had said as they had left, he felt certain that Mrs Small would be on the phone to her friend to arrange her alibi.

So, having entered the address into her Sat-Nav, Shirley followed the route and found herself in a quiet street on the outskirts of town. On both sides of the road, reasonable sized nineteen-thirties houses stood back from the road in tree-lined gardens. She stopped outside the house she was looking for; a double fronted brick built property with lead-paned bay windows either side of a front porch. Beside the house was a recently built garage, a feature that was repeated beside most of the other houses in the road.

Shirley walked up to the front door and rang the bell. There was no answer and casually turning round she noticed that she had an audience. Somebody was watching her from behind a net curtain that was moving in the downstairs' window of the house opposite. Shirley tried the bell again and looked up at the upstairs windows in a bit of exaggerated play acting for the benefit of the watcher. Then she walked back into the road and after looking up and down she went up to the door of the watcher's house and rang the bell. Almost instantly it was opened by a small woman with short grey hair and gold rimmed glasses wearing a navy blue skirt and a light blue cardigan.

"Can I help you?" she asked with a smile.

"Yes" said Shirley "I was hoping to visit my friend in the house opposite. It is a bit unexpected and I did try ringing her earlier. I had intended coming here two weeks ago, but my plans were changed unexpectedly. Now I find myself in the area and I thought I would look in on the off chance that she might be at home. It seems as though I've missed her, I'll have to come back later, I suppose she's out at work or something."

"Yes, I think she must be. It's a good job you didn't come a fortnight ago, because you would have been disappointed then as well."

"Really, why is that?"

"Well, she was away on holiday in Tenerife, didn't get back here until the beginning of this week."

"Really, well thank you for your help, it's been nice meeting you."

"Shall I tell her you called?"

"No, I'll give her a ring later. Bye."

With that Shirley got back into her car and drove back to the station. While she was there DS Tom Watson called her over and said

"I've got something that might interest you. One of the members of that gang that Bosworth helped to send down was released from prison in Munich six weeks ago. His name is Dieter Hoffman. A casual watch was kept on him for a while, but he disappeared off the radar about a month ago. He may have gone anywhere in the EU, border controls aren't what they used to be. He's short, five foot eight, well built. Looks like a prize fighter from all I can gather."

Shirley thanked him and made a note to ask in the village if anyone matching that description had been seen lately. Then she went and collected Newman who had been having a cup of tea in the canteen. She told him about the news from Germany and asked

"Did you manage to find out anything more about Mr and Mrs Cash?"

"Not really, apart from the fact that they were definitely the parents of the girl who killed herself. I've had a good look on the internet and I can't find Bosworth's name anywhere on the Cash 4 U website. If he is the man in charge he doesn't advertise the fact. It seems to me that they were down here for a few days' break and it was a total coincidence that they were staying near to Bosworth's home on the night that he was killed. Sergeant Watson says he has a friend in the force up there. He will make a few discreet enquiries, but I don't think they have anything to do with it."

"Well I guess we were right about the Smalls hiding something from each other. Mrs Small was not visiting her friend as she said. At least she wasn't visiting the person whose name she gave us, because that person was away on holiday in Tenerife."

"So what are we going to do now then Sarge?"

"We're going back to the village and I'm going to drop you there. While you make a few more enquiries in the pub and the shop, as to who was around there between half past five and seven o'clock, I'm going to have another word with Mrs Small......on her own, if I can."

As they drove up onto the moor the clouds thickened and the patches of sunlight decreased. Very few of the trees standing up on the hedges had any leaves left, and their dark shapes seen in silhouette against the sky looked like dancing skeletons.

"I still say this landscape looks threatening" said Shirley with a shudder.

""Wait 'till you see it in the spring or early summer on a bright sunny day, you'll think differently then."

"Maybe, right now it just looks cold and unfriendly."

They drove into the village and Newman got out.

"I'll see you here later" said Shirley, and with that she drove off towards Grimstone and the two cottages. She parked in front of the second one and walked over to the door. This time the door was not opened as she approached it. She knocked on it loudly and waited. From within she could hear the boisterous barking of their Springer spaniel. After a few minutes and a second knocking she heard footsteps and the door opened. Angie stood, bent over holding the dog by its collar. She was dressed in jeans and an old sweater and looked as though she had just come in from cleaning out the stables.

"Oh, it's you.....I was half expecting someone else......come in."

She led the way into the cluttered front room. The magazines on the tables didn't seem to have been moved since Shirley's last visit and the pile of coats on the chair in the corner if anything had been added to.

"Is your husband in?" asked Shirley.

"No, he's out riding, I doubt if he'll be back for an hour or more. Was it him you needed to see?"

"No, its you I wanted to talk to. I need to clear up something you said last time we were here. You gave us the name of the lady you had lunch with on that Tuesday, the twenty fourth; is there anything else you would like to add to that?"

"I don't think so......why?" she said with a slightly nervous look on her face.

"Well, the problem is, on that specific day and until recently, the lady in question was in Tenerife on holiday. So quite obviously you couldn't have spent time with her. If you were meeting someone else, who can vouch for your whereabouts on that day, it would be better if you told me now. Otherwise I might think that you could have been involved in the death of Mr Bosworth."

The indignant look on Angie's face quickly turned to concern and then to resignation. She pulled a chair out from the table and slumped down on it. Shirley remained standing, waiting for the inevitable excuses followed by a confession that she felt sure was about to come.

"Will what I tell you have to come out in court, or be made public? I mean, if I tell you where I was on that day can it be kept just between you and me?"

"That depends on where you were" said Shirley.

"I was with a gentleman friend of mine."

"Is he married as well?"

"No, he's a widower. He's an old friend and we meet occasionally, generally at his place. I suppose you'll want me to give you his name."

"Yes."

"He's called John, John Trimble."

She got up from her chair and walked over to the window and looked out. She stood there for a while, deep in thought as if deciding what to do. Then she took her mobile phone out of her pocket and dialled a number. Shirley watched, guessing what was about to happen. When the phone was answered Angie said

"I've got a Sergeant Ashton here who would like to have a word with you."

With that she passed the phone over to Shirley. Without saying why she needed to know, Shirley got him to say what he had been doing on the Tuesday in question. The fact that it had been Angie who had made the call seemed to indicate to him that he should tell the truth and he happily admitted that she had been with him. Shirley thanked him and passed the phone back.

"When we were last here I could tell that your explanation was more for your husband's benefit than for mine."

"Will he have to know? It's not what you think...."

'No, it never is' thought Shirley who was not in the least surprised at the revelation. She had been expecting it. But nothing would be gained by upsetting the relationship that existed between them. Too often she had seen marriages broken and families disrupted when police enquiries pulled dark secrets out into the open; secrets that would otherwise probably have remained hidden for ever without harming anybody. She had found out what she needed to know, Angie was not involved. Whether her husband Joe was or not was another matter. But it was not her job to break up their marriage.

"I see no reason why I should make your secret public; it has no bearing on the case. But if you do know of anything else that might help us I expect you to tell me."

"Thank you" said Angie, a look of relief spreading over her face. Then as Shirley started to walk towards the door she added

"Would you like a cuppa before you go?"

"No thanks."

The dog, sensing that people were about to go outside and that a walk might be next for him, jumped up and danced excitedly around the two women. They all walked out into the yard where Shirley shook hands and then drove off towards the village. As she went she wondered just how many seemingly happy couples had secrets that they kept from each other. Did Martin have secrets that he kept from her? She hoped not, but then, their relationship was purely business.

Back in the village she found Newman talking to Ben Fuller outside the shop. He came over and got into the car with her.

"So, what if anything have you found out?"

"First, no sighting of a well built German prize fighter, but there are a couple of things that may be of interest. Our friend Joe Small was in the pub from six till seven that evening. We thought that he was keeping something from his wife, maybe she's none too keen on his drinking, who knows. But if he was here in the pub until seven that means he couldn't have shot Bosworth at six thirty.

The other thing I got from Ben Fuller. It seems that Terry Cooper, the plumber chappie, had a very good reason for disliking Bosworth. Cooper wanted to buy the Old Mill, a property that was for sale by auction. I'm not sure of the exact details, but Bosworth made him pay ten thousand pounds more than he needed to and then laughed at him. It was something to do with a bill where Cooper had charged him extra for a late call out. This was Bosworth's way of getting his own back; with interest I should say."

"So now we've got to see Cooper and find out what he was doing that evening. D'you know where he is working at the moment?"

"Yes, he's doing an annual boiler service for Phil German at Manor Farm, just down the road from here. I got that bit of information from a chap in the pub."

"Right; we'd better go and see him right now, then we can go back to the industrial estate and see the watchman fellow."

FORTY THREE

Phil German had farmed Manor Farm all his life. He had taken over the tenancy from his father and when, due to death duties, a large part of the estate had been sold off he had bought the farm. Since then he had enlarged it by buying the land of the farm opposite, the buildings of which were now the holiday complex.

Shirley and Newman drove into the yard and parked in front of the old farmhouse. A little further on in the yard Phil was talking to Jeff, his workman, who was sitting in his tractor. Two collie dogs were beside Phil, one lying quietly at his feet. The other, probably younger, was standing watching the newcomers leaning forward slightly. Every now and then it would look back at Phil as if waiting for the signal to rush at them barking furiously. As the two detectives walked towards them, both dogs growled gently and Phil told them to be quiet. He recognized Newman and stepped away from the tractor saying

"Hello again, how can I help you?"

"We understand that you have Mr Cooper working here" said Shirley. "Would it be possible to have a word with him?"

"Yes, come on up to the house" said Phil. Then after a few more words to Jeff he led them out if the yard and through a small gate into the front garden of his home. It was a big house, some two hundred years old, set on a slight rise above the farmyard. Formerly it had been the home farm of the manor. It was built in Georgian style with an arched granite porch over the front door. It replaced the old farmhouse, which was to the side of the yard and was now occupied by Jeff.

Phil led them into a large kitchen in the centre of which was a large scrub-topped table surrounded by six chairs.

"Take a seat while I go and see if Terry has finished what he's doing."

Shirley looked around her. A large Aga stood in what had at one time been a huge open fireplace. The lintel of the chimney breast above it was a huge piece of local granite and above it the stonework had been cleaned of plaster and had been beautifully pointed. All the rest of the walls were painted an off white which helped to give brightness to the room. On the opposite wall under the large window there was a full length work-top with a double Belfast sink let into it, and built-in cupboards underneath. On another wall stood a Welsh dresser with blue and white plates displayed on its shelves and against the fourth wall was a large settee and a small table. The whole room gave out an aura of warmth and well used homeliness.

Phil returned with Terry who was carrying a large bag of tools. He stood looking down at them with a slightly pained expression on his face.

"We need to ask you some questions, Mr Cooper, if that's alright."

"Yes, I've just finished here; I was testing the system when Phil came to get me. What is it you want to know?"

"As you may know, Mark Bosworth has been found murdered" said Shirley. "We have to question everybody who had any dealings with him. I understand that you and he were not exactly the best of pals so I need to know what you were doing on Tuesday the twenty fourth of October between the hours of six and seven."

"Am I a suspect?" asked Terry with a look of dismay on his face that very shortly turned to a broad smile.

"It would help to eliminate you from a list of possible suspects" said Newman.

Terry put down his bag and looked inside it. He took out a small book which he opened and leafed through. After studying it for a short while looked up and waving the book at them said

"This is my work diary. On that day I was installing a new bathroom suite in Beech Cottage. It's a holiday cottage owned by some folks from London. I thought it was a good time to do it while they were away."

"Was anybody there with you?"

"No, I work alone."

"And when did you leave work?"

"I stayed 'till I finished, and that was about eight o'clock."

"Then what?"

"I went home; I was living in the annex of a friend's house then. I hadn't moved into my own place, in fact I've only just moved in now."

"So nobody can vouch for you, give you an alibi" said Newman.

"No. Does that mean I'm still a suspect?" he said, still with a smile playing on his lips.

"You don't seem to be particularly worried" said Shirley.

"Why should I be?"

"We understand that after Mr Bosworth caused you to pay a great deal more money for your new house than you intended or planned, you were heard to say that he ought to be shot and if you had a gun you'd be the first to do so. Am I right?"

"I may have said that. I reckon I was speaking for nearly everybody in the village. He was a most unpleasant and hated man. He seemed to delight in upsetting people. I'm not at all surprised that somebody killed him, but one thing I do know....it wasn't me. I can't prove that it wasn't me, any more than I can prove where I was that evening. By the same stamp, you can't prove that I killed him, can you?"

"If you didn't do it you have nothing to worry about" said Phil, who had been standing with his backside resting on the rail in front of the Aga.

"It's all a matter of elimination" said Shirley. "As you say, too many people in this village and elsewhere would have been happy to see Mr Bosworth dead. It's my job to find out who did it and bring him to justice."

"Justice!" said Terry with a laugh. "Justice has been done, if you ask me. Killing that bullying bastard was justice....and just retribution. He cost me a pretty packet, just out of spite. Everything he did was just to show that he could, because he had plenty of money. He didn't care who he hurt, he seemed to think that his money gave him the power of a god over the rest of us mortals. Justice.... huh!"

He picked up his bag and turning to Phil said

"I think you'll find that's all OK for another year."

"Thanks Terry."

"Thank you Mr Cooper" said Shirley. "I do understand your feelings. If you should think of anything that will help us in our enquiries please get in touch with me."

With another grin on his face Terry turned back to face her as he walked to the door and said

"Don't wait up; it'll be a sad day when I turn in the man who killed Bosworth"

With that he left the room and the three people who were left let out a sigh in unison.

"I didn't expect that" said Phil. "I knew he was upset, but I didn't think for one minute that his feelings ran that deep."

"Mr Bosworth certainly knew how to upset people" said Newman.

"You don't think he's guilty do you? I realize it sounds bad, the way he talks and all. And not having an alibi doesn't help, but...."

"Sometimes having an alibi is no proof of innocence" said Shirley.

"Well" said Phil. "I've known Terry since he was born. He used to come here for haymaking in the summer, like many of the local kids. He was always first here for work and last to leave. A good, honest, hard working boy and he's grown up to be a good, honest, hardworking man. He's had his share of knocks, but he's got over them all by his own efforts. I would trust him with my money, my house, my wife and my life. In fact, if he says that on that Tuesday evening he was in Beech Cottage and you say that you have information that he was seen coming out of Cleave Farm Lane, I would believe him rather than you. OK?"

There was silence for several minutes as Phil, obviously upset by Terry's outburst stood waiting for a response from Shirley with a pained look on his face. Finally she said

"We only need to eliminate him from our enquiries. There are so many people who had good reason to hate Mr Bosworth, and so many who cannot account for their movements between six and seven.

It's our job to find the guilty person, the last thing I want to do is to arrest the wrong man."

She got up from her chair and signalled for Newman to follow her. Then she went over to Phil and said

"I'm sorry if this has been difficult. It's not our intention to upset people. Thank you for your help, I hope we won't have to bother you again but if you should think of anything that might help us please get in touch."

With a smile, Phil held out his hand and said

"I wouldn't have your job, Sergeant, not for all the tea in China, not in this village at any rate."

FORTY FOUR

"We'll go and see if that young boy at the café is at home. It would be good to hear what he has to say about the man he spoke to who wanted to know the way to Grimstone Court."

"Right ho Sarge, and after that are we going to see the watchman at the bottling factory?"

"Yes, there's still a lot there that needs clearing up."

They stopped outside the café and went in. Jacqui came out from the back to serve them and was disappointed to find that they were not customers.

"We were hoping to have a word with your son, is he home from school yet?"

"Yes, but he's at home, not here. We live at Braggator with Mick Cribbett."

"Oh right, well we'd better go there then."

They drove on through the gate and down the lane to the old mine and the mine captain's house. Two collies came to meet them, as they parked outside the house, wagging their tails and barking in a friendly manner. In a field behind the house two horses, a grey and a bay, and a stocky pony were grazing contentedly. As they got out of the car Mick came out of the house to greet them.

"Good afternoon Mr Cribbett is Timmy here we need to ask him a couple of questions, he may be able to help us in our enquiries."

Mick turned, opened the front door and called to Timmy who came out almost immediately. Shirley guessed that he had been watching them from indoors.

"Hello Timmy. I understand that you gave directions to a gentleman who wanted to know the way to Grimstone Court."

"Yeah tha's right."

"Could you describe him to me?"

"I dunno....tall....smart', I mean smartly dressed, like a salesman type, or a bank manager. Short darkish hair, going a bit grey at the sides like."

"That's a very good description Timmy, not many people remember as well as that" said Shirley.

"Did he have an accent of any kind, was he local would you say?"

"Hard to tell, he didn't have no accent, not like Mick here or London talk like me" he said with a grin on his face.

"Could it have been our friend from the nursing home Sarge?" said Newman in a soft voice.

"That's a point" said Shirley digging in her bag to take out her mobile phone. She tapped it and flicked across it a few times until the photograph of Clive Luscombe came up on the screen. Then she passed it over to Timmy and said

"Could it have been this man?"

After a long look at the small picture Timmy said

"Yeah, could have been, it's a job to remember, it was a while ago and that's a very small photo, but yeah, it could be him. Why....did he kill old Bosworth?"

Mick gave a brief laugh and said

"Timmy, I don't think you should ask questions like that. It's up to the Sergeant to ask the questions."

"That's alright Mr Cribbett, Timmy has been most helpful and I can understand him wanting to ask questions." Then turning to Timmy she continued

"We don't know who was responsible, not yet any way. But we have to eliminate everyone who was in the area at the time, that way we may be able to find the guilty person."

"D'you want to join the police when you leave school?" asked Newman, smiling at Timmy.

"Dunno, I never thought about it, haven't really thought much further than my GCSE's next year."

"Well, the force could use a bright young kid like you, someone who sees things and notices what he sees. You've got good powers of observation."

"If you do remember anything else" said Shirley, trotting out the usual phrase as she was about to leave. It came out parrot fashion and sounded very false to her ears; although she realized that to everyone she spoke to it was new. Then she asked Mick

"Did you see anybody unusual that day, strangers to the area?"

"No, I can't say as I did."

"Oh well, we must be on our way, thanks once again."

As they drove up the lane Shirley said

"Smart kid that, not local though. Obviousely Mick Cribbett isn't his father."

"No, he and his mum came down from London a couple of years ago when her marriage failed. Her parents own the café. Timmy made friends with Mick but then one night he stumbled on a crime here while he was out badger watching. Surely you remember it, some gang growing cannabis in a barn near here.

Timmy got beaten up, left for dead. Mick found him and....love blossomed and now Jacqui is Mick's partner."

"They're lucky, Mick seems a really decent bloke."

They arrived at the entrance to the industrial estate just after the watchman had closed the gates. Leaving the car outside they walked in through the small gate for pedestrians and were met by a middle aged man in uniform. His grey hair was slightly too long to be either fashionable or tidy and his eyes looked tired, but his smile when they spoke to him was warm and friendly.

"Are you Colin?" asked Shirley taking out her warrant card to show him..

"Yes, I was told you might be coming. What's it all about."

"We would like to know what you were doing and everything you saw here on the evening of October the twenty fourth."

"Let's go in the office a minute" said Colin leading them into his small building.

"October the twenty fourth, it's hard to remember...."

"That was the evening of the Barcelona match" said Newman.

"Oh yeah, great game, did you see it? That second goal was pure genius......"

"No, I didn't see it, I was on duty" said Newman.

"Can you remember, now you know which day we are talking about?" asked Shirley. Colin thought for a moment, holding his chin between the finger and thumb of his right hand. Then he said

"Well, I closed the gates after everyone had gone; I suppose that would have been at about five thirty. Then I did a walk around, just to see if anybody was still here working."

"And did you see anyone?"

"Yeah, there were a couple of girls at the printers, but they were just leaving."

"In a car?"

"No, they walk, catch the bus outside. Then I saw Jez."

"Jez?"

"Jeremy from the water bottling factory; he was outside having a fag. We had a brief word. And then I came back here."

"Was that the only occasion that you did a tour of the place and did you see anyone else then or later."

"I went around again a bit before half six, it must have been about then 'cos I got back here in time for the local forecast on ITV and that's a bit before six thirty."

"Did you see anybody that time?"

"No, it was all quiet."

"Was the bottling plant working?"

"I think so, you can't tell when the door's shut, but Jez's bike was outside. Then I went round again at about seven o'clock or maybe a bit after that. It was getting dark and I wanted to lock up before the football started."

"And did you see anyone then?"

"Yeah, Jez was putting some rubbish in the bin, cardboard and stuff. The bins get emptied on Wednesday mornings, see."

"And that was the only person you saw then"

"Yes."

"Are there any other gates to this compound, or is this the only way in?" asked Newman.

"This is the only gate for vehicles."

"What about pedestrians?"

"Well, there's a gate behind the tile place, next to the bottling factory, but it's never been used so far as I know."

"Why on earth would they have a gate there if it's never used?"

"It was all to do with the ramblers or some such lot. There used to be a cottage on this site, farm worker's cottage for the farm down the road. When the planning application went in these people protested, said the right of way had to be maintained, public footpath and all that. Well it wasn't a public footpath at all, just a short cut for a bloke going to work. But they got their way and the site couldn't be developed unless there was a gate in the fence for the footpath. Ridiculous really, because when the planning was passed the first thing to happen was the cottage was knocked down. Mind you, it would have fallen down if they hadn't knocked it down. It had been derelict for years."

"Has this gate ever been used do you know, and is it kept locked? I presume it would be if you lock these gates."

"I've never known it to be used. There's a key somewhere, probably on a peg by all the others."

He went over to the back wall where, beside a wall chart showing the rota of who would be on duty, there was a row of small brass pegs on which were various keys. Each peg had a white label above it with the name of the key in question. One peg was marked Side Gate and on it was hanging a long old-fashioned key.

"Here it is Sergeant, all present and correct."

FORTY FIVE

Grace was at home cleaning some of the shelves in her kitchen. Having been away for some time staying with Hilary she noticed how dusty the place had become. Also with the autumn sun low in the sky it tended to show up the cobwebs. Because she was so short and because there was rather a lot to be done she had asked Lisa to help her and she was busy upstairs giving the bedrooms a good going over. She had to admit, if only to herself, that elderly eyes like hers didn't always see what needed cleaning.

When she got to the point on the worktop where the electric kettle was standing she decided that it was time to make a cup of coffee, so she filled the kettle and switched it on. Then she went out into the hall and called up the stairs to Lisa that it was time for a coffee break.

They sat facing each other across the kitchen table, drinking their coffee and eating ginger biscuits. Then Lisa said

"How is Mrs Bosworth, have you seen her lately?"

"She seems to be bearing up quite well. It has been a considerable ordeal for her, first the uncertainty of not knowing where her husband had gone and then to find that he had been murdered."

"And it doesn't seem as though the police have any idea who did it. Terry said they were quite nasty to him, almost accusing him, as if he would do a thing like that."

"Oh dear me no....Terry wouldn't do anything like that I'm sure....no......it certainly wasn't him."

"Well, he didn't have an alibi for the time of day that they think the murder was committed. Because of that he felt they were accusing him. I always thought that in this country you were innocent until proved guilty. It sounded as though they were saying that he was guilty until he could prove otherwise."

"Oh, I don't think so.....no.....that Sergeant Ashton is a kind and understanding person, from what I've seen of her. No, I don't think Terry needs to worry.....no.....it wasn't him...."

"You sound as though you know who it was, do you? Is he out there still, is it someone from this village and is he likely to kill again? One hears of these psychopaths who seem to kill for the sheer fun of it."

Lisa shivered at the thought and looked anxiously at Grace, repeating her question

"D'you mean to say that you know who the murderer is?"

"Oh yes, I think I know.....mmm......but I can't say anything yet because I don't have any conclusive evidence.....any proof."

"So is he likely to kill again?"

"No, I don't think so.....you see my dear....this was a hate crime.....a very personal thing. So you see, your Terry needn't worry."

"I don't know that I would call him my Terry exactly, we are just good friends, as they used to say in the papers."

"But you do rather like him, don't you? In fact.....I would say that you rather fancy him.....am I right?"

"Mrs Russell, really! I never thought I'd hear you using that sort of expression, I mean...."

"Just because I was the wife of a vicar and a Christian believer, it doesn't mean that I don't understand human feelings and desires. I'm very glad for you and Terry....yes....you certainly seem to be meant for each other."

"Well, I'm not sure that Terry feels that way, he doesn't have a great deal of trust in women."

"Well, he has good reason.....he was greatly hurt and deceived by his former wife....mmm....yes.....it's up to you to restore that trust, and....yes.... I think that you could be just the one to do it."

FORTY SIX

"As I see it" said Shirley "there's one more person to interview and that's Mr Clive Luscombe. Let's hope he's home from work by now."

"Alright for some Sarge, he may be home for the evening; we have to go on working."

"I don't suppose it will take long. You'll soon be back at home with your wife and kids."

Clive Lucsombe was at home when they knocked and introduced themselves. He had not long got home from work and was just drinking a hastily made cup of coffee. So with a slightly puzzled look on his face he asked them to come in and led them into a sitting room that felt rather cold and smelt slightly musty. Shirley got the impression that it was a room that hadn't been used for several days if not weeks. But then if he was living on his own, what with his mother in a nursing home, she guessed that he probably lived in the kitchen for most of the time that he was at home.

"What can I do for you?" Clive asked as he sat down in one of the armchairs, motioning them to do the same.

"We need to know what you were doing on the evening of October the twenty fourth; from half past five onwards, if you can remember."

"Is this to do with the death of Mark Bosworth?

"Yes."

"Just one minute while I get my diary." He stood up and left the room and Newman looked at Shirley with one eyebrow raised. Before either of them had time to say anything Clive came back into the room with a large dark blue office diary in his hand.

"Here we are" he said, flicking through the pages to the relevant date. "Yes I was working north of the moor that day, Launceston and Okehampton. I drove back over the moor, it was a nice evening and I find the scenery relaxing after a stressful day's work."

"Did you stop at all?"

"I was running a bit late, I usually visit my mother on Tuesdays. She's in a nursing home. I wasn't sure if I would have enough time to do any paperwork before I called in on her."

"So you wouldn't have had time to stop and talk to anyone?"

"Err.....yes I did, come to think of it. I stopped in a village to ask directions. There's a nice old lady in the next room to my mother. Her daughter Hilary and I have become friends, thrown together by the fact that our mothers are friends. Well, she gave me her address some time ago, Grimstone Court. I have never visited her; I wasn't sure exactly where Grimstone Court was, so when I was passing through the village that evening I stopped and asked a young lad for directions. Nice lad, a Londoner I would say by his accent, and most helpful. "

"What time would that have been?"

"Shortly after six I would think."

"And did you go there, did you visit Grimstone Court that evening?" asked Newman.

"No, I didn't have time, as I said I was running late as it was. Besides, what would be the point? By that time Hilary would be at the nursing home visiting her mother. Like me she always visits on Tuesdays."

"So after your brief stop in the village, what then?"

"I drove home. I had a quick cup of tea and did the necessary paper work before dashing off to visit Mum."

"And what time did you get to the nursing home?"

"Oh I was late getting there; it must have been nearly half past seven I should think. Hilary was just leaving, so we had a quick word but we couldn't stay chatting. For one thing, they don't like visitors after eight o'clock."

"And have you seen Hilary since then?"

"Oh yes, poor girl, I feel so sorry for her. First of all her husband goes missing and then it turns out he's been murdered. What a shock for anybody. Yes I saw her at the nursing home the next Tuesday."

"Have you been to her house?"

"No, not yet, I was thinking of going there this evening. She needs all the help and support she can get."

"Well, thank you Mr Luscombe, you have been most helpful. We may need to call on you again."

"Of course, that will be fine."

He stood up and led them to the door. As they got there he asked

"Have you got any idea who did this, I mean do you have a prime suspect? I believe that's the correct term, I watch a lot of those crime stories on telly." He gave a sort of embarrassed laugh.

"Not as yet" said Shirley "but we will find out who did this, they always make a mistake that catches them out."

FORTY SEVEN

As soon as Shirley and Newman left, Clive went upstairs and showered and changed from his business suit into more casual attire. Jeans and a sweater he felt would be more appropriate for this evening. He had never visited Hilary at Grimstone Court, or anywhere else for that matter. They had met several times at the nursing home, but that was as a by-product, so to speak, of seeing their respective mothers. On two or three occasions they had shared a drink and a meal on the way home after these visits, but again they were not planned meetings. Now for the first time he was going out with the sole intention of meeting Hilary. It almost felt like a date, and that was something that he hadn't been on for more years than he cared to think.

As he drove out onto the moor he thought about how he should approach Hilary. She had just lost her husband, an abusive and sometimes violent man who had dominated her and her life ever since they had married. So now that he was dead she would be bound to feel relief that that painful ordeal was over. Yet feeling relieved would be bound to give her feelings of guilt. She would also be feeling lonely, life would be more than a little empty without the constant need to attend to Mark's needs and wishes. He remembered how after his father died he had found his mother sitting on her bed and crying her heart out one day. When he asked her why, she had taken his hands and between sobs had said

"I know it sounds silly after all he put me through, but I miss him.....I miss him being here......I miss having to do things for him.......I miss him

216

shouting at me.....yes.....and even in a strange way.....I miss him hitting me."

He would have to tread carefully, let Hilary lead the way so to speak. Although he had set off feeling almost as though he was going on a date, he realized that he was just a friend and a casual friend at that. If Hilary should wish for their relationship to go any further, would he be pleased to give it a try? She was a nice person and he felt that they had several things in common, but it was very early days as yet.

So it was with a few butterflies in his stomach that he drove down the long drive to Grimstone Court. Hilary had told him, he thought jokingly, that it was a rather posh house, but he was still impressed with what he saw as he arrived in front of it. He thought it looked like a miniature Elizabethan manor house or stately home, with its granite mullion windows and ornamental chimney pots. He parked on the gravel apron in front of the house beside a smart silver Range Rover. Then he rang the bell beside the large studded oak front door.

There was a long pause and he was about to ring again when the door was opened and Hilary peered somewhat anxiously around the side of it. As soon as she saw who it was she pulled the door fully open and said

"Clive, how wonderful to see you; is there some special reason for this visit?"

"No, I just felt it was high time I came to see you, and as I've never been to Grimstone Court before I thought 'why wait until Tuesday?'"

"Well this is a nice surprise, come in. Let me get you a drink."

She led him into the lounge and went over to a small cabinet from which she took out two glasses from the top shelf. An array of bottles was lined up on the shelf below, but as she reached for these Clive said.

"Before you pour out any drinks, have you eaten yet?"

"No."

"Well, nor have I and I was wondering, well hoping, that you might like to come out for a meal with me tonight, perhaps in your local pub which I hear is a good place to eat with excellent food."

Hilary put down the glasses and turned to face him with a surprised yet pleased look on her face. Smiling a little shyly she said

"Well, I don't know, I haven't eaten and...."

"It was just a thought......" said Clive, a trifle embarrassed, as he felt they both were, by his invitation.

"And a lovely thought. Yes, why not, it will do me good to get out."

"You're not worried that people will think it a bit odd, or too soon after Mark's death."

"No doubt some of them will think that, no doubt some will think me a callous bitch. Some may even think I killed him. There were times when, if I had had the strength and the will power, I would have done. But I was always too weak, too afraid. Perhaps it would be better if we went somewhere other than our local pub" she paused and then said "no, why not, we'll go to our local, The New Inn, its good there. Let people think what they like."

"Well, if you are sure.....it's a big step."

Hilary walked over and stood looking down at him with her head slightly on one side and a gentle smile on her lips.

"Two people have shown me kindness since this all happened" she said. "Two people who haven't judged me or told me what to do; you and Grace, the late vicar's widow. Everyone else seems to be afraid to come near me; they all avoid me as though I've got the plague or something. But having said that, it's probably just as much my fault, few people here know me, I haven't mixed much in village life since we moved here."

"Perhaps we are the only two people who understand exactly what you've been through" said Clive; pleased, surprised and relieved at her positive attitude.

"Perhaps so; I'll just go and slip into something more suited to going out. Please, help yourself to a drink; I'll try not to be too long."

And with a smile and a little wave she left the room with a spring that was almost a skip in her step.

Over their meal Clive was careful not to lead the conversation too much. Hilary seemed to have conquered her shyness to a great extent and he let her talk as much as she wanted to and on any subject. The only question he did ask was

"What about the funeral arrangements?"

"I've been told that they will release the body next week. I intend to have him cremated; I don't want there to be a grave that has to be maintained. Besides after him being in the Reverend Russell's grave it wouldn't feel right somehow."

She gave a short laugh and looked down at her hands that were on the table on either side of her plate. Clive noticed the old embarrassed gesture that he had seen her use many a time and waited quietly for her to continue. She obviously still had a long way to go.

"I know that I have to move forward. Jeremy has been very supportive; he's wonderful, as he always has been. But he has his work to do running the water bottling plant. There is so much to do, especially regarding Mark's business interests. I really don't know where to start, thank heavens I've got Paul to help, he's a godsend. Then there are a number of people in the village whom Mark has hurt. I would like to try to put things right with them if I can. Like Mr and Mrs Small, I know Mark turned off the overflow water that went to their field. Well they could have that re-instated. And then there's their neighbour, Mr Moore who used to use the path through our place until Mark stopped him. As far as I can see there's no reason why he can't use it again, it doesn't bother me him walking through our back garden."

"That sounds like a very good start, if I may say so" said Clive. He wanted to ask about the plans for the new building that had recently been passed on appeal, and whether she intended to go ahead with it. But he felt that he had better leave that subject, again he didn't want to push her too much.

The one question that he really wanted to ask her but couldn't, was did she have any thoughts as to who could have killed Mark.

FORTY EIGHT

Lisa was getting ready to go to dinner with Terry. She had decided on a pair of pale blue jeans and a grey blue jumper. Although for work she normally wore shorts all the year, like a lot of the local postmen, she felt that evenings demanded a more formal dress code.

Like Terry, she had also suffered from an unsatisfactory relationship. She had lived with her former boy friend for six years, although it hadn't taken her that long to discover that they weren't suited, and they had eventually parted. Fortunately they had never married and there were no children, but like Terry it had made her very wary about getting involved in another relationship.

She had seen him around the village, had even cleaned up after him in one or two houses where he had been plumbing. Not that that was really necessary, after he had done a job he always cleaned up what little mess he had made very well. But the owners of the houses often liked to ask her to come in, using the fact that Terry had been working there as an excuse. She sometimes thought that they really only wanted her to call for her company. In fact, many of her customers kept her talking and drinking coffee for longer than she worked.

What she had seen of him and the recent conversations that they had had, pleased her. So she was glad that they had become acquainted, first with the cleaning of, and then his moving into, the Old Mill. But did she fancy him, as Grace had suggested? Perhaps; he was good looking sure enough, and kind. He liked fair play, or maybe it would be more truthful to say that he didn't like unfairness. This had been obvious when he had told her about the way Bosworth had run up the price that he had had to pay for his new home. And also he had got very cross at the way the police had seemingly assumed that because he had no alibi for that Tuesday evening, he could be guilty.

It was a cold dry evening, but she threw a rain cape into her carrier and cycled the mile and a half to the Old Mill. Terry met her with a huge grin on his face and led her into the sitting room. Little had been done since she was last there, but he had a fire roaring away in the grate and a couple of rugs on the floor, which all made the place seem not just warm but a bit more lived in. A small wooden box stood between the two armchairs, acting as a coffee table, and on it was a copy of Dartmoor News and two small dishes. In one were some potato crisps and in the other were stuffed olives.

"Can I get you a drink?" asked Terry, "I've got Gin and Vodka or a glass of wine perhaps. I'm sorry, I don't even know if you do drink."

"A glass of wine would be lovely, thank you. I think gin and tonic is best on a warm summer's evening, sitting outside on a terrace and watching the sun go down, preferably into a warm sea."

"You've been watching too many 'chick flicks', all hearts and flowers and happy endings."

"Well, what's wrong with that, I like happy endings, don't you?"

"Yes, but life just doesn't seem to send them my way."

"Don't be such a pessimist; see how your luck has changed just recently."

"How d'you mean?"

"Well, I'm here for a start" she said, giving him that smile which transformed her face and caused his heart to skip a beat. He turned away, so as not to let her see his face, and went into the other room to get the bottle of wine. They both had a glass and after eating a few of the nibbles Terry said

"I need to see to the cooking, would you like to come through and watch or would you prefer to read that magazine?"

"Oh, I think I'd much rather watch you cook."

The meal went well and after it they went back into the sitting room with their coffees. Sitting looking at the fire, now burning a little less brightly but still just as warmly, Lisa asked

"So what's the next thing you have planned to do here?"

"Well, the first thing I want to do is to rip out that old Devon grate. They were all the rage back in the fifties. Candy's of Heathfield made thousands of them; sent them all over the country. They come in three pieces; the tiled surround, the tiled hearth and the fireback. They are very efficient, the fireback is so designed that it throws the heat out into the room."

"It certainly does that alright; it's lovely and warm in here."

"People had got fed up with sitting by the old hearth fires that were big enough to sit in. In fact, that's what you often had to do to keep warm. And even then most of the heat went up the chimney."

"So what will you do if the big old hearth fire is so inefficient?"

"Clean it up, and then put a wood burner here. There's plenty of wood out behind here, I didn't realize there's nearly half an acre of woodland that goes with this place." Terry looked across at Lisa as he spoke, his eyes sparkling as he thought about the improvements he would be making.

"Sounds like it'll be a pretty dirty job, loads of soot and allsorts, probably a dead bird or two" said Lisa with an impish grin.

"Well, whatever. That will be the first job, the rest of the work, which is mostly upstairs, will have to wait until I've got a bit more cash saved. That Mark Bosworth has a lot to answer for; who ever it was that did him in deserves a medal in my opinion."

Lisa's eyebrows lifted at this, then she said

"I was talking to Grace, you know, the late vicar's wife"

"Widow"

"Yeah right, widow. I told her about your conversation with Sergeant Ashton, how you felt that your lack of alibi shouldn't mean that you were guilty, even if she thought that you could be. Well she says that you don't have to worry, you didn't do it, but she seems to think that she knows who did."

"How on earth can that funny, little old woman know who murdered Bosworth, when the police don't seem to be able to suss it out? What does she know?"

"You may think that she's just a funny, little old woman, even a bit strange and out of this world. But I can tell you that she has a better understanding of human beings and human nature than anyone I've ever met before."

"Well, let's hope she's right and the police don't bother me any more."

There was a pause in the conversation as they sat and watched the fire, lost in their respective thoughts. Terry working out in his mind's eye how he would tackle the removing of the fireplace and Lisa wondering who Grace thought was the killer. Finally she said

"D'you want a hand with the job, taking out the fireplace I mean?"

"That would be great, those things are quite heavy. I'll need to borrow a set of sack trucks to wheel it outside. When can you start?" he asked, and realized he sounded like a foreman taking on a new employee.

"Tomorrow evening, if you like" she said, and wondered if she had sounded too eager.

"I'd like that very much, but I'm sorry, I can't cook a meal as well. You'll have to make do with a snack 'cos I'm just a poor helpless man and I can only do one thing at a time; unlike you women who were born to multitask."

They both laughed and Lisa gave him a playful punch on his arm.

"I'll see you tomorrow then, at about seven."

She got up from her chair and looking him straight in the eye said

"I have had a truly lovely evening, you cooked a perfect meal and I've enjoyed your company. Thank you very much."

She stood up on tiptoes, put her hands on his broad shoulders and gave him a kiss on the cheek. Then she walked towards the door, he managed to get to it first and opened it for her saying

"I should thank you, for all your help. Both what you've already done and what you have promised to do."

She gave him one of her amazing smiles and stepped out into the night. After she had gone Terry went back into the kitchen area to do the washing up. As he did he thought about Lisa and what he was feeling regarding her. She was attractive, although physically not in a way that he would previously have considered attractive. She had a great sense of humour and obviously enjoyed work. In the few hours that they had spent working together, as in the time spent tonight, he felt that they had both been comfortable in each other's company. He certainly no longer felt that no woman could ever share his life again.

"Terry you daft fool" he said to himself "be honest, you fancy her, don't you?"

FORTY NINE

When she got home that evening, Shirley found on her answer-phone that she had had another call from Martin. He had found two more properties that he thought might be suitable for her and wondered whether and when she would like to see them. So she rang him back and arranged to meet him at his office again the next day. She then rang Newman and told him that she wouldn't be in until the afternoon. She suggested that he go to Exeter and have a look at the security camera tapes. She didn't think they would show anything of use, but they needed to be checked to be certain. With so little to go on and no clues as to who could have committed the murder, any straw was worth clutching at.

The whole case was getting her down and she again was wondering which way her future was headed. She had hoped that the challenge and the excitement of working on a murder case would have given her a more positive outlook. But the team seemed to be one of all boys together, chumming up with Stormin Norman, as they called DI Smith behind his back. They went for drinks in the pub together after work and all that, and she felt more than a bit left out. Not that she really wanted to be included, not if it meant swilling back pints and being 'one of the lads'. Another thing, she didn't like the confrontational attitude adopted by some officers towards the general public. Perhaps it was as a result of dealing with criminals for so long that they had become cynical. She preferred a more tolerant approach; liked to listen and hear the other person's point of view. Newman Chaffe was alright, she didn't have a problem with him, in fact she hoped that he would soon get promoted to Sergeant; he certainly deserved it and he'd passed the exams.

She was beginning to feel that the job wasn't fulfilling enough. She needed something more in her life. As a teenager she had almost decided that she would never follow the path that her mother had taken, getting married and having children. For her the important thing was a career, preferably in a job where she could move up the promotion ladder, be a success and feel that she had achieved something in her life; which was why she had joined the police. Now her thoughts turned to Linda Narraway, living in that isolated farm out on the moor with her husband and that delightful little girl. She seemed to be extremely happy, seemed to have it all. Perhaps she ought to take up her kind invitation and go and spend some time with her, have a chat with her. She might get some ideas there.

But for now she needed to forget her worries and the case and get herself something to eat. Then, after a good night's sleep she could go with Martin to look at the houses he had found. That could be fun.

The first house that they went to see was just outside of town. Several years before, three fields there had been developed into a large housing estate. Just outside this estate were two cottages, semi-detached, that had been previously used as farm workers housing. As the farmer's land had been reduced and mechanisation had taken away a lot of the need for farm workers, the cottages had been sold off. They were well built, spacious three bed-roomed houses with good sized gardens. The couple who were leaving were elderly and had decided to go and live with their daughter, hence the sale.

Shirley had a good look around and although there was nothing wrong with the place, apart from the fact that it was probably too big for her needs, she wasn't too happy at the idea of living in a semi. One of her reasons for considering moving was to get away from close living neighbours.

"I'm not sure about this next one I'm going to take you to see" said Martin. "It may feel a bit too far out 'in the sticks' as you might say. But it is without doubt a lovely little property, and it's not that far from town, not really. It is not on the market yet, I have only just received instructions, so you are getting a preview as it were."

"Now you've got me worried as well as interested" said Shirley.

They drove away from town and towards the moor. As they started climbing to the higher ground they came to a crossroad where a lane to the right led off through a wooded area. This they followed through large trees which were all bare of leaves, and looking to right and left Shirley was pleased that she could see through the trees, clear of undergrowth to daylight beyond. Suddenly the wood ended and they were out in a small valley. Fields fell away from the road to the right and on the left, in a bend in the road some two hundred yards from the trees, stood a small slate roofed cottage. It looked absolutely idyllic, with three windows upstairs and one each side of the front door downstairs, it was every small child's drawing of a house. The walls were painted white and the front door was sky blue.

In front was a small garden area and joined onto the far side of the building was a lean-to garage which had previously been a cart linhay and was painted to blend in with the rest of the house. Behind was a large garden set mostly to lawn, but there was a small vegetable plot in one corner. Inside the cottage it was bigger that it appeared from the outside, largely because a previous owner had added a further lean-to area along the back wall. This made space for an office and a smart new kitchen. Upstairs were two bedrooms, each with their own en suite bathroom.

Behind the garden the open moorland rose up to a large area of down land with an impressive rocky tor at its top, almost a mile away. From the front windows, as from the garden, there was an amazing view down across the valley over the town to the sea, several miles below.

Martin left Shirley to look over the whole of it while he sat on a wooden bench in the rear garden. The last thing that he wanted to do was to in any way influence Shirley. He knew, from their previous conversations, that this house was possibly too far out of town for her. But he also knew from his years of experience in the trade, that it was the sort of place that came onto the market very very rarely.

Finally she came out to join him and he could see form the sparkle in her eyes that she was excited by what she'd seen.

"Well" he said "what d'you think?"

"I don't know what to think. It's beautiful, it's idyllic in a lot of ways it's every thing I could wish for, but....."

Martin watched her, waiting for her to continue. He could see that she was finding it hard to make a decision. The change in this property from her previous set of demands for an area where she could live was great, although the house itself was perfect.

He guessed that she would need to talk it over with some one, maybe with a friend or her parents. And although he hoped that she looked upon him as a friend, he knew that he couldn't advise her.

"I need some time to think about it, talk it over with some one. Do I have much time? I would imagine that a place like this would sell very quickly once on the open market."

"I can give you three days; it could take me that long to get the details and the photographs done. I can see you like it, but I guess it's the isolation and the distance from town that are worrying you. Am I right? And what about the price, am I still within your price range?"

"Yes, the price is fine and I'm not too worried about the isolation. Although I live in a block of flats, I don't know or have anything to do with my neighbours, like most people in town. And the distance from town isn't too great really. Although driving through that wood made it feel like I was going into a different world. I seem to have a strange sort of fear of Dartmoor, which I don't understand and is quite ridiculous I know, but I have it nevertheless."

"As I say, it won't go on the open market for three days, I'm sorry I can't give you any more time than that."

"That's fine, it's very good of you to give me any preferential treatment at all, I appreciate it."

She smiled at him and he found himself thinking, not for the first time,

'I'd like to get to know this girl a lot better'.

FIFTY

Back at the incident room DI Smith was going over the case with DS Tom Watson, trying to find a suspect from the many names of those who had any real grudge against Mark Bosworth. Shirley joined them but regretted that she had little to add that would help.

When Newman came back from searching the tapes in the office of the security firm at Exeter he also had little of use to add. On the evening in question several lorries had been in and out of the industrial estate up until half past five. Then there had only been two vehicles. Most of those that worked there had left around half past five and Jeremy had entered the site just before four o'clock. He could clearly be seen riding his bicycle, wearing jeans and what looked like an old army sweater. As he passed through the gate he had looked towards the small office, probably to say something to Colin, and smiled. It was then that it was possible to see his face, which until then had been hidden under his cycle helmet.

Watson reported that the German, Dieter Hoffman, had turned up. He had apparently been on holiday near the town of Antalya in Turkey. As to the Cash couple, all decided that their visit to the village was a total coincidence.

"We need more background checks on these characters like Armand and Luscombe, and those two possibles in the village, Hunt and Cooper. Also Bosworth's old acquaintances from his time before he came to live in Devon and we must include all his so called chums here."

"Does that include the ACC?" asked Tom Watson with a grin.

They all laughed at this, showing the little respect they felt for their superiors. Then DI Smith asked Shirley how Hilary was getting on.

"She seems fine Sir, The lady who was staying with her, the late vicar's widow, has gone back to her own house to live now, but she visits most days. Then there's her brother who works at the water bottling place; he calls in now and again. And there's a friend whom she met at the nursing home where her mother lives. His mother is also there. I think he calls in from time to time."

"She must be a very wealthy woman now. Which leads me to wonder two things; did she arrange for someone to kill her husband, she obviously didn't do it 'cos she has a good alibi. Did this boyfriend, Luscombe, do it in order to get in with her and all her money? This is the sort of thing we need to look into, who is this Luscombe fellow and just what is his role in all this? And what about the PA fellow, the one you say looks like a tortoise? Is his looking after her, more than just her business affairs?"

"Right Guv" said Tom Watson "I'll see what I can find out."

But when she left that evening Shirley's thoughts were not on Luscombe or the case, she was thinking about the house beyond the woods. She needed to talk to someone who was a bit like herself, and yet who obviously loved Dartmoor. So she rang Linda and asked if she could take up her kind offer.

"Yes, come and have a bite of supper with us, it wont be anything grand, but there'll be plenty and you'll be most welcome to join us."

"Thank you, that's most kind I'd love to; what time?"

"Come as soon as you like, we generally eat at about seven."

"I'll see you then."

FIFTY ONE

Terry had arrived home early from work. One of the advantages of being self employed was that he could arrange his work day to suit his personal needs. This usually meant that he worked all the hours God gave in order to pay the bills. But this evening Lisa was coming again and they were going to take out the Devon grate in the sitting room and see just what was behind it. He had moved what little furniture there was into the kitchen and had started chipping off the plaster on the chimney breast. As he did so he got to thinking about Lisa, wondering why she was so keen to help. Apart from the first time of asking, that day at The Old Rectory when he was servicing the boiler for the Cameron-Hydes, he hadn't ever asked her to help; she had always offered. Like the previous evening, when as she was leaving after their dinner, she had asked him if he would like help to take out the grate.

He smiled at the thought of her boyish figure with her well toned muscular arms and legs, lifting the heavy pieces of the grate. The more he thought about her the more he realized that, yes, he did fancy her. She was fun to be with and they seemed to think along the same lines about so many things. But did she have any similar feelings for him, and was that why she wanted to help? Or was it just that, like him, she was fascinated by the old building.

She arrived, dressed in her usual shorts but with a pair of stout boots on her feet and a bandanna tied around her head to protect her hair. Straight away, without the need for Terry to say anything, she grabbed the wheelbarrow and started shovelling up the old plaster that Terry had knocked off the wall.

Then they set to work on the grate. The largest piece was the tiled surround and once loosened from its fixings, they carefully lowered it onto the sack trucks and Terry wheeled it outside. He was glad of her help as it was quite a heavy piece. Then they took out the tiled hearth and finally the fireback. There was still a lot to remove, brickwork that had been built in to reduce the size of the old hearth, and it was a good hour later that they finally could see the full extent of the old inglenook fireplace. Sand and soot and several small twigs were piled up on the large flat granite stone that had formed the base of the hearth. They got to work, clearing that away and found, as Lisa had predicted they might, the remains of a dead jackdaw.

"There've probably been several jackdaw nests up in the top of this chimney" said Terry. "I expect it's completely blocked."

Then when all was cleared away they were able to look at where centuries of fires had burned.

"You can't help but wonder at the way they used to live in the old days" said Lisa. "Just imagine, cooking all your meals on an open fire, heating any water you needed for washing, and drying your clothes in front of it on a typical wet Dartmoor day."

Terry picked up a torch and stooped as he went into the aperture to look up the chimney. His voice from inside sounded strange and ghostlike as he said

"This chimney will need a damn good clean, the soot looks to be several inches thick, it's a wonder they didn't have a chimney fire here. There's a bar across the chimney for the crooks" he said as he came back out into the room. "You know, those crooks that looked like saws with big teeth, on which they used to hang the cooking pots. I had hoped that they might still be there, but whoever put in the Devon grate probably sold them, they are quite sought after by antique dealers and the like."

"Are you going to do any more tonight, or shall I make a cup of tea now?" asked Lisa.

"I'd like to just clean the walls of the fireplace a bit before we stop. Then tomorrow I can have a good look at what's here, in daylight."

They scrubbed and scraped the walls, getting themselves thoroughly dirty in the process. An hour later, with all the mess cleared away, they stopped and looked at each other and roared with laughter. Sooty smears on their faces made them look like soldiers in camouflage going on exercise. Having gone outside and brushed off the worst of the dirt they went into the kitchen for a good wash.

"I'd offer you a shower, but there wouldn't be much point unless you had a clean change of clothes to get into" said Terry.

"You only want the opportunity to offer to wash my back" replied Lisa, grinning happily.

Terry grinned back and then got some cold meat and cheese out of the fridge. This together with a loaf of bread he laid on the table.

"I said it would only be a snack, is this alright?"

"Lovely, can I come again tomorrow?"

"You really are a glutton for punishment. Yes of course you can, but I'll never be able to repay you for all your help."

"Who said I wanted payment? I like coming here, and it's fun."

As they tucked into their simple supper Lisa found herself looking across the table at Terry and thinking

'Looking at him, I always used to think he was a bit of a rough sort. With his cropped hair and the fact that he's big.....yeah.....he is big. He looks a bit of a bruiser, the sort that would pick a fight for no reason. Now I find that he's exactly the opposite, kind and considerate, except where Mr Bosworth is concerned, and I realize how wrong I was. I'm beginning to....well....I look forward to seeing him again.'

FIFTY TWO

Shirley drove up onto the moor, following the now familiar route that she and Newman had taken so many times. As she drove through the village, sleepy in the fast fading evening light, she couldn't help thinking that it seemed impossible for a brutal murder to have been committed there. She drove on and, with the dark bulk of Brown Tor on her left, dropped down into the valley of the Redacre Brook. She crossed it on the granite bridge and turned left up the lane that led to Wistworthy farm. When she got to the point where the field hedges began, she stopped and got out of her car. There was still just enough light to be able to see and she walked out onto the old stone clapper bridge. It was constructed of two huge flat lichen encrusted granite slabs of rock, resting on stone piers, built at both banks, and a huge square rock in the middle of the stream. A bridge that was almost as old as time, built high enough to be out of the reach of the water, even when the stream was in flood.

She stood for several minutes watching the water flowing beneath her. It swirled and bubbled along, tinkling and laughing as it passed over the rocks on its way to join the big river in its journey to the sea. Like many before her she found that she could watch the ever changing movement for hours, marvelling at the patterns in the water and the strands of weed that waved like a girl's hair. But it was getting increasingly dark and she went back to her car and drove on to the farm.

Linda was watching for her and waved from inside the window as Shirley walked up the course to the door. Inside the kitchen she was struck by the warm friendly atmosphere of the room. It wasn't just the heat from the Aga cooker; the room seemed almost to have a comforting personality of its own. A large saucepan was sitting on the stove, filling the room with a lovely slightly spicy smell.

"Jasmine's next door with her Gran" said Linda, "she likes to go up there and play for a while. This is two houses see, Frank's grandfather converted an outbuilding into a dwelling when Frank's dad was married. It's very useful; it means that I don't have any difficulty getting a baby sitter. They'll join us later and Frank won't be here for another hour at least. So we can have a drink and a girly chat before we eat. It's going to be spag-bol; I hope that's alright with you."

"Lovely" said Shirley, as she now recognised the aroma coming from the pot on the cooker.

"Tea or coffee, or would you rather go straight into the wine now?" asked Linda.

"I think coffee" she said with a bit of a laugh, "if I start on the wine now, you'll have to give me a bed for the night."

They sat at the table with their mugs of coffee and Linda asked

"How's the case going? Or am I not supposed to ask."

"Well, I'm probably not supposed to tell you; in any case I'd rather not think about it, let alone talk about it. It's a nightmare; we don't seem to be getting anywhere. No, what I wanted to ask you is more personal."

Linda sat back in her chair and looked across the table at her new friend. What could she possibly want in the way of advice?

"I've come to the conclusion that it's time to move house. I have an acquaintance whom I met years ago on a case, he's an estate agent and he's been looking out some possible properties for me. The other day he came up with a fantastic cottage that had absolutely everything I could wish for. Quiet, secluded, wonderful views, the only trouble is...." she hesitated, realizing that what she was about to say could sound silly, "it's rather too close to the moor. In fact, the garden backs onto moorland. For some reason, which I admit I can't understand, I am sort of afraid of the moor."

Linda remained quiet, wondering what to say and if she should wait until Shirley asked a more specific question. She had also got the feeling that Shirley's estate agent could be a bit more than a business friend. Shirley was sitting with her hands clasped around her coffee mug, watching the steam rising off the warm drink deep in thought.

"Did you always live on the moor" she asked.

"Yes, born and bred in this parish."

"So you like it here, I mean just because you've always lived here it doesn't follow that you like it here."

"Oh I love it, I love Dartmoor."

"You don't find it at all threatening? The dark tors and the wildness of it all."

"No, far from it; I find it comforting and reassuring, like being wrapped in velvet or a warm duvet. Frank probably loves it even more than I do, he calls it his church. If he has a problem.....some decision that he is finding hard to make.....he'll go up on the open moor and talk it over."

"What, with himself?"

"Yes, or with whatever and whoever he feels is out there as his god. But it always seems to work because he gets his answer; anyway, he comes back with the problem solved."

Shirley thought about this for a while and felt that Frank's approach, though obviously working for him, wouldn't work for her.

"Have you ever been up onto the moor, for a walk or a picnic as a child or anything?"

"No I haven't"

"Perhaps you should go and re-visit this lovely cottage you were telling me about, and maybe you could go for a walk from there with your estate agent friend. What's his name?"

"Martin, I don't know if he's into walking."

"Would you like to find out? I'm getting a feeling that you could rather fancy him, am I right?"

"Yes, I suppose I do. God, you don't miss much do you?"

"And are you feeling that you need a change of perhaps more than just the place where you live? Is the job getting you down?"

Again there was a long pause while Shirley thought of the time she had spent with Martin and what she had recently been thinking about her job.

"Before I answer your question d'you mind if I ask you one?"

"No, go ahead."

"How long have you and Frank known each other and been married?"

I've known him since we were kids in primary school. We were best friends then, but when we moved up to big school it changed. I suppose, like a lot of boys at that age, it wasn't cool to be with a girl. Then when he reached sixteen he changed again and we became boyfriend and girlfriend. We were just about to get engaged while we were still at school."

"So you've been married for quite some time then" said Shirley, wondering, because she remembered that Jasmine was only three years old.

"No, it's a long story. When Frank was seventeen his dad got Huntington's disease. I didn't know about that at the time. Frank and his dad never got on too well. Frank always wanted to be a mechanic, while his dad, quite understandably, wanted him to stay on the farm. Well, Frank up and left for the Army without giving any explanation, almost without saying goodbye."

"God, that must have hit you hard."

"It did. I mooned about like a lost soul for months, years almost. Then I married Eric, a teacher from the comprehensive school. He was very keen on sport and was always helping the kids with extra games after school. The trouble was that his bit of overtime was another teacher called Sheila."

"So you were doubly let down then?"

"After fifteen years, Frank's dad died and Frank came back. Just after that I learned about Eric's affair. Friends of mine had suspected for years, but they always say that the one involved is often the last one to know. Frank was around, still a friend but sort of at arms length, if you know what I mean. Then there was a dance in the new village hall, after it had been converted from the old primary school. We danced together for the last waltz and....." She stopped talking, tears filling her eyes at the memory, "and we just knew, we knew we couldn't live without each other."

"So it all turned out alright in the end then?"

"Well no, not exactly. You see, Huntington's disease can be hereditary; that was why Frank had left in the first place. He couldn't possibly marry me because he couldn't bear the thought of my having to look after him, as an ill man, for years. He was about to go off, back to the Army I suppose, when he found out that he wasn't carrying the disease."

"So then you finally did get married."

"Yes" said Linda, a huge smile breaking across her face.

"And by the looks of you, it's good."

"Oh yes, it's good alright, it's good because I have someone to share life with. That's what matters, that's what makes it work, sharing. A problem shared is a problem halved and a good thing shared is twice as good for the sharing. So when you are thinking about Martin, and whether you ought to follow your heart and get more involved with him; just think of that, think about sharing and the benefits that it can bring to your happiness. But never forget, you have to share your thoughts and your feelings as well, it's no good having secrets. If you do, they are bound to come out one day and could spoil everything."

"Are you acting as a matchmaker for Martin, have you met him?" asked Shirley, grinning from ear to ear.

"No to both questions, but you came here with a problem, and that problem was quite obviously what to do now that Martin has come into your life and you have strong feelings for him. I just say, give it a try. What have you got to lose? As to the cottage, don't rush into anything. Go and take another look, get the feel of the place and the whole area around it. If your gut feeling is good, then go for it, but if not.....d'you see what I mean?"

Before Shirley could answer, the door burst open and Jasmine came running in and jumped onto her mother's lap. Behind her at a more sedate pace came Frank's mother, Blanche. Linda introduced her to Shirley while Jasmine busied herself proudly laying the table for supper. As soon as Frank's van arrived in the yard Linda put on the water for the spaghetti and ten minutes later they all sat down to eat.

It was a lovely meal, shared with a lovely warm family, and as Shirley drove home she felt that she could understand what Linda had said about the importance of sharing and why she had said it. But whether it could influence her decision regarding Martin was something about which she wasn't sure.

FIFTY THREE

Terry was back from work early again the next day. He had called in at his parent's house and borrowed his dad's chimney sweeping rods and brushes. Once he got home he changed out of his usual working clothes into an old boiler suit and a pair of old trainers. He knew that he would get very dirty sweeping the chimney and the fewer items of filthy clothing that he would have to wash the better. Then having fixed an old blanket across the front of the hearth he got behind it, inside the fireplace with his tools and a torch, and started work. Centuries of soot was stuck on the inside walls of the chimney, in places it was several inches thick. It was a wonder that there hadn't been a chimney fire.

He remembered how, when he was still a young boy at school, a neighbour's chimney had caught on fire. Smoke was pouring out of the top of the chimney and even through the cracks in the stonework. It was a quiet day with little or no wind and the smoke seemed to fall out of the chimney and drift down the valley only a few feet off the ground.

The neighbour, an elderly widow, had come running to them for help. So Terry's dad had gone, muttering to himself that it was their own fault. He had offered to sweep the chimney for them on several occasions when her husband was alive, but they had always refused. They were probably hoping to save a bit of money. When he had got to the house he had asked her to fill the kitchen sink with water.

"Should I call the fire brigade?" she had asked.

"No, they'll only go up with a hose and pour water down the chimney. It may put the fire out but you'll have a hell of a mess to clear up. Have you got a couple of large old towels?"

These she had produced and, having soaked them in the water, he had shoved them into the throat of the fire place. Almost immediately, with no air to breath, the fire had gone out. When he had got back home and was telling his wife and Terry all about it, he said that there were lumps of white hot soot, the size of a man's fist, falling down the chimney and into the grate. The next day the old lady had come over and asked him to sweep the chimney.

So Terry started work on his chimney. It was warm work and several large pieces of soot and even small stones fell down onto his head. He was glad of his hard hat and thought that there were some aspects of 'health and safety regulations' that made sense. But after a while he could push the brush no further, for some reason it was stuck. He went outside to see if he could see anything but he soon realized that he had not pushed up enough rods to reach the top of the chimney. So he went back inside and pulled down the rods, counting them as he went. Only seven, 'I must be about three rods short of the top' he thought. So he took off the brush and pushed up just the rods. With a struggle they went on through and when he had pushed up ten rods he went outside again. There, to his delight, he could see that one rod at least was poking out of the chimney pot.

So he went back in again and before he did anything more he shovelled up the soot, three buckets' full, and put it on the piece of ground in the garden where he was hoping to have a vegetable patch. Then he pulled down the rods and fixed another device on the top of the first rod, it looked like a double corkscrew which he thought was probably used for clearing blockages in drains. Up this went and after seven rods had gone up Terry found that he had to push and twist for about five minutes before he managed to get it to go any further.

Suddenly, mixed with soot, a shower of twigs and leaves came rattling down on him. Bits of wool and horse hair and a few soft feathers added to the huge pile by his feet. It was an old jackdaw's nest. They would drop twigs down a chimney until one stuck. It might be several feet down from the chimney pot, so the birds would keep dropping twigs and leaves and bits of grass until the nest was nearer to the top.

Finally Terry was able to push the brush right up past the obstruction. He went out and looking up gave a little cheer at the sight of the brush sticking out of the pot at the top.

He finished clearing up the mess and then had a shower and put on some clean clothes. He had only just come back down when Lisa arrived.

"I've brought fish and chips for our supper. D'you want it now or later."

"You didn't have to do that" Terry said. "Thank you very much, let's have it now while they're still hot. They're never the same, warmed up in a microwave."

So they sat in the two armchairs and ate their fish and chips straight out of the wrapping, licking their fingers and smiling at one another as they enjoyed their supper. After they finished eating, Lisa went over to the fire place to look at what Terry had been up to.

"What's this here" she said, pointing to an area of stonework to one side of the hearth that looked different to the rest. Terry went over to look, and picking up a brush scrubbed at it. The cement looked lighter than the rest and it wasn't because there was less soot on it. Terry started scratching at it and it came away easily.

"This is different mortar, not particularly good, not like the rest here."

"There's a long stone here at the bottom, and a bit further up it almost looks like an arch" said Lisa.

"It's an old bread oven; there was an old bread oven here" said Terry, his eyes shining with excitement. So piece by piece, poking and scratching away with an old screwdriver and a small stone chisel, they took out all the stones. At last they had the opening clear.

"Get the torch, let's see what's inside" said Lisa "this is where we find the treasure. Could it be gold, pirates doubloons d'you reckon?"

She was almost jumping up and down with excitement and could hardly wait for Terry to shine a light into the hole. When he did all they could see at first was what looked like an old piece of cloth. Lisa put her hand in and started to pull it out.

"Gently!" said Terry "the treasure might be breakable."

Suddenly Lisa let go of the cloth and jumped back saying

"There's bones in there, lots of bones, I don't like it Terry."

He put the torch in the oven so that he could see, and then ever so gently moved the piece of cloth. It came away easily, as though it had just been laid on top of the bones. And then he was able to see clearly what was there. He stepped back with a shocked look on his face saying

"Bloody hell, it's a skeleton; there's a human skeleton in there. I saw its head, I mean skull, at the back of the oven."

"What do we do?"

"I suppose we've got to call the police, though I'm none too happy with them at the moment. That Sergeant Ashton seems to think I could have killed Bosworth."

"Well, if you tell her about this, she'll probably change her mind about you. D'you want to ring them now?"

"No, I can't get a signal on my mobile down here. Besides, that body's been here for years, a few more hours aint going to make any difference. I'll ring her in the morning."

"I wonder who it was" said Lisa, going over to take another look. "It doesn't look very big, d'you think it could have been a child?"

"Judging by the size of the skull I think you could be right. Ah well, that's all we can do tonight. I'll ring the sergeant first thing, I expect we'll have police swarming all over the place tomorrow."

"Are you happy sleeping here, knowing what's in there?"

"Well he didn't do me any harm before, and it's not as though he's going to get up and bite me now that we've opened the door, so to speak."

He laughed, and Lisa, at first horrified at what he had just said, finally saw the funny side of things and burst out laughing as well. They stood laughing and giggling endlessly, finally catching hold of each other. Terry's chin was resting on top of Lisa's head, and when she at last stopped laughing, she looked up at him. Their eyes met and for a few seconds they just looked, then he kissed her on the forehead. She gave a sort of sigh and he kissed her again, this time on the lips, a kiss that lasted a long time and said so much. After what seemed like an age they pulled apart and Lisa said

"I was hoping you'd do that."

"I've been thinking of nothing else all day" said Terry.

"Oh, you old tease you."

They laughed again and hugged each other. Then Lisa said

"You may not be able to get a signal on your phone here, but you can take photos with it. Once the police are here you won't be allowed to get near it. Think of it, you might even be able to sell the pictures to the newspapers."

"You're right, you hold the light I'll get my phone and take a few photos."

Later, as they were saying goodnight, Lisa said

"I'll come down again after work tomorrow, see you then."

"Yeah, if that sergeant hasn't arrested me."

FIFTY FOUR

Shirley was waiting in the car park for Newman when he arrived the next morning.

"Jump in" she said "we've got another corpse in the village."

"He hasn't struck again has he Sarge."

"No, nothing to do with Bosworth's killer. That plumber chap, Terry Cooper, he's been doing up his house; the old mill down below the village. Well he took out a modern grate and found a blocked up old bread oven in he inglenook fireplace. When he unblocked it he found a skeleton of what sounds like a child."

"Well I never."

"I reported it to DI Smith and he said to get out there and hold the fort until the SOCOs team arrives. He's also told Dr Hall, though if it's a skeleton I can't see what he will be able to do to estimate time of death."

They drove on in silence up onto the moor. A fine mizzle was falling and the tops of the higher tors were lost in cloud. A lone gorse bush in full flower was beside the road and Shirley asked

"What's that bush doing out in flower, doesn't it know that summer's over?"

"That's a gorse bush. It's the only plant that I know of that has two names; gorse and furze. Locally they call it vuzz. It flowers twice a year, early in May and then early in September. In May when huge banks of gorse are in flower the scent given off is just like the smell of coconuts. A month later, the seed pods burst and you can hear them cracking away like little machine guns going off. Then in September when the heather is out it's a wonderful sight of purple and yellow. But no matter what the time of year, you can always find a bit of gorse in flower somewhere."

"I'm learning a lot about Dartmoor from you Newman; thank you."

When they arrived at the mill Terry was waiting for them. He had had to go up into the village to phone, but he had not told anybody about the find in his bread oven, and he had asked Lisa to keep quiet about it as well. He told them to come in and asked them if they wanted a cup of tea.

"That's very kind of you Mr Cooper. I fear we didn't get off to a very good start the last time we met."

"Well you can be sure of one thing; I didn't kill this kid in here. I reckon he was dead long before I was born."

Dr Hall was the next to arrive, closely followed by a van load of police officers. The skeleton was studied and photographed from all angles and then it was carefully taken out of its resting place to be taken to the lab.

"How long d'you think it has been there Doctor" asked Shirley.

"No idea, at least fifty years, maybe a hundred or two, it's hard to say."

"Any idea of the cause of death?"

"Again it's too early to say, but I noticed a small hole in the skull, might mean something, might mean nothing."

He picked up his bag and left, following the police vehicle that was carrying the child's remains. Then the SOCOs team spent a while probing and looking all over and around the fireplace.

"I've just swept the chimney and given the whole hearth a good clean" said Terry "so I don't suppose you'll find anything."

"No, I doubt if we will" said one of the officers, "but we have to make sure, for the record that is."

Shirley and Newman had been standing back while the others got on with their searching. Terry was standing close by, fascinated by their thoroughness. Shirley eventually said to Terry

"You must have the deeds to this place, could you possibly give me a list of the previous owners."

"Yes, they are with my solicitors. I should be able to do that for you. It might take a day or two; you know what lawyers are like."

"Thank you, it might be useful to know who was living here and when."

"Will the press be able to get copies of those photographs that your boys took?" asked Terry.

"No, not unless we need to issue them to help us to identify the deceased."

"Good" said Terry, smiling to himself.

Some two hours later, after all the police had left, there was a knock on the door. Terry opened it to find two men standing on the doorstep.

"We understand that you have found a body here" said one of them."

"Oh yes, and who are you?"

"Press, we're from the local paper, and this is my photographer. A young lady phoned a short while ago and told us, said her name was Lisa."

"Oh, right."

"Can we come in, take a few photographs and do a bit of an interview."

254

Terry stepped outside and closed the door behind him.

"I'll be happy to give you an interview but no pictures. I have taken photos of the scene, before and after I discovered the body. Actually it is only a skeleton. If you want pictures you will have to pay for them, OK? I can show them to you and then when you agree a sum, I'll e mail them to your office."

He took his phone out of his pocket and showed the pictures to the waiting reporter.

"With these we could do quite a spread. What about TV coverage?"

"Fine by me, you might have to check with the police though."

"We already have" said the photographer.

FIFTY FIVE

That evening the talk in the pub was all about the skeleton in the bread oven. When Terry and Lisa walked in for a celebratory drink they were bombarded with questions. He pretended to be none too keen to answer, but underneath he was quite thrilled that Lisa and he were the centre of attention. He told them what he had done, how he and Lisa had taken out the modern grate, exposing the old inglenook fireplace. How he had swept the chimney and cleaned the hearth, and how Lisa had noticed the difference in the stonework which had led them to discover the bread oven.

"Any idea how old this child could have been?" asked Ben Fuller.

"The doctor chappie said it could have been about seven."

"I don't suppose they know whether twas a boy or a maid" said Charlie, who was sitting at the bar, quietly enjoying his customary evening pint.

"No" said Terry "he told the sergeant that he would possibly have more information for her after he had done his examination, what ever that might be."

"Sounds very fishy to me" said Sidney. "And how come there were only bones left, where had all the flesh gone?"

There was silence for a moment as the men looked at one another, hoping to hear an explanation. No suggestion was forthcoming and then

"Blow flies" said Charlie, taking another pull at his pint.

"What d'you mean Charlie?" asked Ben.

"Well, I've no doubt there was a crack or two in the mortar and a blow fly could have got in and laid his eggs. Over time, and it would have taken quite a while I know, the maggots would have eaten all the flesh away. Then they would have hatched into flies and.....buzzed off." He laughed at his little joke.

"Two murders in our little village" said Sidney "what ever is the place coming to."

"Who said it was murder?" asked Bob the landlord, who had joined them and was leaning on the bar.

"Well, if it was a natural death" said Ben "you wouldn't go hiding it in a bread oven and then bricking it in would you? Say Charlie, could it be that boy you were telling us about the other evening; the evacuee lad that disappeared."

"Maybe....Zach he was called, I found out later that he was Jewish. He came from the East End of London, Whitechapel I believe. You know, thinking about it, the police should have a record of it somewhere. After all they never found him, so the case has never been closed, or shouldn't have been."

"You best ask that lady sergeant fiend of yours" said Ben nudging Sidney and winking.

"I might do just that" said Charlie quietly, as he took another drink from his pint.

FIFTY SIX

In the incident room the mood was sombre; no matter how many leads they followed the result was the same; a dead end. All of Bosworth's contacts from his former life in the London area had drawn a total blank.

"We must try to find a link, however tenuous, between him and those he dealt with in this area. Wherever he went and did his business dealings, he made enemies. He bought and sold a number of properties down here. Contact estate agents, see what you can find. Ashton..."

"Yes Guv."

"You had occasion to have dealings with an estate agent a few years ago on some case or other, didn't you?"

"Yes guv."

"Well get in touch with him, see if he knows anything that might shed light on the matter. And what about the widow, are you still giving her the necessary support."

"Yes Guv."

"Right then, all of you get on with it, I need results, the ACC is getting restless."

Shirley went back to her desk and rang Martin. When DI Smith had started talking about her having dealings with an estate agent, she was worried in case he was aware of her personal relationship. If Martin was in any way connected with Bosworth, in a close business manner, it could mean that she wouldn't be able to see him again socially. That would not be good, especially with the cottage through the woods being so much on her mind at the moment.

When he answered she had to put on her police sergeant's voice, introducing herself as Sergeant Ashton. Fortunately he cottoned on quite quickly and like her became all business like.

"It is to do with the case we are investigating Sir, the murder of Mr Mark Bosworth."

"Oh yes, I read about it in the papers."

"We need to know if you had any business dealings with him."

"Yes I think we may have, I believe we sold him a property some years ago, I would have to look it up in the files to see exactly when. Is it important?"

"Was the deal friendly? Was he satisfied with his purchase?"

"Yes, as far as I know."

"He didn't come back complaining or anything like that."

"No, I can't remember if I ever saw the man again."

"You wouldn't happen to know if there are any of your fellow estate agents who have had difficult or acrimonious dealings with him."

"I haven't heard of any, but I could ask around for you if you like."

"That would be very kind of you Sir; I may look in your office later today, if that's alright with you."

"That will be fine; I look forward to seeing you Sergeant."

"Thank you Sir and goodbye for now."

Although the conversation had been a little awkward and formal, Shirley had found that her spirits had lifted since talking to Martin. Hearing the sound of his voice she could visualise his face, and see his lips moving. She was looking forward to seeing him again, not least because she wanted to have another look at the cottage. She really needed to see it in daylight and perhaps if she were to go for a walk on the moor behind it, she might find that her fear of Dartmoor was unfounded.

But before she saw Martin she felt that she ought to go and visit Hilary again. There was still a nagging doubt in her mind about the woman. She needed to spend a bit more time with her, listen to her and watch her for reactions.

She went over to Newman's desk and told him where she was going.

"D'you want me to come too, Serge?"

"No, I want you to find out all you can about Jeremy Armand; his service career etcetera, OK?"

"Right ho Sarge."

When she arrived at Grimstone Court she wondered just how many more times she would be coming to the place. She even wondered whether Hilary would be staying there or whether she would be selling this large unfriendly house. To her mind it seemed to be far too big for one person, even though she had Paul there in the office to keep her company for five days a week.

There was another small car outside which she recognized as belonging to Grace and she was glad to see that Hilary was still getting that support. So she wasn't at all surprised when Grace answered the door to her ring.

"Oh, hello Sergeant, do come in. I was just about to leave."

"Please don't go on my account Mrs Russell. My visit today is more personal than professional."

Oh, very well then....mm....yes well do come in, Hilary is in the office, I'll call her for you."

"No don't bother, I'll go to her rather than make her come to me."

She went down the long hall and found Hilary sitting in front of her computer, busily writing away. Her fingers were flashing over the keys and for some reason Shirley was astonished by her expertise.

"My word, Mrs Bosworth, I never realized that you were an expert typist."

"Yes" she said, smiling as she looked up from her work. "I trained in shorthand and typing many years ago. That was how I met Mark you see. I was his secretary for some years before we married."

"So you married the boss. I bet there were several other girls in the typing pool who envied you."

"They may have done then, I doubt if they would now."

'Maybe not' thought Shirley 'but I bet they would have liked even just a portion of Bosworth's money'.

"So what is it that you are so busy typing, may I ask?"

"It's a manuscript; an article, one of three, that my brother is writing for a magazine. Their editor commissioned him to write it."

"Really, and what is it about?"

"Afghanistan, and his days there as a service man in a strange and foreign country. There's a lot about the people there as well, it's very interesting. And it's not all guns and killing. Jeremy doesn't type you see, and I haven't got a great deal to do here now; Paul seems to have most things well in hand. So I offered to do the typing for him."

"And so you work from his manuscript do you? I hope that you are able to read his writing."

"Oh no, he doesn't write it down in long hand. He records it all on this little gadget."

She held up a small item no bigger than a mobile phone.

"It's a Dictaphone. I listen to it, take it down in short hand if necessary, and type it. The beauty of it is that I can pause it if I need to, or even go back, and then play it again. When I've finished a section he reads it through, there are always a few corrections and alterations, but I don't mind. All the profits are going to a forces charity, something like 'Help the Heroes'. I think it's wonderful of him, but then he always was a very feeling hearted man."

She got up from her chair and walked confidently around the desk to Shirley, a smile on her face and holding herself up straight.

'And you certainly seem to have gained some confidence since I last saw you' thought Shirley. 'Is that through having somebody asking you to do a job for them, giving you a purpose in life? Anything would be better than being Mark Bosworth's virtual slave, as you had been. Or is it because you have a new friend in Clive Luscombe? The not terribly romantic Mr Luscombe.' She turned to Grace and said

"And how are you Mrs Russell? It's very bad of me to neglect you. After all, you have suffered a great loss and a tremendous upset as well."

"Oh you mustn't bother about me....I'm fine thank you....Of course, I find it a great help to come up here and hopefully be a comfort to Hilary. But she is making great strides....mmm....yes....almost a full recovery."

262

"I'm delighted to hear that. I wish I could bring you some news, but I regret to say that we are no further on in our investigations."

"It must be very frustrating" said Grace.

"I'm sure that you and your team are doing all you can" said Hilary. "Now let me get you a nice cup of tea. Grace here has just brought me a beautiful cake, I'm sure you can help me to eat it, can't you?"

"Thank you, that would be lovely, but I'm afraid I can't stay long."

Hilary then led the way across the hall and into the lounge, chattering away as she went.

"But you must tell us all about this body, or what ever it was, that Terry found in his fire place."

"There's not a lot I can tell. It was the skeleton of a child, probably about seven or eight years old. We have no idea how long it had been there. It's a real mystery."

"Charlie Blundell suggested to me that it might be the remains of a little boy who went missing during the war" said Grace "He was one of the many children who came down here as evacuees from London."

"That sounds interesting" said Shirley.

"Yes, he said the police searched for the boy.....they never found him though."

"I'll have to see if there's any record of it. There should be, but a lot of old records unfortunately have gone missing."

FIFTY SEVEN

Having finished her tea and cake, Shirley made her excuses and left. Once in the car she rang Martin again and asked if he could meet her at the cottage beyond the woods.

"It's coming up to lunch time, would you like me to bring a couple of sandwiches with me?"

"That would be lovely, I'll get some orange juice or something and we can have a picnic."

She drove up to the cottage, the first time that she had done so on her own. The clouds were racing across the sky and the low sun shone through the wood, lighting the moss covered tree trunks like a wooden cathedral. Out in the open she stood in the front garden, looking down over the fields and rich farmland towards the coast. There was no doubt, it was a beautiful view, but was a view enough? She started walking towards the back garden when she heard a car coming, and soon Martin appeared.

"Have you come to a decision?" he asked.

"I'm still not sure about the moor."

"Well, let's take a walk up the slope onto that piece of open moorland and see what it feels like. Have you got any boots in the car?"

"Yes,"

"Right, let's go then."

They both changed into wellington boots, walked through the back garden and through a small gate onto the moor. The ground was dry, and the short grass cropped by generations of sheep and ponies was still green. Under their feet it felt like a thick soft carpet. A few hawthorn bushes were dotted around and clumps of gorse made a useful bit of shelter from the breeze for the animals.

Suddenly Martin grabbed her arm and pointing straight ahead said

"Look, a deer, d'you see it?"

Bouncing away towards the woods, its white scut flashing at them like a signal, was a roe deer hind. In a few bounds it reached the woods and leapt over the fence to disappear amongst the trees. Shirley was amazed and delighted at the sight.

"That was beautiful; the only deer I've ever seen up to now were those that had been knocked down on the road."

They walked on to the top and turned to look at the scenery all around them. Shadows of clouds were scudding across the hills, and the wind made a hissing noise as it played with the grass and the gorse bushes. Overhead a lone buzzard was circling, seemingly unaffected by the wind, while nearby a pair of ponies picked at the short grass. Martin put his arm around her shoulders and pointed to the surrounding tors. One by one he told her the names of them all.

"I never knew that they all had names, I just thought of them as hills I suppose."

"Oh yes, they all have names and even some of the bigger rocks, that are a kind of landmark, have names. After all, the farmers who run their animals up here need to be able to say to a neighbour exactly where their animals are."

"There's a lot more to this place than I ever thought"

"Let's go back to the cottage and have our picnic" said Martin. It was easier going down and, holding hands, they almost ran down the hill. Once inside, with faces flushed and hair all awry from the wind they sat in the kitchen and took out their food.

"I think you enjoyed that, I think that you have seen things today that you didn't realize existed. Has it in any way altered your view of Dartmoor?"

Shirley looked at him and took another mouthful of sandwich. She needed more time to think before answering, more time to be sure that she wasn't rushing in like a fool. True, she had seen a totally different aspect of the moor; it had certainly seemed more friendly and less frightening than she had previously thought. While she had been up on the top, she had imagined that she could begin to feel a little of what Linda had spoken about. Finally she said

"D'you know, I honestly think I could live here. There's a sort of peace up on the moor, even on a blustery day like today. I never realized it before"

"That's great; I hoped that you might change your mind."

"I fell in love with the cottage the first time I saw it. For some silly reason I was just afraid of the nearness to the moor. But now that I realize that my fears are groundless, well I think I could go ahead and buy. All that now remains is for me to sell the flat."

"I don't think that will be a problem" he said.

She looked over at him with a huge smile on her face and a feeling of relief. Then they finished their picnic and as they were walking towards their cars Martin said

"You were asking about Bosworth earlier. He bought a property through an agent whom I know vaguely. It was a large place, in need of a lot of work, almost dilapidated. Bosworth was intending to redevelop it and then there was a fire. The whole place was burned down to the ground. He put in a claim to his insurers and they sent out an assessor. Unfortunately for Bosworth, the insurers claimed that it was arson, traces of accelerant found apparently. So they wouldn't pay up, because the cover didn't include arson, Bosworth wasn't a happy man at all, blamed the assessor."

"Sounds like he didn't read the small print on his policy."

"Well, there's more to it than that. You see, my secretary, nice girl called Lorna, was going out with this insurance assessor. Somehow or other Bosworth got to hear of it. He couldn't get back at the man legally, but he made sure that Lorna was made aware of a nasty rumour. The assessor helped a lot with the local scout group. And the rumour, which Bosworth had probably made up, was that the assessor preferred little boys. Somehow Bosworth saw to it that Lorna heard of it in gruesome detail. She was devastated, packed in her job with us and moved back to live with her parents in Southampton."

"Did she give any explanation to the boyfriend?"

"Not as far as I know; in fact he not only didn't know why she dumped him so suddenly but may not even know that it was Bosworth who stirred up all the trouble."

"Poor chap; the more I hear about Bosworth the more I'm not surprised that he got killed. How is that insurance chap now, d'you know?"

"He's still working for the same company; I don't suppose they ever heard anything about the accusation. It was totally false in any case."

"What was his name, d'you remember?"

"Yes, it was Luscombe, Clive Luscombe."

FIFTY EIGHT

As Shirley drove back to the station her mind was in a whirl. The walk up onto the moorland with Martin had been exciting and exhilarating. She had certainly learned a lot, both about Dartmoor and about herself. But she wasn't entirely sure if it was the fact that she was less afraid of the moor, or Martin's company that had made her feel the way she did. There was no doubt that she found his company enjoyable. He seemed kind and considerate and didn't try to push his ideas on her. Also the more she had looked at the cottage the more she had felt that it would be right for her. Well, she would be seeing him tonight, to start the ball rolling so to speak. He had suggested meeting him at his office, to see to the necessary paper work, and then perhaps they could go for a meal somewhere, an idea that appealed to her.

"No, better still" he had said, "I'll bring any paperwork with me and I'll pick you up at your place."

But the other thought running through her head was to do with the story he had told her about Clive Luscombe and his girl friend Lorna. The more she thought about it the more of a puzzle it seemed. If Bosworth had somehow encouraged Lorna to believe his tale that Clive was into little boys, why had she just up and left so suddenly and without a word? Until that moment their relationship had been strong; in fact Martin felt that an engagement had not been far away. So why had she not challenged Clive to see if the story was true? It would have been logical to give the man she loved the opportunity to defend himself.

And did Clive ever find out, not only why she had dumped him but that it was Bosworth who had told her the malicious lies about him? Had he ever found out? If he had, then it could be said that he had a good motive for hating Bosworth, enough to want to kill him even. But why had he waited for so long? After all, it was six years since Lorna had up and left. Maybe he had found out only recently, but how and from whom?

Once back in the station the first thing she did was the obligatory paper work and then she sought out DI Smith. She told him what Martin had told her and that she had written it all down in her report.

"I've asked Martin Travers to come in and write a signed statement. He said he would be happy to do so, but could he write the statement in his office and bring it in here and then sign it. I said that would be OK."

"Fine; so you now have a prime suspect in Clive Luscombe do you?"

"Well, I'm not sure that I'd call him a prime suspect Guv, but he certainly has some questions to answer. The main two being, did he know why his girl friend Lorna had left him and did he ever find out who told her the tale about him liking little boys? If the answer to both of them is no, as Martin Travers seems to think, then I'm not so keen to call him a suspect."

"Have you checked out with the local Scout group if there is any truth in the allegation?"

"Not yet Guv"

"Well I suggest you do. Then perhaps tomorrow we will bring Luscombe in for questioning."

It took Shirley several minutes and several phone calls before she discovered who in the local Scout group she needed to talk to. Once she had the identity and the address of the man in question she went to see him. It was a difficult subject to broach. The last thing she wanted to do was to imply that the rumour was true. In view of the recent scandals regarding celebrities accused of indecently assaulting underage girls and children in general, she realized that she had to be very careful.

As it turned out, the scout master was a man of the world and knew only too well that people like him and Clive, who worked with young boys, were always a target for those sorts of malicious rumours and scandal mongering. It meant that only too often it prevented good people from volunteering to work with children. He said that he had always had complete faith in Clive and dismissed the whole story as a pack of lies.

So why had Lorna believed Bosworth? What could he have said to make her believe him?

As she drove back to the station her phone went. She let it ring and the caller left a message. Once back at the station she saw that it was a message from Charlie; he wanted to have a word with her. She rang him and after several rings Sal answered

"He's not in any trouble is he?" she said.

"No, he rang me earlier, only I was out. I'm just returning his call."

"I'll see if I can find him, he's out in the garden, in his shed I'll be bound."

She put the phone down on the table with a bang that echoed down the line and made Shirley jump. Then Shirley could hear her shouting from the kitchen doorway

"Charlie, you'm wanted on the phone, 'tis that police lady…..hurry up, she hasn't got all day."

Charlie finally came on the line, puffing from the exertion of running up through the garden.

"You asked me to call you, what is it Charlie?"

"Well, it may be naught, but 'tis to do with that there skeleton what Terry found."

With that he proceeded to tell her all about the young evacuee who had gone missing during the war and how the local police had searched for him.

"I dare say 'tiv got nought to do with it, but I just thought you ought to know."

"Thank you very much Charlie, we are always glad of any information. I'll look into it straight away."

So, armed with the details that Charlie had given her, Shirley set off to search in the records section for any light that could be shed on the matter. It took her well over an hour to find the relevant reports, in fact she had almost given up, fearing that all the records of that era had been lost or destroyed. However, at last she found what she had been looking for.

The boy Zach had been put with a Mr and Mrs Wilson at Town Mill, as it was then known. He had gone missing in September nineteen forty two. All attempts to find him had failed, though it did look to Shirley that maybe the search could have been a bit more thorough and for a longer period. However, she realized that it had been wartime when no doubt there were many other far more important things to do.

The boy had come from the Whitechapel area of the East End of London. Thinking that he might have gone home, a brief search in that area had been made, though it also had failed to find him. Sadly, what that search had discovered was that his parents had been killed, along with several others, when a bomb had landed on their street. If the boy Zach had managed to return home he could have perished in a bomb blast as so many had done.

To find out how the child in Terry's bread oven had died Shirley then went to the morgue to see Dr Hall. He had the remains on a table and was studying them carefully.

"What d'you know Doc?" she asked, having stood patiently beside him for a minute or two.

"Not a lot Shirley. My guess is that it is a male child, though that is only a guess. As to how he died, he was either hit on the head with a sharp object, or he fell and hit his head on something which had a sharp corner, such as a fire place. There's a small hole in the skull. A blow there could have been fatal."

"Any idea as to how long ago he was put in the bread oven?"

"Not really, at least fifty years I would say, but again, it's only a guess."

"So it could have been an accident, or a parent being a bit too heavy handed with the discipline. Then to get rid of the evidence, the body was hidden in the bread oven."

Shirley then told Dr Hall the story that Charlie had told her about Zach and his somewhat unhappy stay in the village with the Wilsons.

"It would seem that this could be that missing boy who disappeared back in nineteen forty two. Or are we just putting two and two together and making five. "

"It certainly could be what happened" said Dr Hall. "How's the other case going, have you got a suspect yet? You must have had several to choose from."

"We may have, but I'm none too sure. One thing, this skeleton is nothing to do with that."

As she walked away she thought 'how odd, in the last two weeks I have been involved in two cases of a missing person, both of them ended up probably murdered and both had their bodies hidden. There's nothing new is there?'

FIFTY NINE

Back in the incident room Shirley found Newman writing his report on what he had been able to discover regarding Jeremy's service career. He had served with the 'paras' for fifteen years, first in Iraq and then for several tours in Afghanistan. Between his tours abroad he had spent a good deal of time at Hereford, but Newman had found that it was not possible to get any details. Had there been a specific charge brought against Jeremy, maybe more details would be made available.

"Sounds to me like he could well have been in the SAS Sarge, Hereford and all that; they have to keep their identities and personal details secret I suppose."

"What rank did he achieve?" asked Shirley "Staff sergeant I suppose".

"No, he was a commissioned officer; Captain J M Armand."

"Coming back into civilian life and running Bosworth's water bottling plant must have been pretty tame after that" said Shirley. "I wonder, could he be the fellow....you know....the boy friend of the girl who committed suicide? The daughter of that couple who stayed in the holiday complex; what were they called again?"

"Cash, Mr and Mrs Cash."

"That's it, they said their daughter had a boy friend who was a captain and he had a French sounding name. We thought that he must be a sailor, either in the Merchant or the Royal Navy. And another thing, if you pronounce Jeremy's surname *Armon* rather than Armand it does sound French. Too much of a coincidence is it?"

"But the only person who can tell you if he was the boyfriend, is Jeremy himself. The girl is dead and the parents never met him. And if he is a suspect for the murder of Bosworth I doubt if he will admit to that."

"Because it would give him a motive" said Shirley, finishing Newman's thought process. "But how could he have done it? He was in the bottling plant, remember? He rang his sister from there; she heard the noise of the machinery and asked him to move outside so she could hear him better."

"Yes, but he certainly had a good motive, what with his girl friend killing herself and Bosworth beating his sister. Who knows there may have been more? And don't forget, if he had been in the SAS he would certainly have been trained to kill, with his bare hands if necessary."

"We're not sure about that, you are guessing at that bit of his service career."

"I still think he's a pretty sure suspect Sarge, don't you?"

"You could be right; at any rate, he's the most likely suspect we've got at the moment, based on motive. But how he did it and how we are going to prove it, I'm damned if I know."

SIXTY

Lisa was at Grimstone Court cleaning, as she did every week. It was a large house and Mark Bosworth had felt that Hilary needed the help. Although she now had enough time on her hands and could have done it all herself, Hilary was glad of Lisa's company if nothing else.

They had just stopped for a coffee when Grace rang the doorbell and with a call of 'only me' walked in and joined them.

"So how is Terry since his new found fame?" asked Grace.

"He's fine; the money he got for selling his story and the photos may not have been a vast sum, but it will help a lot. Now he can do a great deal more of the renovating to the house."

"Oh good, I am pleased for him, and you too. What a sad ending for that poor child....to be hidden away in a bread oven...."

"And I don't suppose we'll ever know how it happened or who was responsible" said Hilary. "The police are having enough difficulty finding out who killed Mark, and that was only a few weeks ago. This poor child has been dead for years."

"You know who killed Mark, don't you Mrs Russell?" said Lisa "You said it couldn't possibly be Terry, when I was worried 'cos the police thought he could. You said then that you knew who killed Mark."

"Yes....well....I also said, if you remember, that I had no proof, and no way of proving it. But yes....I think I know. It's all so sad.....the hurt some people inflict on others.....the hatred that arises from that....and the evil doings....mmm...."

"But if you know, surely the police will find out in time, won't they?"

"Perhaps" said Grace, looking at Hilary with a wistful smile on her face.

"Well you could always tell that Sergeant Ashton couldn't you? Then she could look into it a bit more."

"Oh I'm not sure that I could do that....oh no. You see dear, I may be totally wrong....the person may be innocent.....It can be too easy to give a dog a bad name.....and mud sticks."

SIXTY ONE

That evening Shirley was sorting out what to wear for her date with Martin. She had just tried on a slinky red dress but had found pulling up the zip difficult. Over time, her dress size had increased to a fourteen, but some fourteens, she told herself, were definitely smaller than others. She returned the dress to the wardrobe and tried on a few more. It was a job to know what to wear. What would Martin be wearing? He was always dressed in a suit for work, so he would probably favour something a little more casual. Perhaps she could wear her smart jeans? She tried them on and decided that....well.... perhaps not....a bit too casual. So she went back to the skirt and top that she had put out on the bed before she went for her shower.

She had just finished and was checking her reflection in the mirror when there was a knock on the door. Martin was standing there, holding a bunch of flowers and smiling broadly. As she had thought he had chosen a more casual outfit than his daytime business suit, and was wearing a pair of brown trousers and a dark green corduroy jacket with a cream shirt. She took the flowers saying

"These are lovely, thank you so much."

She went back into the kitchen to find a vase for them. Then, slipping on her coat and grabbing her handbag, she joined him to go out into the dark November evening.

Martin had chosen to come by taxi; he enjoyed a glass or two with a meal, and had no intention of putting Shirley in a difficult position by drinking and driving while on their first evening out. They drove out of the town and up onto the edge of the moor to a small hotel. As they pulled up the headlights of the taxi lit up the red Venetian creeper that covered the walls of the building.

They went in and Martin led her to the small cosy bar area. A fire was burning brightly in the grate and with a gin and tonic in her hand Shirley looked through the menu. She felt totally at ease and thoroughly spoiled, saying to herself

"I could get used to this; it would be no effort to put up with this sort of treatment."

After their drinks and nibbles they moved into the dining room. Linen table cloths and napkins and sparkling silverware and cut glass gave the tables the look of class. Heavy drapes at the windows and a deep pile carpet helped to keep the noise level down. Because of this all the diners were talking in muted tones and this, together with the décor, gave the room an atmosphere of discreet nineteen thirties elegance. Shirley expected to see Miss Marple sitting at one of the tables, which then made her think of Grace.

Later, as they ate their meal they talked and exchanged brief autobiographies. Martin told her of his failed earlier marriage and of his grown up daughter.

"So you never re-married?"

"No, I was always too busy working, never seemed to be able to spare the time for anything except work. That was what had caused the break-up in the first place, I suppose."

"And do you get to see your daughter often?"

"Not very often, she lives up in the Midlands. Youngsters today have to go where the work is and her husband's job is based in Dudley, just outside Birmingham."

There was a pause in the conversation as they ate their delicious puddings, then Martin asked

"Have you ever married....?"

"No, much like you I was always too busy working. I suppose you might call me a career girl, always chasing promotion. Anyway, a policeman's life is not suited to a happy marriage. I have seen too many of my fellow officers whose marriages have ended in divorce; sad really."

"So you never wanted the home life.....a husband and two point four children?"

"No, I never even thought about it" she said, smiling at him as she looked into his eyes.

"And now, do I get the impression that you are having a slight change of heart?"

"You mean the change I'm making, moving out to the country?"

"Yes, at a guess, I would say that you are putting yourself and your personal interests before the job, probably for the first time."

"You could be right, I hadn't really thought about it that way, but I must admit, I have been taking stock lately. The job doesn't give me quite the satisfaction that it used to do. Maybe that's just because I'm getting old."

"You're not old" said Martin, reaching across the table to put his hand on hers. "But do you think that you would ever give up the job, maybe even get married.....?"

"I don't know" she said as she gazed pensively up at the ceiling. "We none of us know what's around the corner. I think the best answer to both those questions is.....never say never."

They had finished their meal and moved into the lounge. A waitress came and asked them if they wanted coffee. Shirley felt the need to stand or walk around for a while and started looking at the photographs on the wall. Several of them depicted a group of cyclists and one young man in particular receiving a trophy. In the bottom right hand corner of all the pictures there was a design or logo which was of circle in which was a three pronged fork with a letter S entwined in it. Shirley felt sure that she had seen this design somewhere and decided to ask the waitress. She returned with a tray on which was a pot of coffee and a dish with various delicious looking chocolates. Shirley asked her about the photographs and the logo but the girl knew nothing about them. However, she said

"I'll ask the chef, he's a keen cyclist, he will probably know."

Some minutes later the chef joined them. His first question naturally was

"Did you enjoy your meal?" They both said how lovely it all had been and then he said "I understand you were asking about the cyclists in the pictures."

"Yes" said Shirley. "I was also interested in the logo on the bottom corner of the pictures, it seemed familiar to me, though I'm not sure why."

"We had a cycle race back in the summer, a race that started and finished here. It was sponsored by a company that makes Lycra clothing, the sort used by cyclists. Stanfork they are called, that's their logo on the pictures."

He stayed chatting about the race for a few minutes and then, after he had gone, Martin asked

"What's with the design on the pictures?"

"I really don't know, it's something I have seen recently, but I can't think where. I'm sure it will come back to me, it probably isn't important."

But she was still puzzling over it all the way home. Once there Martin escorted her to the door and gave her a hug and a kiss on the cheek. She felt warm and happy and said as she looked up at him

"Thank you for a lovely evening; I don't know when I last enjoyed myself so much. I hope we can do it again sometime soon, perhaps you could come here and I would cook a meal for you?"

"That would be very nice, I'd like that."

As he stepped back his hand, which had been resting on her shoulder, slid down her arm and took hold of her hand. He held it for a brief while, then with a squeeze he let go and went down to the waiting taxi.

SIXTY TWO

The next morning Clive Luscombe had been brought into the station for questioning. DI Smith and Newman were conducting the interview, while Shirley was watching and listening through the glass. She was far from sure that he was their prime suspect but DI Smith was adamant, and wanted to get the case cleared up as soon as possible.

As the questioning progressed he became more forceful.

"So, you admit that you stopped in the village on October the twenty fourth at about six o'clock."

"Yes" said Clive.

"And that was to ask for directions to Grimstone Court, from a young boy."

"Yes."

"And what was your reason for wanting to know these directions?"

"I just wanted to see if I was in the area where Mrs Bosworth lived."

"So you then drove up to the house, right?"

"No" said Clive, feeling surprised and somewhat annoyed that he should be doubted in this way. "I drove straight home."

"I put it to you that you went to the house."

"Why should I? Hilary would be at the nursing home in Dawlish at that time, so what would be the point in my going there. Besides I was already late and had paperwork to see to before I went to see my mother in the nursing home."

"I know that you went to the home, you arrived there at seven thirty. That gave you plenty of time to drive up to Grimstone Court after getting directions as to how to get there. You saw Mr Bosworth pull into the little lane at the bottom of the field. As he walked up to survey his planned development you ran down through the field next to the one he was in, found the shotgun in his car and waited for him."

"No, I tell you I went straight home."

"Then you challenged him, had words with him and then shot him."

"No I didn't, this is nonsense; what reason would I have for shooting the man? To the best of my knowledge I've never met him."

"Oh you had plenty of reason. You have formed quite a relationship with his widow and you felt a good deal of enmity towards him for the way he was in the habit of beating her. Apart from that there is the matter of your former girl friend Lorna."

"What about her, what's all this got to do with her? I haven't seen her for five or six years."

"She left in a hurry didn't she? Never gave you any explanation as to why she left, did she? She never told you that Bosworth had told her that in your capacity as a scout master you were sexually abusing boys?"

DI Smith was leaning forward looking straight into Clive's face.

"That's a dreadful lie, I never...."

"Oh I know that isn't true, I know that your behaviour in the scout troop was always exemplary. But she didn't and later...when you heard that it was Bosworth who had started that rumour, told her those lies, well..."

Clive threw his hands up in the air in a gesture of disbelief, leant back in his chair and looked around the room as if for help.

"Why don't you listen to what I am saying, I never went near the house, I went straight home, had a quick cup of tea while I caught up with my paperwork and then went to the nursing home. I met Hilary there then, at about half past seven."

"We know that, and while you were talking to her she told you that she was going to the funeral of the late vicar the next day. That gave you the idea of hiding the body in his grave."

"I never went to Grimstone Court, I never met Mark Bosworth, I never shot him, why don't you believe me?"

"You may not have intended to kill him" said Newman, taking over the questioning "You had the gun loaded and pointing at Bosworth, threatening him. Then he grabbed it, hoping to take it from you and as he pulled it, your fingers were on the triggers and the gun went off."

"You could probably persuade a jury that that's what happened and get away with the lesser charge of manslaughter" said DI Smith.

"This is ridiculous, why can't you understand, I was never there? You've got the wrong man, can't you see?"

"Take him down to the cells Chaffe; a few hours in custody may help him to realize that it's no good to keep on telling us his lies."

With that he stood up and left the room. A uniformed constable came in and together with Newman took Clive, protesting vehemently, down to the cells. Shirley, who had watched the whole thing, was not only dismayed, but disgusted at the heavy handed approach used by DI Smith. She felt sure that they had the wrong man. The circumstantial evidence might point towards Clive Luscombe being guilty, but the whole case against him relied too much on supposition. Somewhere, somehow they had missed something.

She went into the interview room and found Newman and DI Smith talking about Clive.

"He just doesn't seem guilty Guv, worried, perplexed even, but not guilty.

"Rubbish, the man's a good actor that's all. When you've interviewed as many villains as I have, you'll know when they're lying.

"I think Chaffe has got a point Guv" said Shirley, joining in the conversation. "According to Martin Travers, he Travers, was the only person, other than that Lorna girl, who knew of Bosworth's allegation that Luscombe was abusing little boys. He says that Luscombe was never told."

"I still say that a spell in custody will help him to see reason and tell us the truth" said Smith, as he walked off into his office.

SIXTY THREE

The cell door shut with a dull clang; to Clive it sounded like the bell of doom. 'Why am I here, and how on earth did I get into this mess?' he thought. He couldn't understand why the Inspector didn't believe him. He looked around at the walls, remains of half washed off graffiti showing in places, and he thought of all those who had been there before him. How many of them were guilty, more to the point, how many like him were innocent? He had read in the papers of people being falsely convicted, rotting away behind bars for years. Was that what was going to happen to him? His heart beat faster as the terrible thought took hold in his mind.

And what about his mother, how would she cope, what would she think when she heard the news that he had been locked up for murder? He sat on the hard raised area that served as a bed. He was shaking, almost in tears and his heart was racing. He heard a noise as the tiny window in the door opened.

"You alright in there?" a voice said.

"No I'm not, I feel sick and I can't stop shaking. Can I see Sergeant Ashton? I need to talk to her."

"I'll see what I can do" the voice said and the window closed. Clive waited, hoping that Shirley would come. He trusted her for some reason; he thought that she was kind and understanding. But nobody came, certainly not Shirley. He could hear voices occasionally and he thought at one time that he heard her voice. Then there was a lot of shouting and arguing and the sound of the cell door next to him clanging shut as another person was locked up.

Finally, when he had almost given up hope of ever seeing Shirley or the outside world ever again the door opened and she was there.

"You wanted to see me?"

"Yes, you're the only one who understands me. I shouldn't be here, I haven't done anything wrong. Why won't they believe me? Will I ever get out of here?"

He was almost in tears and Shirley, who felt somewhat responsible for his predicament, said

"Of course you will. You can only be held for thirty six hours without charge. But you have to realize that you are the only person who can help you. The reason the DI doesn't believe you is that you cannot explain where you were and what you were doing from six o'clock until seven thirty when you arrived at the nursing home. Try to calm down and think; where did you go and what did you do. Did you meet anybody, talk to anybody who might remember you? Sometimes we do things so routinely that we forget that we even did them. I can't help you any more, but I am in the station here this morning and if you do manage to think of anything that might help call the duty officer. I'll tell him that you may call, and that if you do he is to get me, OK?"

"Thank you Sergeant, I'll try."

He sat back on the bed, his head in his hands, as Shirley left and the cell door shut with that terrible dull clang. But try as he might all he could think of was the predicament that he was in. He would get up and pace around the small cell and then sit down again. Eventually he calmed down a little and began to think rationally. What was it the sergeant had said, think of what he had done and where he had been from six o'clock until seven thirty?

Well, at six o'clock he had stopped in the village to ask directions and had spoken to that polite young man. Then, because he was running late he had driven home and on the way he had…..yes, the memory was coming back. Of course, just like the sergeant had said, a routine occurrence.

He called through the cell door's little window and after what seemed like an age Shirley opened the door.

"I've remembered something Sergeant, I don't know if it will help."

"What is it?"

"Before I got home, it must have been at about six twenty or twenty five; I filled up the car with diesel."

"Where was that?"

"That little garage just outside town, by the recreation ground."

"Will they remember you? Did you talk to anyone there? How did you pay? D'you have an account there?"

"No, I always pay as I go, and I pay with my credit card. That way I get two receipts, one when I pay and another when the bill comes."

"And where is your credit card now, is it in your wallet?"

"Yes, and the man who took all my belongings when they locked me in here put it all in a big envelope."

"I'll go and have a word with DI Smith, this may change every thing. I won't be long"

Once again the cell door clanged shut, but this time for some reason it didn't sound so ominous.

SIXTY FOUR

Once again it had seemed an age before Shirley came back to the cell. It had taken her some time, first of all to find DI Smith and then to persuade him to listen to what she had to say.

"Right, bring him up and get his possessions. You and Chaffe can interview him."

In the interview room Shirley and Newman faced Clive across the table, the envelope of his belongings in front of them.

"I hope this isn't a wild goose chase Serge" said Newman.

Clive emptied the envelope out onto the table, his watch, a bunch of keys, a handkerchief, a small packet of chewing gum and finally his wallet. This he opened and took from it a credit card and several receipts. He passed them all to Shirley saying with a sudden return of confidence

"If the details are not on the receipt, the card company should be able to tell you where I used the card and when."

"Yes, you're right, this receipt shows where you were and the date and time; twenty fourth of October, eighteen twenty three hours."

"So that proves that I couldn't have killed Mr Bosworth, doesn't it?" he said with great relief in his voice.

"Newman left the room to report the matter to DI Smith and came back a few minutes later saying

"OK Mr Luscombe, you are free to go, thank you."

Delighted to be free, Clive didn't argue or question whether there would be any compensation for his being held for so long. He just said to Shirley

"Thank you Sergeant, if it hadn't been for your advice I wouldn't be going anywhere."

With that he scooped up his belongings and left the room.

A short while later in the incident room Shirley was saying to Newman and Tom

"We've missed something, you know. Somehow somewhere we've missed a vital clue and I can't think what. There are times when I feel I knew exactly what it was and now I have forgotten it. Then I think it was all a dream. That's the trouble now, I find myself dreaming about the case. Then I wake up thinking that I've found the answer, but it's all just been a load of nonsense that I dreamt up."

"You need to get right away from it for a while, to sort of clear your head" said Tom Watson.

"It's no good; we've got to go through all the statements again."

"I'll do that Sarge" said Newman.

"Good, there's a couple of things I need to look into. If you make a start on the statements and anything else that you can think of, I'll get on."

SIXTY FIVE

She left and drove over to the small industrial estate. She parked outside and walked in. Then having checked in with the man on duty she walked over to the tile warehouse near to the bottling plant. She walked around until she was behind the building and, stepping over a few old broken pallets, reached the boundary fence. Walking along beside it she soon came to the small gate. The lock was stained around the keyhole, making that part of it slightly darker than the rest. Perhaps, she thought, with oil. She looked around her, there was nobody about so she took out a nail file from her bag and put it into the keyhole. She remembered seeing the key hung up in the watchman's office and had seen that it was a very simple sort of lock. After a few pokes and twists, there was a satisfying click and the door was free to open. She walked through into a small wooded area. From the noise she could hear she knew that she was not far from a road. She followed a track and soon came to a small but fairly busy road. She stood looking around her trying to get her bearings. After walking a hundred yards along the road she worked out where she was. A side turning led into an estate of houses and flats.

So she retraced her steps and shut and locked the gate. For some reason, locking it was easier than unlocking it had been. As she sat in her car she rang Newman.

"Do we have the home address of Jeremy Armand?"

"No Sarge, all we have is his work address."

She then drove into the estate, to the bewilderment of the watchman, and parked outside the bottling plant. The same girl was in reception and she called for Jeremy. When he arrived Shirley said

"I've got just a couple of questions Mr Armand, if you don't mind. When you finish work how difficult is it to switch off this operation"

"No problem, I just have to wait for the line to finish and then switch off."

"Can you switch off before the line is finished, if you needed to?"

"Oh yes, we have to be able to stop it any time for safety reasons."

"The other thing, we don't seem to have your home address, could you let me have it please?"

"Certainly." He wrote down the address and Shirley thanked him and left. When she got back to the station she got out a map and studied it for a while. Newman came over, curious as to what she was up to. Shirley pointed to the map, indicating the industrial estate. Not very far from it, in the housing estate was the address of Jeremy's flat. The road from it to the industrial estate went a long way round; making the distance travelled at least four limes longer than if taken through the small wood and the side gate.

She took a magnifying glass out of her desk and then drove out to the small hotel where she had dined with Martin. She went in and, having shown her warrant card, asked the receptionist if she could go into the small lounge where they had enjoyed their coffee. She spent a long time looking at the coloured photographs of the cyclists. Finally she took one of the pictures down off the wall and studied it carefully with her magnifying glass. One figure in a maroon suit looked familiar, but his face was turned away from the camera. It was a casual photograph of a group on their bicycles, apparently laughing and joking together.

As she looked at it the chef came into the room.

"Back again, still interested in our cycle race? What is it, d'you want to take part in the next one?"

"No, I was hoping that you might be able to tell me who this man is". She pointed to the figure in the maroon Lycra suit. The chef bent over the picture and took the glass from Shirley.

"It's a bit difficult to be sure, he's got his face turned away, but the names are all on the back" he said, taking the picture from Shirley and turning it over. She studied it for a while, then with a smile and a thank you she hung the picture back in its place on the wall.

She then drove on to the village and to the house where Grace lived. It had crossed her mind that Grace would be up at Grimstone Court keeping Hilary company, and that her journey might have been wasted. But after a couple of knocks the door was opened.

"Oh it's you Sergeant, do come in. What brings you here" she said as she led the way into the kitchen. Outside, the sun low in the sky was flooding the room with light. A newspaper was on the table, open at the crossword page and a pencil lay beside it.

"Will I make you a cup of tea, I was about to make myself one?"

"Thank you, that would be very nice" said Shirley. Grace busied herself making the tea, asking as she did

"How are your investigations going...are you any further on?"

"Yes, I think that at last I am. But I need some help, and I have come here to ask if you can do me a favour."

"Oh I say...a favour......well yes...of course I will....if I can."

"It may not be too easy, but I hope that with your powers of persuasion....."

"Me, powers of persuasion....I really don't know."

"What I would like you to do is to get Hilary, Mrs Bosworth to hold a Sunday Lunch party."

"When?"

"This coming Sunday."

"And who is to be invited to this lunch?"

Shirley handed Grace a piece of paper with a couple of names on it.

"Will you be coming as well, with that nice young constable? He does seem so young doesn't he?......I say, this is exciting."

"If possible, yes; I'll ring you to find out if you have managed the arrangement and I'll let you know then if we will be able to join you. By the way, I forgot to ask, how is Hilary these days? You have been a wonderful help to her, notwithstanding your own bereavement."

"She's very well; she seems to be coping with it all very calmly now. To start with she was so upset....almost panicking....I think that Paul has taken a lot of the strain off her...the business side of things....yes.."

"Will she be staying at Grimstone Court d'you know? It's such a big place for just one person."

"She did say something of the sort the other day, but then she also said that she didn't want to make a hasty decision. She needs time, don't you think?"

"Sometimes we don't have the time" said Shirley wistfully. "Well. I'll see you on Sunday, all being well."

Shirley finished her tea and drove back to the station. She walked through the incident room and knocked on the door to DI Smith's office. Once inside she said

"I don't need to tell you Guv that this case has got us baffled. I hate to admit it but we just don't seem to be making any progress at all. Any person who looks at all like a suspect has a cast iron alibi, as was proved this morning."

"So?"

"I have an idea, you may say it's a crazy idea but it may work. All our evidence is circumstantial. We don't have facts, we have suppositions. Nothing that we have would stand up in court, in fact I doubt if the Crown Prosecution Service would even let us make a case of it and take it to court."

"So what's this crazy idea of yours?"

"Well" said Shirley and proceeded to tell him. At first he sat shaking his head as she outlined her plan. Finally after she had gone into all the details she could think of, he said

"It sounds a bit too much like Hercule Poirot to me. Still, it just might work. You do realize though, that it may still never get to court?"

"Yes Guv."

"OK then, just be careful. Should there be any comeback it's on your head. I'm not sure that I ought to wish you luck but..." he grinned at her in a conspiratorial way and for the first time Shirley saw him in a new light. She left his office with a beaming smile on her face and rang Martin.

"Would you care to come over for a bite to eat this evening? It wouldn't be as good as the other night, but I'm in a good mood and want to share it with you. Will seven o'clock be alright?"

"That sounds great, I'd love to. I feel honoured that I should be chosen as the recipient to share your good mood."

SIXTY SIX

On her way home Shirley called in at the supermarket to get some things that she needed for the meal that night. She had never considered herself to be a particularly good cook, so she had decided to keep it simple and do a dish that had always worked for her, chicken in a honey and mustard sauce. As for dessert, she had noticed that Martin had chosen the less sugary of the sweets on offer the other night, so she was going to do lemon solid, which was an old recipe of her grandmother's.

Once home she set to work on the preparation. She felt quite excited at getting a meal ready for two; it was something that she hadn't done for a long time and it made her feel good. Was this an example of what Linda had said about the pleasure gained from sharing? Perhaps it was; and perhaps this was what she needed, and more so. Or was it that her mood had been lifted by the fact that she had finally found the answer to the murder case. Certainly her reservations about the job had faded, she felt a lot more relaxed about it all now. And then there was the cottage and the excitement of moving. How much of that was the cottage and how much Martin? She had to admit that he had been in her thoughts lot recently, more than anyone else had ever been before.

With the table laid and everything ready she sat down in her favourite armchair and looked around. It was a good little flat and her time in it had been good, it had served her well. Admittedly of late she hadn't bothered too much, certainly not as much as she should; pictures on the walls were often askew and it was far from tidy most of the time. When she had first moved in she was so proud of it and had kept it like a show home. It was obviously time to move on and the cottage and Martin seemed to have come into her life at the right time.

He arrived on her doorstep, a huge smile on his face, a bottle of wine in one hand and a box of chocolates in the other. She took these from him and while her hands were full he held her shoulders and kissed her on both cheeks.

"You said that you were enjoying a good mood; tell me about it, what has brought this on?"

"The case, it's this case I've been on."

"The murder case?"

"Yes, it has had us all baffled for so long. Too many possible suspects, all with plausible motives and most of them had perfect alibis. There have been just too many variables. But now I think I have the answer. I can't go into detail but I can tell you that the feeling of relief is great."

"I can see that, and I'm very pleased for you. I can also tell you that your purchase is going through without a hitch, it will take a week or two, these things always do, but you can start making definite plans now."

The meal was a success and afterwards they sat together on the settee talking about the cottage and what she might do to it.

"Well I certainly don't intend doing anything for at least a year. It's absolutely lovely as it is and anyway, I think one needs to live in a place for a good while to find out what, if anything, needs changing."

"I think you are very wise" said Martin. He felt like saying 'I think you're very lovely', but he wasn't too sure. He didn't want to push his luck and spoil things. This was the first time for many years that he

299

had felt this way for a woman, any woman, and it made him a bit cautious.

Shirley was watching him, looking at his lips and his eyes. And she liked the look of his hands, sensitive long fingered hands that moved a lot as he talked. She was beginning to feel that this relationship was meaningful. She took his hand and said

"I'm sure that a lot of my good mood is due to you and the way you have helped me. It's not just with buying the cottage, but also the way that you showed me that there's nothing to be afraid of on Dartmoor. And I definitely enjoy spending time and sharing things with you."

She stopped, afraid that she might have said too much but she needn't have worried because he smiled and said

"I'm so glad, because I have enjoyed the past few days enormously." He leaned over and kissed her, first on the cheek and then on the lips. Then he stood up and taking his phone out of his pocket said

"I'll just ring for my taxi. This has been a lovely evening, but it's getting late…."

Shirley wanted to say 'You don't have to go, you can stay the night'. But she feared that it might be too soon for that. There'd be another time, she was sure of that. Instead she said

"Would you like another cup of coffee while you're waiting for the taxi? I can easily make one."

"Yes, that would be very nice."

So they sat and drank coffee, but somehow the atmosphere had changed. It was as though they both were aware of thoughts that had nearly been put into words or actions. When the taxi arrived they stood up and Shirley said

"When will I see you again?"

"Soon I hope; I'll ring you tomorrow."

He took her in his arms and kissed her again. Then he pulled away, and as he went out through the door she thought,

'I should have asked him to stay'.

SIXTY SEVEN

At Grimstone Court although Hilary was the hostess for their Sunday Lunch party, Grace was very definitely in charge, not only in the kitchen but ushering the guests into the lounge for a pre-dinner drink. Newman was wearing a pair of grey trousers, a white shirt with a red tie and a navy blue blazer. Shirley had on a light blue dress and jacket and a pair of shoes with heels, she felt that the increased height might help to give her a bit more authority.

Jeremy was standing protectively next to Hilary while Clive, who was standing at the other side of the room talking to Newman, never took his eyes off her. Shirley walked into the kitchen to see Grace.

"You managed to get them to come."

"Oh yes, I have always found that men who live on their own will always take up the kind offer of a good, home cooked meal……yes….especially if it's roast beef. It will soon be ready to bring out, I was going to ask Jeremy to carve, what do you think?"

"I think you are right. Shall I go and suggest to Hilary that she ask them to take their places? Then I'll help you to bring out the food."

"That will be lovely. When do you propose to do your piece?"

"I think after we have eaten and are back in the lounge."

Once they were all seated and as Jeremy was carving the joint he said

"This is an interesting gathering, may I ask why we are all here and why we are honoured by the presence of our two friends, I hope, from the police?"

It was Grace who answered, it being she who had organised every thing.

"I think Sergeant Ashton wanted to tie up a few loose ends...yes...it's sometimes better in a more....informal atmosphere."

"How exciting" said Jeremy.

"I don't know about exciting" said Clive "but it should certainly be more pleasant than my experience in the formal, and somewhat frightening, atmosphere of a police station."

"Oh I say" said Jeremy in a silly camp voice "is somebody going to be arrested?"

"You will just have to wait until after our meal. I'm sure that Sergeant Ashton will explain all in due course" said Grace.

The meal progressed in near silence with only a minimum of small talk. This may have been due to the fact that the food was delicious, but more probably it was because there was a definite air of tension in the room.

Coffee was taken in the lounge and with everyone seated comfortably Shirley stood up in front of the fire place, where she could see them all, and began.

"I appreciate that this is not usual police procedure, but this has been a most unusual case. For Hilary here it has been traumatic and for everybody connected it has been a long and worrying time. We in the police have found it particularly baffling. First of all we had a missing person, a strange case which had no rhyme or reason to it. Had Mark been kidnapped, had he run off of his own free will, or what? Then, thanks to the observance of Charlie Blundell, we found Mark's body and the case became one of murder.

So who could have committed the crime? Who had motive enough? Who would benefit from Mark's death? The obvious beneficiary is Hilary, but she was visiting her mother at the time and there were several people who were there with her. We did briefly consider the possibility of her hiring a hit man to do the job for her, but I think you will all understand when I say that that idea didn't last very long.

There were many people in the village who had good reason to hate Mark, but hating somebody and hating that person enough to murder him are two very different things.

Then there was the problem of how was the murder committed. We know Mark was shot at close range, using his own gun, but was that planned, or did the murderer have a previous plan which he then changed when he saw the gun in the back of the Range Rover?

My theory is in favour of the latter. I suggest that the murderer, let's call him M, came here to meet with Mark and have it out with him. But when he arrived Mark wasn't here, in fact he was in the field below, looking at the site of his proposed new development. So M ran down through the next field, hidden from view by the blackthorn hedge and found in the back of the Range Rover a shotgun and a waxed jacket with cartridges in the pockets. How convenient, what could be better than to use the victim's own gun? Mark came back down the field and met M who threatened him and then shot him. It is possible that Mark tried to grab and take the gun away, and in pulling it caused it to discharge, thus virtually causing his own death.

304

Then M replaced the gun and the jacket and drove the Range Rover back up here where he parked in front of the house, the wrong place incidentally, and put the keys on the hall table, also the wrong place. M then went away, home perhaps or back to his place of work. Later, probably around two o'clock at night, he returned and using the wheelbarrow and shovel that were near the body, brought Mark to the churchyard and placed him in the grave that was all ready for the funeral the next day."

"So who is this M, are you going to tell us?" asked Clive.

"My theory, and I call it a theory because although I am sure it is correct, there is no way that I can prove it, my theory is that you Jeremy are M."

Jeremy's mouth opened in what could have passed for amazement and then he burst out laughing.

"I've never heard anything so ridiculous in all my life" he said. "I was working at the bottling plant, you remember Hils" he said, turning to his sister "I rang you from there, didn't I?"

"Yes you did" said Hilary, "you spoke to mother."

"Oh yes, you spoke on the phone, your mobile phone, but it wasn't from the water bottling plant. It may have sounded like it to you Hilary, and that's what had us fooled for so long. I only realized how you managed that trick of being in two places at once, when I came here the other day and Hilary was typing your article. You were working from a small Dictaphone, weren't you Hilary, and that's how it was done. You made a recording of the factory working and played that next to the phone just after you shot Mark. You may even have left a similar recording playing through the office computer in your factory to simulate that work was still in progress."

"So how did I get here, the watchman in the industrial estate saw me there, he never saw me leave until eleven o'clock, or thereabouts?"

"You left through the little side gate behind the tile place. The little side gate that few people know about, that is normally kept locked. Curiously that lock has recently been oiled. That little side gate is no more than a few hundred yards from your home. You may have left a bicycle there in readiness. To ride from there to here would not have taken an expert road racing cyclist like you very long. When you came back later in the night to bury the body I think you were wearing your maroon coloured Lycra suit. The one you wore in that race last year. Unfortunately for you the cover from the end of the zip came off and was found in the grave with the body. It was a small round bit of plastic, the size of a five pence piece, maroon in colour and with a design on it of a three pronged fork with a snake entwined in it. That, as you probably know well, is the logo of the firm that made Lycra cycling suits. There is a photograph of you, wearing just such a suit, in the coffee lounge of a hotel near here, the hotel from which that cycle race started and finished last year. D'you still have that suit Jeremy, or was it so covered in blood that you had to get rid of it?"

Hilary gasped, recalling how soon after Mark had disappeared Jeremy had come to see her, dressed in a new suit which was light blue and yellow. She had said that she preferred the old maroon one, liked the colour better. To this Jeremy had replied that the lighter colours were better for the winter, brighter for other road users to see.

"Er, no I think I may have got rid of it, I think it may have been damaged."

"Convenient that the refuse collection for the industrial estate is on Wednesday mornings, the day after Mark was killed. Also I find it very interesting that the only time you have ever rung your sister at the nursing home, was when you needed an alibi, an alibi that placed you at the water bottling plant when in fact you were by the ruins of Glebe Farm."

"But why on earth would I want to kill him?"

"Two very good reasons spring to mind. First, he was, and had been for a long time, mistreating your sister. It started as verbal bullying and later became quite violent physical abuse. I noticed several bruise marks the first time I met Hilary and I can't believe that you were unaware of her ill-treatment. I suppose you thought that you were doing her a favour. But would she wish to get rid of a violent and abusing husband and find that she now had a murderer for a brother? Then secondly, the girl Ann Cash, with whom you had formed a relationship, even as far as proposing marriage I believe, committed suicide. She had made the mistake of borrowing money from Cash 4 U, a firm which was owned by Mark. You held him responsible for your fiancée's death.

The idea of concealing the body in Quentin Russell's grave was brilliant. Did the idea come to you when Hilary told you, that evening on the phone, that she was going to his funeral the next day? It would have worked if it hadn't been for Charlie. He knew that it was supposed to be a double grave, but when they lowered the coffin into the ground it didn't go down far enough."

"Very clever Sergeant, a very plausible hypothesis; I can't fault your logic" said Jeremy who was lying back in his chair trying to look unconcerned. "But can you prove it? That's what matters; can you take it to a court of law and get a conviction?"

"Is it true?" said Shirley in reply, looking him straight in the eye.

"Oh Jeremy, no surely not, you didn't did you?" said Hilary.

"If I had done, it would have been for your sake Hils, and if I did d'you think I'm likely to admit it. I doubt if anyone will disagree with me that the world is a better place without him."

"But you had no right" said Clive, with a look of astonished incredulity on his face. "You may have killed when you were a soldier, killed legally, but.....you can't play judge, jury and executioner.....its wrong."

"I always thought that you were the only person who could have killed Mark" said Grace. "You see, it was a matter of character....and personality.....and ability of course. With your army training...mmm....So what happens now?" she asked turning to Shirley.

"I'm sorry that we couldn't bring you a more satisfactory conclusion" said Shirley, turning to look at Hilary, "but unless Jeremy wishes to confess it will remain on file as an unsolved case. But don't forget, that doesn't mean that the case is closed."

"Oh dear me" said Grace "I feel so sorry for you Hilary. You were just beginning to gain a little strength and confidence....and....now this.....It's dreadful. Well......for what it's worth.....you can rely on my support....mmm...yes." Then she got out of her chair, a little grey haired woman in her late seventies, and went and stood in front of Jeremy. She looked down at him with great sadness in her eyes.

"As for you young man.....You may not have been convicted," she said. "But there's a judge and jury in your head, and they will remind you every day of what you've done. If you think that you have got away with this....well.....you will find that you have made....a grave mistake."

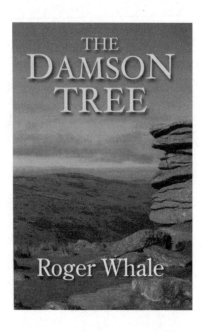

THE
DAMSON
TREE

Roger Whale

Frank Naraway is home on leave for his father's funeral. Friends and neighbours all seem to think that he will now come back to live and help his mother run the family farm on Dartmoor.

Does he have the expertise and the self-confidence to take on his father's job?

Will his love of the moor be great enough for him to give up his career in the Army that he has followed for the past fifteen years? Will he miss the camaraderie of the regiment?

He knows that he will receive a warm welcome in this small community, and in some ways feels that he owes it to his mother, but is this reason enough?

And what about Linda?

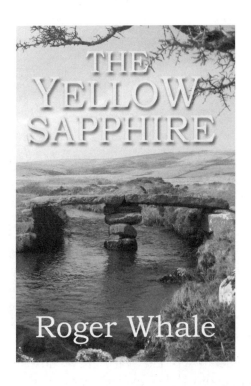

Piers Silverton from San Francisco is visiting
Dartmoor to see if he can find where his ancestors
lived. Can an old heirloom of his grandmother's and a
family portrait provide the clue?

He is lucky enough to enlist the help of local
girl Beatie who is also researching her family tree.

They are not the only ones in the village to
find surprises in their family cupboards.

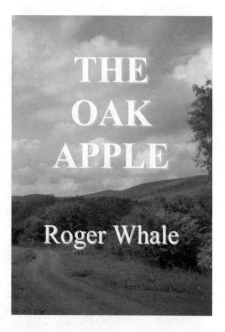

THE OAK APPLE

Roger Whale

Jacqui has left her abusive husband in West London, and with her twelve year old son Timmy has come to live with her parents on Dartmoor. Despite the unfamiliar surroundings Timmy soon falls in love with the open spaces of the moor and its wild life. But his natural curiosity gets him unwittingly caught up in a crime. Fortunately he has been befriended by Mick Cribbett, a white-haired mystery man who lives on his own and never mentions his past, giving rise to much speculation.

Mick is not the only member of the community who has built a protective wall around himself.

Can a young boy help to break down these barriers?

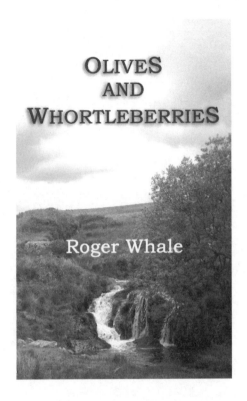

OLIVES AND WHORTLEBERRIES

Roger Whale

Jenny finds herself unexpectedly pregnant. This puts added pressure on an already strained relationship with her partner. Remembering her uncle's expression

"You don't learn everything by stopping at home" she hopes that a move away and a holiday may help her to see her problem from a different angle, and possibly provide a solution. She is by no means the only person to try this approach.

A chance meeting with an old acquaintance from her college days gives her further insight into how best to tackle her problems.